SO-AUG-036

DEATH as a
CAREER
MOVE

Other Chico Cervantes mysteries by Bruce Cook

Rough Cut
Mexican Standoff

DEATH as a
CAREER
MOVE

BRUCE COOK

St. Martin's Press
New York

DEATH AS A CAREER MOVE. Copyright © 1992 by Bruce Cook. All rights reserved. Printed in the United States of America. No part of this book may be used or reproduced in any manner whatsoever without written permission except in the case of brief quotations embodied in critical articles or reviews. For information, address St. Martin's Press, 175 Fifth Avenue, New York, N.Y. 10010

Production Editor: David Stanford Burr

Library of Congress Cataloging-in-Publication Data

Cook, Bruce
Death as a career move / Bruce Cook.
p. cm.
"A Thomas Dunne book."
ISBN 0-312-06946-4
I. Title.
PS3553.O55314D4   1992
813'.54—dc20   91-40915
CIP

First Edition: March 1992

10 9 8 7 6 5 4 3 2 1

For Susanna

One

Even though from where I was sitting I couldn't see Hollywood Boulevard four stories below me, I knew it was there.
The noise from the midmorning traffic drifted up to where I
was sitting, my feet up on the desk and my hands clasped
behind my head. You might say I was bored.

This was the way it had been ever since I had taken an office
there in that building at Hollywood and Ivar. Typical day: I
get in about 9:30, make coffee, check the answering service for
calls (usually zero), then settle down with a book. Right then
I was about halfway through the Samuel Putnam translation
of *Don Quixote* by my famous ancestor. I'd read it long ago
in Spanish, too young to get much out of it, my father marking
my progress with tests in the form of little discussions to make
sure I'd gone as far in it as I'd said. Miguel de Cervantes
Saavedra had no legitimate children, so how my father could
be so sure we were directly and legitimately descended from
him I don't know. But it was more than a tradition in our
family, it was the law. So look at me. Here I am twenty-five
years later, reading this book my father used to treat like the
Bible or something, only this time I'm enjoying it. It's funny,
and sad, and true, and I wasn't old enough or smart enough
to know that the first time around. It probably also helped
that I was reading it in translation—and if you understand
that completely, then you understand more than I really do

1

about myself. Let's just say that Antonio Cervantes has this little identity problem that pops up from time to time.

Like one night Alicia turned to me in bed—turned over and looked at me—and she said, "Chico, when did you stop to be Mexican?"

She said it in English. She'd been getting pretty good with the language. But that annoyed me—cómo no? I sat up and looked at her, sort of—the room was dark. "What do you mean, when did I stop? I *am* Mexican—Mexican-American."

"Which?"

"Both."

"But how much one, how much the other?"

"How do I know? I don't keep count."

Then the baby began sniffling and snorting. If she woke up, she'd probably start crying. We both knew that. Alicia told me to be quiet. I tried to go on, talking in a whisper, but she shushed me and said we'd go into it later or words to that effect. We didn't do that, but now I think I know what she was getting at.

The baby was why I was stuck away here in the office. Oh, I wasn't blaming her. Who could blame a kid four months old? But what had been not just my apartment but my place of business had been turned into this . . . this nest of women. I felt like—well, I felt like old man Cervantes must have felt in 1584 with his houseful of women—"two sisters, his illegitimate daughter, his niece, and a maidservant, in addition to his wife." (I always read introductions, too.) Well, my place wasn't so crowded, but with Alicia, and the baby, and Pilar to take care of them both, it just wasn't the right spot to wait around for the telephone to ring, so I got out and took an office. Sure, Pilar left every day about the time I got home, but the kid—call her by her name, Marilyn—she was at that time in her young life when she couldn't quite make it through the night without a feeding, and so with just the three of us in that four-room apartment it was still kind of a strain.

Money wasn't a problem. I wound up the Toller business counting the zeros on the biggest check I'd ever held in my hands. Not only that, but when the Tollers took over Majestic

Pictures they put me on a retainer as security consultant. That took care of the office rent—and then some. All I had to do to earn it was show up once every couple of weeks, talk to the chief of studio security (who kind of resented my little visits), walk around the lot, and end the session shooting the shit with Casimir Urbanski.

Casimir had left the LAPD, just as he said he would. He was now in a middle management position at Majestic—upper middle. If the security chief didn't take kindly to me, you can imagine how the holdovers from the old regime at the studio took to this funny-talking ex-cop from Detroit. Or maybe they just accepted him according to that honored tradition in Hollywood: the son-in-law also rises. Casimir wasn't quite there yet, but soon—it would be soon. When at last Ursula Toller, as president of the Motion Picture Division, had finished the business of lopping off heads, had wiped her blade and sheathed it, she had let it be known that she and Casimir would be married. In the meantime, the two were living in a beach house in Santa Monica.

Old man Toller, the CEO, didn't like that part of it at all. He saw no reason why his daughter and this Polish person she had chosen couldn't share his castle with him. But he lost that one, just as fathers always will, no matter how tolerant and accommodating. Heinrich Toller was left to rattle around his estate up Benedict Canyon with just his assistant, Hans-Dieter, and his servants to keep him company. Until about a month ago, when he had surprised everybody by returning from one of his regular trips to Europe with an old girlfriend, a Dutch lady of a certain age with beautiful blue eyes and a laugh that could shake walls down. At the age of eighty, he had installed her as the mistress of his castle.

The last time I was at the studio I happened to run into them. He was giving her the grand tour. He introduced us. The lady's name turned out to be Hedvige. I made some remark about that being Hedy Lamarr's real name, and she said something like, "Then it's wasted on me." Which wasn't true. Then she treated me to that laugh of hers. I swear the thin, false-front walls along the standing New York street set began to quiver. I loved it. Hans-Dieter was along. Old man Toller sent them on ahead, and we talked for a moment. He asked me what I thought of her, and I told him it was impossible not to like a woman with a laugh like that.

He nodded eagerly, almost boyishly, and said, "Exactly." Then he frowned and looked at me curiously. "What would you say if I married her, *De Quincey*?"

I thought about that a moment. "Well, I'd say you'd both be lucky." In different ways, of course—but I didn't add that.

He smiled a little smile, then said, "I think a man should have a widow—not just ex-wives." He shook my hand, mumbled some vague invitation about coming for dinner soon with my lady friend, then hurried after Hedvige and Hans-Dieter with that hitch in his step he always had. It didn't seem to slow him down much.

That was my last visit to Majestic Pictures. Today, this day at the office, was to be my next. Only this time it was different. Ursula Toller, hearing from Casimir that I was coming by, had issued a special invitation—a summons—that Alicia come along and bring the baby. We would all have lunch in the executive dining room. I wasn't looking forward to it. At best, Ursula made me nervous. But she was literally the boss and so, with a smile, I complied. Besides, she had a genuine interest in Alicia and the kid—you might say she had a stake in them both. I had to give her credit, she hadn't just dropped them after participating in the drama of the birth. Usually, in Hollywood, they experience their little shiver of reality, marvel at how wonderful it all was, then go on with their lives like nothing had ever happened. But not Ursula Toller. She'd learned more than moviemaking from her father.

I was to swing by the apartment at 11:30 and pick up Alicia and the baby. The more I thought about it, though, the more uneasy I became. Would she be ready? Would we make it to the studio by noon? I wasn't worried about the kid. Pilar would have her diapered, dressed, and all set to go. But Alicia was something else again. We had been out on a couple of shopping trips—once to Bullock's Wilshire and once to Cen-

4

tury City—so she certainly had clothes to wear. That was just the trouble. The greater the choice, the longer she would take to decide. I knew that from experience. I thought about that a moment, looked at my watch—it was eleven o'clock—then picked up the phone and dialed home.

I got Pilar and asked for Alicia.

"She's dressing now, Senor Cervantes." I couldn't get her to call me Chico, or even Antonio.

"Well, call her."

"She's pretty busy."

"Call her."

Pause. A moment later I heard the sound of voices, agitated and shrill. They were at it again. And then a moment after that I had Alicia on the line.

"Oh, Chico," she moaned into the phone, "I have nothing to wear. Absolutamente nada."

"You do," I insisted, "sure you do. You were going to wear the yellow dress. Remember?"

"I put it on. I look too brown in it, like a mestiza."

"Well, what about the black one?" It wasn't quite right for the occasion, but what the hell. No, it wouldn't do, she said. She looked too fat in that one. One by one we went through her entire wardrobe, which admittedly was not huge but should have provided something at least that suited her. But no. Finally I sighed and said, "Listen to me, chica."

"Yes, Chico?"

"Wear the yellow one. You remember I told you about the tanning salons? The women here, the gringas, they go to them and they pay a lot of money to lie under the lamps to look just the way you do in that dress. Believe me, it's right for you."

"You really think so?"

"Claro! I wouldn't say it otherwise. Now, go put it on, and be ready when I come."

All the way on the drive home I thought about her and the baby and our crazy situation. We were doing more than sharing space, but we were less than a family. And it was something besides a marriage ceremony that kept us apart. Sure, you could say that if the kid were mine, Alicia and I would

5

probably be married—and if you said it, you might be right. But every time I had thought about this before, I had thought about it strictly from my angle. Now I thought about her, what she wanted, or seemed to, and I had to admit that maybe the reluctance was hers. Maybe she didn't want to make this thing permanent. I remember I brought it up once not long after she came back from the hospital with Marilyn. I didn't exactly, well, *propose,* maybe, but I certainly opened the subject for discussion. I said something like, "Look, I think we ought to talk about the future—about you and me and the baby."

I don't know, did she get the idea I wanted to get rid of them? How could she? Pilar and I had gone out and bought all the kid stuff—a baby bed, a baby bath, a baby this and a baby that—so that it was all waiting for them when they came. I wanted her to feel like she was coming home.

Anyway, all she had to say when I brought up the "future" was that there would be plenty of time to talk about it later on.

Sure, why not? When in doubt—and God knows I was in doubt—just let it slide. It slid and slid. She never brought it up. That made me wonder now, driving down Fountain, winding my way around the left turns, cursing those who failed to signal. I wasn't exactly in a hurry. Providing she was ready, there was plenty of time to get to the studio. But somehow the tension and turmoil about all this that had hit me back around Highland seemed to have spilled over into my driving. I was an accident just waiting to happen. I eased off consciously and took it easy the last mile or so.

Well, she was ready when I got there, they were both ready, and Alicia looked terrific. Pilar had thrown open the door and gestured proudly at Alicia standing just behind her with Marilyn in her arms. Hey, talk about a Madonna and child, the two of them looked as though they'd materialized from some sixteenth-century Italian painting, only a little browner. I was right about the yellow dress, just tight enough and just loose enough in the right places. And Alicia's skin sort of glowed in its natural color, looking better than any tan I'd ever seen on any woman. I felt a little catch in my throat. She could do that to me sometimes.

"Do I look all right, Chico?" she asked, wide-eyed but with just a hint of a smile that said she knew very well how she looked.

Two could play at that game. "You'll do," I said. Then, as her eyes narrowed and the smile vanished, I added in a hurry, "No, you look wonderful, just right. Really. But . . . let's go. Okay?"

Reassured, she laughed and handed me the baby bag. We were on our way.

Alicia had been preparing for this outing for months. Back from the hospital, she began dieting and exercising right away, determined to get back into shape. I bought her that Exercycle I had threatened her with before, and according to Pilar, she spent at least an hour on it every day. And at night she worked on her English.

When Ursula and Casimir moved into their beach house in Santa Monica, we were invited to their first party. Quite an honor, I guessed from the guest list—a number of producers, a few directors, and a couple of actors Alicia recognized immediately. She wanted to talk to them, and one, an actress known for her commitment to Latino causes, wanted to talk to her. But since the actress spoke only "maid Spanish"—and she couldn't very well tell Alicia to do the windows and not to forget to clean under the sink—the conversation was necessarily held to Alicia's limited range of English. I wanted to come over and act as translator, but I knew I wouldn't be welcomed—not by Alicia, anyway. So I held my ground, talking uneasily to Casimir, as Alicia repeated phrases over and over and began using her hands to explain things, and the actress seemed to grow more and more nervous, her eyes darting and her neck tightening in tension. In a few minutes it was over, and Alicia turned back to me with a look of terrible disappointment. We left early—the baby had to be fed—and that night Alicia studied her English even harder.

That was then, but this was now. It was more often English than Spanish between us these days. Sure, she spoke mostly in the present tense and had a pretty heavy barrio accent that was really kind of charming, but she had all the slang and buzz-words from watching television, and you never knew what she might pop out with next. Like when she started calling me "dude" all the time, and the day she looked at me and said, "You're a very private person." (She was surprised and kind of offended when I laughed.)

All this effort had been aimed at today—her first trip inside a movie studio. Alicia certainly hadn't given up on her master plan. She hadn't worked the details out, but she was profoundly, religiously convinced that she was going to be a big movie star. It was an article of faith with her. When I tried to explain to her that there were probably a million girls in Los Angeles who were here for just that same reason, she countered reasonably, "Sí, but I got friends in the beezness." What could I say? It was true. How many beautiful blondes from Emporia, Kansas, could claim the head of a major studio as a friend? It was Ursula Toller herself who had called Alicia up and invited us to lunch, had asked her to bring the baby, and had told her to bring a résumé and some glossies so she could circulate them.

That was when Alicia turned to me in terror and said, "Chico, what's a résumé?"

Well, I explained that it was a record of professional experience, and then I saw the problem. She couldn't put down El Gallo Inmortal, Culiacán, particularly not if someone were to inquire just what she did there. Moaning in feigned ecstasy didn't count as acting except in the kind of movies they show at the Pussycat Theatre. Of course Alicia had told Ursula that she had been an actress in Mexico—stage, a few movies, etc. So I got my typewriter out, and we sat down together and documented her lies in detail. We made up theaters in Mexico City and Cuernavaca, coined directors, and minted some movie titles. Who, after all, would check up on her? Last of all were the glossies. They were no problem. I made a couple of inquiries and took her to the best—or the best I could afford. Anyway, this old, bald-headed gay guy accomplished the impossible—he made her look even better than she looked when

8

I came home every night from the office. The pictures were great. I ordered a hundred.

Though not, come to think of it, any better than she looked at that moment in her yellow dress riding beside me in the Alfa. We made the fifteen-minute drive to the studio mostly in silence. A couple of times I glanced over at her and the baby. Marilyn was awake but quiet, sucking on a pacifier. If it was possible for a four-month-old baby to look like anything but another baby, then she looked like Alicia—quick, bright, and with big, dark, beautiful eyes that roved continually, taking everything in.

Alicia didn't say much to me, but I could tell she was having some serious conversations with herself. She stared straight ahead, but her lips were moving without a sound. I guessed that she was practicing phrases, sentences, whole paragraphs in English in response to questions she anticipated. Reading the tension in her face, I reached over at one point and gave her arm a reassuring squeeze. "You'll do fine," I told her. She relaxed just long enough to flash one of her brilliant smiles, then went back to her silent mumbling. If she had had a rosary in her hands, I would have sworn she was praying. Maybe she was.

They still speak about the movie business as "Hollywood." But not many of the studios are there anymore and haven't been for years. Universal, Warner Brothers, and the Disney operation are out in the east end of the Valley and Burbank. Columbia just took over the old MGM lot in Culver City. Fox is in West L.A.—or is it Beverly Hills? I'm not sure on which side of the line it stands there on Pico. Only Paramount and Majestic are still there in what is literally, physically, and measurably Hollywood. Which is, I guess, a tribute to the continued success of both. Both have had their ups and downs, their good years and their bad, the way all the majors have had, but they've weathered their movie flops with active participation in television. TV pays the rent.

So it wasn't surprising that most of the big billboard signs along the walls surrounding Majestic were screaming the dubious virtues of all the sitcoms produced on the lot. There was

9

just one theatrical represented along the way—the soon-to-be-released *Cold Wind,* the movie biography of the late rock great, Tommy Osborne.

I took a left turn into the gate and came to a stop at the guard post. The studio guard on duty—a black woman, heavy, fortyish—gave me a big smile and what would have been a high five if I hadn't been sitting so low in the Alfa.

"Hey, Chico, how you doin' today?"

"Pretty good, Alta Jean. Meet my lady friend, Alicia."

She nodded. "Lucky lady. You know where to park."

"I know."

"On your way then. There's people waitin' behind you."

Two

I've been inside movie studios so often that I sort of know my way around. Well, at least I know enough not to go through the door when the red light is flashing above it. And I know that not every brick building you see on the studio street is really solid or really brick. And I know enough not to stare.

These three bits of advice I passed on to Alicia in principle as we drove to the parking space with my name on it. I told her to (1) follow the rules; but (2) remember it was all mostly phony; so that (3) she shouldn't be too impressed.

A lot of good it did. I remember I was along years ago when my cousin Pancho took his daughter for her first trip to Disneyland. Cristina is married and lives out in Simi Valley with a family of her own now, but she was about five years old then—and you should have seen her. Once we were inside the place, the kid was in a trance. She didn't say a word, she just looked and kept on looking. Well, that was Alicia from the moment we drove through the studio gate. Her eyes were big and eager, drinking it all in—no, *devouring* it. And what was she looking at then? Sound stages—just a bunch of big factory buildings. Whoever called Hollywood the "dream factory" got it right, believe me.

The studio streets were pretty crowded just then, and you would have thought that Alicia was the big star on the lot from all the looks she got. It was the baby, of course. How many times does real life in the form of a four-month-old kid intrude into this world of adult children? The men noticed, but the women seemed overwhelmed. One of them, matronly and in her forties, came running up to us and blocked our way. She looked vaguely familiar, an actress I guess, and she just *had* to have a look at the baby.

"Isn't she *darling!*" the woman exclaimed.

Alicia smiled and nodded in agreement.

"What's her name?"

With that, Alicia seemed to focus on the woman for the first time and looked at her suspiciously. She spoke up then with an odd sort of defiance in her voice. "Her name is Marilyn. I name her for Marilyn Monroe. She gonna be a big movie star jus' like her mama."

I'd heard that one before.

The woman drew back. It wasn't so much what Alicia had said, but the hard tone in which she had said it. But, a trooper to the end, the older woman managed a smile and mumbled something about "that beautiful baby" before moving on down the studio street.

What was it all about? I was about to ask Alicia when she said, "I know her from "Bitsy."

" 'Bitsy'?" And then I remembered. It was a sitcom. "Oh, yeah."

"I didn' know her at firs'! She's the mother-in-law. She's real mean."

So much for my advice to Alicia. All this was realer than real to her. I hustled her along to the studio commissary and on inside. Off to the left, where everyone above the line ate, we were met at the door by a tall, gaunt man in a dark suit and tie who acted suspiciously like a maître d'. He barred our way.

"Yes, *sir?*" He said it like we didn't belong.

"We're here for—"

"Let me make clear our policy on children," he interrupted.

Whatever it was, I could tell it was intended to keep us out. I'd been in here just once before with Casimir. We usually ate off the lot at a bar down the street. Obviously my single visit hadn't made much of an impression. "Well, let *me* make clear who—"

"Only professional children over the age of five, and none at all below that age, I'm afraid. Unless I'm very sadly mistaken, that child is much, much younger than five, so you see . . ."

"*Chico!*"

It was Casimir. To the rescue. He pumped my hand, gave Alicia a squeeze, and tickled Marilyn under the chin. The guy had the moves. He must have learned them back in Detroit watching the alderman work the street around election time. I was impressed.

He turned to the maître d'. "We'll sit usual," he said, "by the corner booth." No doubt about it. He was in command.

Without a word and just a nod, the tall man in the dark suit led the way to the usual place. We slid in and took the menus he offered. "And Miss Toller?" he asked Casimir.

"She'll be here."

The man vanished.

Casimir turned to me then and shook his head in dismay. "Guy gives me a pain in the ass, you know? Why didn't Uschi fire him along with everybody else?"

"Ask her."

He grinned. "Nah. I leave all that stuff to her." It sounded to me like the formula for a perfect relationship—for them, anyway. Then, to Alicia: "How you doin', huh? Not eatin' so many burritos these days, huh? You look great, kid."

She nodded, lowered her eyes, and batted them in the unashamed, old-fashioned way Mexican women do. "Thank you," she said. "I lose a little weight."

"You go by the gym with Chico?"

"No. At home."

"Well, wherever. It's working, you know?"

She smiled mysteriously. "I know." She knew.

"Let's see the baby."

Then, just as Alicia was hauling Marilyn up from the seat next to her, there was a great squeal from a few yards away. Heads turned up and down the aisle, and Ursula Toller came

13

charging up. She dived into the bench seat beside Alicia and somehow managed to encircle both her and the baby in an embrace. All three babbled at each other happily, Uschi asking Alicia the usual questions about a baby, any baby—like, how much does she weigh, does she crawl, does she try to stand up yet, and so on—and Alicia did her best to answer them. Marilyn contributed her own happy sounds to the racket.

Feeling pretty well ignored, Casimir and I looked at each other and shrugged. We knew there was nothing we had to give to that conversation, so we decided to have one of our own.

"So. Tell me, Chico, how's it going?"

"How's what going? Life? The business? What?"

"Any of them, I don't know. All of them."

I pulled a kind of a long face. "Well, okay," I said, "in four months I've had exactly four cases—two runaways, a bad check operator, and a divorce case. All of them wound up in less than a week, all of them paid in full. I *hate* doing divorce cases, so that'll tell you how desperate I am."

Casimir frowned sympathetically. "Oh, Chico, if you need money, I could prob'ly get you more here."

"It isn't that. I'm bored. The business just isn't coming in. And the little that does come in just isn't very interesting. You know what I think killed things for me? That little item that was in the columns about me working for the studio, like I was some kind of supersleuth giving advice on scripts and stuff. It made it sound like I was on full-time here."

He got a kind of funny look on his face. "Yeah?"

"Yeah. I was talking to Barney McCall—he's a lawyer downtown who used to steer cases to me—and he as good as admitted it, made some remark about me being too busy since I was private eye to the stars now. I set him straight—in a nice way, of course. But then I began to wonder about it. Everybody in this town reads the trades, even the lawyers." I paused, maybe to get my breath, I don't know. I hadn't blown off steam like this for a long time. Finally, I asked, "Who put that item in, anyway?"

14

Casimir looked away. "Well . . ."

"Oh, no! You, Casimir?"

"No, well, you know, the publicity department did it. I sort of gave them, like, the basic information, though. I thought it'd be good for your business, like advertising or publicity. But, like, something got lost in transition, you know? Or maybe it got bigger, you know?"

I nodded. Just then the waiter came and took our orders. Casimir and Ursula had "the usual," which turned out to be a steak for him and a salad for her. Alicia signaled with her eyes that I was to order for her, so I took the easy way out and just said we'd have what they were having.

I wished I hadn't dumped on Casimir in advance the way I did. After all, he was only trying to help. And I could be wrong about the slowdown. Me and my theories. Maybe business had just tapered off with the move and everything. Anyway, Casimir wasn't talking. He just sat there looking guilty.

Ursula had noticed. She looked from him to me and back at him. "What's wrong?" she asked.

"Nothing," I said.

"Oh, I just did something dumb—the usual," the big guy said. He was studying his hands.

"No, you didn't." I cuffed him on the shoulder. She didn't like that. "Things have just slowed down. That's all. I was looking for something to blame it on."

It was one of those moments that perfectly reveal a relationship. She had become tense, hostile. She leaned across the table and fixed me with a stare that must have made strong men weak here inside the studio. "What is this all about? I want all the details."

"Nah, it's nothing, Uschi," said Casimir. Chico and I were just talking."

She put her hand on his and gave him a glance that was both tender and dismissive. It said, I'll handle this. It was the kind of look a mother might give to a child when she was taking his part in a disagreement with an adult. The fierce look she gave me said, You hurt him, and you deal with me.

Casimir didn't say anything more. He just looked miserable.

Could this marriage last? Would it even become a marriage?

Alicia had no idea what was going on. She only knew there was trouble. She looked around the table uneasily and fixed a hopeful smile on her face.

Now, it would be fair to say that at the best of times Ursula Toller and I merely tolerated each other. We had butted heads hard and often in the past and still had bruises to show for it. There was too much of the spoiled child in her to suit me, and too little of common humanity. If she wanted to play mother to Casimir, that was her problem—and his. But I knew I had no intention of going back over what I had just said to him and trying to justify muself to her. I regretted what I had said, sure, but it was more or less an accident. I might even say I was sorry—say it to him, not to her—and not even in front of her. So we sat there, the two of us, and looked at each other for a while.

She repeated: "*All* the details."

Then the baby started to cry. I've read that babies can sense tension in the air and get upset without ever hearing a voice raised in anger. I believe it. At that moment there was enough electricity charging between us to light up L.A. County for an hour or two. So maybe it was inevitable that the kid would cut loose at just that moment.

What was surprising was the way Alicia reacted to the situation. She handed Marilyn to Ursula. Smart girl. Taken by surprise, Ursula looked from me to the kid, then began cooing at her, talking to her in German, and rocking her around a little. In the middle of all this, she looked back at me and said, "We talk about this later." The way she said it, it was a threat.

That was when the waiter showed up with our food. Alicia offered to take the baby back, but Ursula insisted on keeping her, holding her on her lap, bouncing her on her knee, as she attempted to eat her salad. Casimir dug into his steak, apparently recovered from his attack of insecurity. I can't say I went after mine with anything like his gusto—in fact, I didn't eat much of it—but I did manage to catch Alicia's eye long enough to give her a nod and a reassuring wink. She smiled back, apparently relieved.

Marilyn never did really settle down. She wasn't crying exactly, just fussing. I looked around the executive dining room and caught the glances from the other tables. They would have been angry glances if it weren't for Ursula Toller sitting there. She was doing the best she could with the kid, but somehow it just wasn't working.

So Alicia reached out for her and got no argument this time. "I think she is hungry, too," she said. Then, with a smile, she unbuttoned the front of her yellow dress—she had picked it out with this in mind—undid her brassiere in front and gave Marilyn the nipple of her left breast.

Casimir, who was sitting next to her, tried not to look and just kept on with his steak. Ursula stopped eating and stared, entranced, as though some miracle was being performed right there at the table. Alicia kept on eating. She seemed to like the salad.

I couldn't help it. I looked up and around and caught the reaction of the crowd. What were glances before had become looks of astonishment, shock. Maybe they'd never seen anything like it. Across the aisle, a couple turned away almost in disgust and began whispering to each other. At that moment—I'm ashamed to admit it—I was embarrassed.

Then I remembered Alicia's question a few nights ago— "When did you stop being Mexican?"—or however it was she said it. And a second wave of embarrassment swept over me. But not just that—a sense of betrayal, too.

I got out of there as quickly as I could. Oh, I had an excuse to leave, all right. My excuse was Norbert Wiggins, Majestic Studios chief of security. I told them I had something to talk over with him. That part was a lie. Wiggins and I had next to nothing to say to each other. But I figured that if I was a security consultant I should give the chief of security an opportunity to consult with me, so every time I came to the studio I visited his office. He was always there, even ate his lunch at his desk. It wasn't a matter of keeping an appointment, just a way of getting away from that table.

Casimir must have known that. But it was okay with him if I left early. He didn't want a rerun of that confrontation scene between me and Ursula any more than I did. Alicia didn't either. That was why, as soon as Marilyn had had her fill, Alicia hooked up, buttoned up, and handed her back to Ursula. That would occupy her for a while. Still, it seemed like a good time to leave, so I left.

But like the good German she was, Ursula insisted on shaking hands with me as I got up from the table. She gave my hand a manly squeeze—she must have practiced that—looked at me meaningfully and said, "Later."

Yes, probably. As I left the place, catching a smug glance from the maître d', I thought about Ursula and decided that my days as a consultant were probably numbered. If it wasn't this, it would be something else. She considered me a bad influence on Casimir. Why, I'm not quite sure, except that if I had any influence at all, it wasn't hers and was therefore bad. So sooner or later things would come to a boil—and maybe sooner rather than later because I was to pick up Alicia at Ursula's office at two o'clock.

Out on the studio street, it didn't seem quite as crowded as before. Maybe everybody was off eating lunch someplace. I looked at my watch—a little before one o'clock. I was in no hurry to get to Wiggins's office, since I had an hour to kill, and our visits seldom lasted more than fifteen minutes—if that. So I sauntered along, enjoying the sunshine, doing what Californians do best. There was a bulletin board down from the commissary, so I stopped just to see what I could see.

It wasn't too interesting—a few sublets, a few commercial postings for gyms, yoga classes, and one for a karate dojo, and the usual for-sale-by-owner used cars. I was checking the cars out, wondering what I could get for my Alfa these days, when I felt a tap on my shoulder.

I turned and looked. All I can say is that the face was familiar. About thirty-five, lean and hungry. No, not an actor—I'd been through that once before that day. And then I remembered—Barney's Beanery—but that's all I remembered. I couldn't come up with a name.

"Chico?"

"Yeah, right, and you're . . . you're . . ."

"Bill Schmidt. At Barney's."

"Sure. We drank together a couple of times."

"That's right. Remember, I told you that you ought to try writing scripts?"

"Yeah, that's right." (I hear that a lot.)

"Well, have you done any? I mean, that's what they're looking for today, man—authenticity. And you got that coming out your ears."

I hadn't quite thought of it that way. "Yeah, well, I got a couple of ideas, I guess, but nothing down on paper. I just haven't got the time." Absolute barefaced lie. I had nothing but time these days.

"Private-eye work keeping you pretty busy these days, huh?"

"Oh, yeah. Since I opened my new office in Hollywood, it's really something. Have to hand out numbers at the door." Sometimes I astonish even myself. I touched my nose to see if it had grown longer. Evidently not.

"Well, what you ought to do," he said, "you ought to put the ideas down on paper—just, you know, a few pages, even one page. I could help you sell them."

I'd heard that one before, too. "Oh, that's right, you're in the business, aren't you?" Then I laughed. "Well, I guess you are, or you wouldn't be here, right?"

"Right."

"You're a . . . you're a . . ."

"I'm a gaffer. But I've got connections, plenty of connections."

"Oh, sure, right. What are you working on now, Bill?"

"Big feature, the biggest. In fact, it's the only one shooting on the lot right now. *Cold Wind*—you know, the Tommy Osborne biopic." *Biopic*—that was right out of *Variety*. I didn't know people actually said words like that.

But wait a minute. "You said it's the *only* picture they're shooting here now? It looks pretty busy to me."

"Oh, yeah. Well, this is all television. When the Tollers took over, they scrubbed the whole slate, the way new management always does. Everything down the tubes, except for *Cold*

Wind. That would have gone, too, except it was too far along, and the director's too hot—Donny Emmett—also it's sure to make a ton of money."

They're all sure to make a ton of money. You don't think they make all those dogs because they're sure they'll fail, do you? No, if a movie goes into release, it's because the people at the top think it's got at least a 50–50 chance of making a profit. But in this case, maybe Bill Schmidt was right. Twenty years after his death Tommy Osborne was still big—maybe bigger than he ever was. The wild man of rock and roll back in the late sixties was still selling albums—greatest hits, pretty good hits, and now they were down to garage tapes. But his generation—it was my generation, too—kept right on buying. And all these years after his death, he even had the college-age kids buying his albums. Nostalgia for what they were too young to remember. A movie about Tommy Osborne would probably put him over with the teenagers, too.

Yeah, in this case, Bill Schmidt was probably right. *Cold Wind* might even make a ton and a half. I shook his hand in congratulation. "Hey, that's great," I told him. "You guys always like to work a winner, right?" I began backing off down the street.

"Right. But hey, Chico, what're you doing here?"

"Me? I'm security consultant for the studio." Then, thinking ahead, I added, "Special job—just temporary."

He waved. "Well, you have to get it while you can."

I laughed, waved back at him, turned, and headed down the street to Wiggins's office.

I think it was sometime between our first and second meeting that I asked around and found out that Norbert Wiggins had gained all his police experience on the Glendale Police Force. To me that meant he wasn't a real cop. Maybe today I'd draw different conclusions because Glendale's got the same problems as every other community in the greater Los Angeles area—drugs, gangs, murder—but twenty years ago, when Wiggins did his time there, it was a quiet, prosperous little place—tucked up against the mountains, quite separate from the city. It was symbolic of something that what it was most famous for was Forest Lawn Cemetery, which was there just on the edge of town.

I never got around to asking Wiggins why he'd left the peace and quiet of Glendale. Maybe because working security at Majestic Pictures provided even greater peace and quiet. The job certainly seemed to suit his nature. He was a big, taciturn man, grown soft from sitting in his office all day long. I could never figure out what he did, except sign parking permits. He even had a secretary who parceled them out, typed them up, and processed them for him. But he'd survived three or four changes at the top. Nobody ever thought of firing him. After all, if you had a studio security force, somebody had to be in charge, didn't they? And Norbert Wiggins was the man. As he had told me on at least a couple of occasions, "The buck stops here."

These visits had become rather painful occasions for me, mostly because they were so damned wearying. Nothing much was said, and he made it pretty clear that he tolerated my presence simply because he had to. Well, for some reason his attitude changed that day. Maybe I came into his office smelling like defeat from my encounter with Ursula. Who knows? Anyway, he seemed to have decided to tolerate me no longer.

I remember we'd been sitting there looking at each other across his desk for only a couple of minutes. He'd grunted out a few civilities, and then he got right to the point. "Cervantes," he said, "why do you come around here?"

That stopped me cold for a moment. Finally I said, "Well, to make myself available. If you've got a problem, I'm here to help you solve it."

"We don't have any problems here at Majestic. Not your kind, anyway."

"What do you mean, 'my kind?'"

"Well, you're a detective, right? An investigator."

"Sure, right, of course."

"Well, that's major crime. We don't have major crime here. Some theft, sure. There's pilferage all the time. Anything big we call in the LAPD. We have to. You know that as well as I do."

He was really making me feel useful, wasn't he? "Yeah, I know that," I said, "but this is how I look at it. If there is major crime on the lot you call in the cops, sure, but I'm here to represent the interests of the studio."

"Now, wait a minute," he said. "You're going to tell witnesses what to say? You gonna impede the investigation?"

"What investigation? Listen, all this is theoretical until—"

The phone rang. Wiggins picked it up and growled his name into the receiver. I glanced out the window, wishing this conversation was over and I was out of there. When I looked back at him, he was wide-eyed with—what? surprise? fear? He liked to play the tough guy behind that desk of his. But whatever he had heard made him drop that silly pretense. He said, "Right away, yes, right away." And then he hung up, still looking scared.

"There's a dead body in the editing department," Wiggins said. "He's been stabbed. I . . . I guess it's murder."

Three

Norbert Wiggins was actually hurrying. He had pushed himself away from his desk and lumbered out of his office. His secretary, fiftyish and fighting gray with Clairol red, looked up in surprise to see him on foot this time of day. As he moved past, planting one leg firmly after the other with me close behind, he called out to her, "I'll be in Post Production seventy-three!" Just as I headed after him out the door, I looked back at the secretary, and she yelled, "Is he all right?"

I didn't have a chance to answer. All I could do was shrug. Then I rounded the bend and saw that Wiggins was well ahead of me, chugging down the long corridor, picking up momentum as he headed for the stairs. That was where I caught up with him. It looked to me like he might break his neck. Here was this six-foot-three-inch, 280-pound object about to hurtle down a forty-five degree decline. If his big feet failed to keep rhythm with the angle of the stairs, then he would probably wind up a quivering mass at the bottom. But no. He plunged down the stairs and out the door, moving even faster than before. Since I had no idea where, on the lot, Post Production 73 was located, I had no choice except to follow.

I was right along with him when Wiggins jumped into the Jeep Cherokee just outside in the parking space nearest the building entrance. The Jeep was painted black and white and looked almost like LAPD property.

There I was in the passenger seat beside him as he twisted the key in the ignition and started away. He seemed almost surprised to find me there. Flustered. "Well, I guess it's all right if you go along." But he didn't seem quite sure about that.

"You bet it is," I said. "Come on. Let's go."

You'd have to be at the studio a long time to really know your way around. Even though the streets are laid out more or less in a grid, there are too many dead ends, too many buildings tucked off in out-of-the-way corners for the short-term employee to learn his way, much less a visitor. I couldn't have gotten us to our destination even with a map. But Wiggins certainly knew the way. The Jeep screamed and hurtled around the narrow corners, rattling my teeth as it hit the speed bumps. He honked at pedestrians to clear the way. The yellow flasher on top was going, not that anyone would have noticed in the daytime, and if he'd had a siren, you can be sure he would have used that, too.

"Hey," I yelled at him, "are you sure you really want to attract this much attention?"

"Whatta ya mean?"

"You don't want to attract a crowd where we're going, do you?"

He thought about that a moment, then slowed down and killed the flasher with a switch. We drove the last couple of blocks at a speed that would be termed reasonable and proper.

We pulled up at a building tucked off in the northeast corner of the lot. Call it nondescript and you'd be kind. I hadn't seen much of Majestic Pictures except for the glassy, shiny new office buildings up near the gate and the former admin building where Norbert Wiggins had his office. The soundstages were pretty grungy on the outside, but what did you expect? These old buildings in the back fringes of the lot were something else again. Built in the twenties, if not before, they were stuccoed and Spanish-tiled. Except that the stucco was many shades grayer than the last coat it had been given, and looking at the tile roof three stories up on the Post Production Build-

24

ing, you could be pretty sure it would leak in the unlikely event of rain.

Anyway, that was how I sized it up when I jumped out of the car and followed the chief inside. As I'd guessed, number 73 was up on the third floor. Wiggins was a lot slower going up two flights than he was coming down one. He turned to me about halfway up to the top and asked, "You're not carrying a gun, are you?"

It seemed an odd question under the circumstances. "No," I said.

"Neither am I."

"Well, if it *is* murder, you wouldn't expect the guy to hang around, would you?"

"You never can tell."

This guy was scared to death—not that somebody was going to jump out and stab him, not that there was some mad killer loose who'd kill somebody else in the next five minutes. No, he was afraid he might do something wrong. This was probably the first real break in his routine in years, and his only taste of the real thing since . . . Glendale. *(Glendale?)*

When at last we reached the third floor and I looked down that long corridor, there could be no doubt which of the doors was Room 73. A small group—four or five—had gathered outside a place about halfway down. There would have been more there, probably, except that it was still lunchtime on the lot. They stood around, looking the way people always do in such situations—glancing inside, talking in low tones among themselves—three men and a woman.

Wiggins blustered through them, growling something like, "Security, security, one side, step aside," and I followed close behind through the wide-open door.

A studio guard was there, one I'd seen at the gate. He stepped aside for Wiggins but moved to stop me.

"Tell him, Wiggins," I called out.

He turned, looking puzzled. "Oh, uh, yeah. He's okay, I guess."

The guard let me past.

It was a workroom—postproduction—editing, I guessed.

There was one window. The place was small and kind of dingy. On the long worktable there stood a computer, a row of numbers and codes on the screen in green, and just to one side a machine that looked from the front like a TV set with the guts exposed—a screen but no tube, film on spools instead. I sort of halfway recognized it as a moviola, the basic tool of film editing since year one but now mostly replaced by a fancier item called the KEM Table. The moviola screen held the image of a young man with long hair and a wild look, an actor whose picture I'd seen in the paper. He was frozen in a medium shot, naked from the waist up, his mouth open wide as if he were shouting a warning.

The corpse was almost hard to find. He was tucked down beneath the table, lying awkwardly half on his side. There wasn't much blood beneath him. Although I couldn't see the wound, or wounds, because of the position of the body, I would have bet they would have been right in front, with direct entry into the heart. It would have stopped pumping immediately. Whatever blood was on the floor had simply leaked out.

There was no evidence of a struggle. It looked like the assailant had simply walked in, gotten close, and let the guy have it while he was still sitting in the chair at the worktable. The victim had tumbled from the chair to the position under the table. No blood smear. He hadn't been moved.

All of which meant that the assailant had come in very quietly and surprised the guy where he sat; or he was known to him, and his entry was routine or expected.

Wiggins was doing the same once-over I was. I had no idea what conclusions, if any, he drew. But at last he nodded, very businesslike, and turned to the guard. "You touch anything?"

"Oh, no, Chief. Not me." Then he hesitated. "Well, I did use the phone to call you."

"Well, you ought to know. Don't touch *anything!*"

The guard was nearly as big as Wiggins, but he hung his head just like a kid. It didn't really matter much. I doubted that the guy who did the number with the knife had hung around to make any phone calls.

"And I touched him, too," the guard confessed, indicating the figure under the table with a nod of his head. "You know. To make sure he was as dead as he looked."

"Well . . ." Wiggins decided to give him a pass on that one.

"But I left the door open, you know, for prints on the inside. Then I just stood here, waiting for you."

"Did you find the body?" I asked.

"No. That guy there."

The guard pointed out a young guy in the group at the door—two more had joined them. He was dressed in jeans but had a hundred-dollar haircut. He sort of shrunk back, like he'd been accused of something. A natural reaction under the circumstances, it seemed to me. I gave him what I intended to be a reassuring nod. Then an uneasy notion struck me. I turned to the guard. "You said you called him."—Wiggins— "You did call the cops, didn't you?"

Before the guard could open his mouth, Wiggins said, "I'll take care of that."

"Well, do it."

"There's somebody in administration I'm supposed to call first. In emergencies."

"Yeah, and I'll bet his name is Hans-Dieter." The Tollers' little fixer, the one who tries to orchestrate everything. "Well, okay. You take care of that. I'll take care of something else."

Then I left, Wiggins and the guard looking after me. As I walked out the door I hooked the guy with the hundred-dollar haircut and asked him if he had an office on this floor, some-place with a phone.

"Just down the hall," he said.

"Isn't it awful?" the woman in the group muttered as I passed.

"Yeah," I said, "and it may get worse. Stick around."

I followed the guy to Room 78 and happened to notice he was carrying a sandwich in a wrapper. I guessed the sight of the corpse took away his appetite.

He threw the door open and then followed me inside. The room was a lot like the one I had just left—but bigger and brighter. There was a computer, but instead of a moviola it had a more complicated setup, with a screen above a long, flat table with a ribbon of film running the course of it on spindles. The KEM job.

The phone was next to the computer. I went right to it, dialed 911 and reported a homicide at Majestic Studios, Post Production Building, Room 73. I gave my name and said I'd be there. Then I hung up.

"I'm glad somebody did that," the guy with the haircut said. He was leaning against the table, looking very serious and maybe a little dazed.

"How come you didn't? I understand you found the body."

"Yeah, that's right. I found him." Full stop, just like he'd answered my question.

I decided to try another approach. I stuck out my hand to him. "My name's Cervantes," I said. "I'm a security consultant for the studio. Which means, I guess, when something goes seriously wrong here I'm supposed to look into it."

After a moment's hesitation, he put out his hand to me, found it held the sandwich I'd noticed, then with an ironic chuckle laid it aside on the table. I noticed the bread was squished. He'd been holding it tight. Finally, he shook my hand. "I'm Tom Beatty," he said. "That sandwich. I got it at the snack shop for Jimmy. I guess I've been carrying it around ever since."

"The deceased's name was Jimmy . . . what?"

"Worley. James Worley. He's a music editor. Or was." He hesitated. "So am I."

I had a notebook in my pocket. I fought the impulse to start writing down names and details. Later. Right now, keep it cool, keep it conversational. "What was he working on?"

"*Cold Wind.* We both were."

"Isn't that unusual? I mean, two on one picture?"

"Not really," said Beatty, "not for a movie like this. For one thing, it's big. For another, they're in a hurry. And it's kind of a musical."

I nodded. Made sense.

"Besides," he went on, "we were working on different pieces of the picture. I'm doing the background stuff. You know, heavy violins for the love scenes and so on. And Jimmy, he's doing the source music. Or was."

"Uh, what's that? Source music?"

"That's when the people on the screen are singing or playing or whatever. Or in this case, seem to be singing. None of the actors on this show do their own stuff. It's all dubbed from original Osborne tapes. I mean, the actors are miming with the music, but even so, it's tricky. For that kind of matching, Jimmy was an expert—the best."

"And that's what he was working on when . . ."

"Yeah. On the moviola. That's what he learned on. That's what he used."

"I see." I didn't, really, but I wanted to keep him going.

Tom Beatty struck me as a pretty reasonable kind of guy. Now that I had him talking, he didn't seem in the least dazed. He was good-looking, not much over thirty, with a sort of studious manner. Dressed just a little differently, he might be taken for junior faculty at a local university. Except for the haircut—that was pure Hollywood—perfectly layered, just short of collar length, the sides waved back and down so that they covered just the tops of his ears. But there was something about him, something that seemed kind of elusive. Not like he was hiding anything. Just something.

I cleared my throat and gave him a nod of encouragement. "Could you tell me the details? You might start with the last time you saw Worley alive."

He hesitated just a moment. Then: "Sure. Okay. Around noon we broke for lunch. I stuck my head in the door of his room down there, and I asked him, oh, how it was going, and what kind of sandwich he wanted. The usual, and then—"

"Wait a minute," I interrupted him. "Was this the customary thing? He didn't go out for lunch? You always brought him back something? He always worked right through lunch?"

"Well, yes."

"How come?"

"I told you. This is a big picture. Because it's the kind of picture it is, there's been a lot of pressure on Jimmy. He's been very . . . conscientious."

"I see." There it was again. Something. Only this time I did have the feeling he might be holding back. "Go on."

He sighed, collecting himself. "So I went off and had lunch at the commissary." He gave a weak smile and touched his stomach. "I want to tell you it's churning around in there right now. Oh, yeah. I ate with Marty Weinstein, one of the editors on the second floor. If you should want to check."

"Not me. Mention it to the cops, though."

He nodded. "Then I stopped off at the snack bar and picked up the sandwich—cream cheese and avocado on whole wheat." He pushed it toward me. "See?"

He was delaying, putting off the moment he didn't want to remember. I waited him out.

"So I came bounding up the stairs like some eager little puppy—I had some gossip for him—and I threw open the door. At first I didn't see him. The chair was empty, and I called out his name, 'Jimmy.'" His throat had tightened, and his voice had dropped to not much more than a whisper. "Then I saw him—his body—under the table, and this time I yelled his name out and ran over to him. Well . . ." He stopped a moment, took a deep breath, and plunged on: "Well, I could see he was dead, the blood and all, and the way he was lying, and so I just got out of there. I probably should have called the police right then, but I don't know, I suppose I didn't want to take responsibility. Maybe that was it. Anyway, I knew there was a guard right down at the entrance to the building—in a little side office there. So I ran down and told him. And I guess he called you."

"Yeah. More or less."

Beatty was panting by the end of his recital. I noticed him holding tight to the edge of the table, so tight his knuckles were white. I believed him. I believed it happened just like he said. But a couple of things stuck out. One was that phrase like "some eager little puppy." Not the kind of thing that pops out every day when some guy is telling how he found a stiff. The other thing was the gossip. I wondered about their relationship—Beatty's and the victim's.

"What was the bit of gossip you had for Worley?" I asked.

I put it to him in a flat, direct tone. No smile, no pat on the shoulder.

He relaxed, audibly. A sigh slipped from him, and he shrugged. "Oh, that. Nothing really, just something I heard at lunch."

"What was it?"

"I'd rather not say."

I looked at him. He turned away from me and glanced out the window, then he began staring down at the floor.

"You don't have to," I told him. "You don't have to tell me a damned thing. But I've taken you through this for your own good. The first time you tell anything, it's the hardest. Now, the cops are going to take you through this over and over again. You can trust me on that. If there's any inconsistency they're going to find it. If you hold anything back, they're going to get it out of you. You can't tell them you'd rather not say, not unless you're willing to plead the Fifth. And if you do that, you're immediately suspect. If that's what you intend to do, there's the telephone. You better call your lawyer right away."

I waited. Beatty raised his eyes to me at last. He looked, well, not so much frightened as very unhappy. Even miserable.

"Look," I said, "the whole point of this exercise is to get you prepared for them, the cops. If you tell it all to them in the beginning, there it is, they've got it. But like I say, if they have to pull it out of you, it can get nasty. Believe me, I've been there."

"On their side?"

"Well . . . yeah."

What he said next surprised me. "You seem like a decent person."

I didn't quite know how to respond to that. Finally, I shrugged. "I try to be."

He didn't say anything for a long time, maybe half a minute. Then he sort of exploded: "All right, all right, all right! If you want to know what the gossip was, it was who was fucking who. It was just gay gossip. The subtext to all this is that I'm gay and so is Jimmy. Or he *was*. Yes, Jesus, *was, was, was!*"

At last he gave in to the tears that had probably been crowding him since we started talking. They streamed down his cheeks. He sniffed back hard, set his jaw, and kept right on talking: "Oh, it was no secret. I've been out of the closet since I was twenty. I mean, if anybody wondered. And Jimmy! Jimmy was just totally up-front about it. But . . ."

"But what?" Quietly. Just to keep him going.

"He had it."

"It? What do you mean?"

"Oh, you know—goddamn, fucking AIDS."

Four

Hans-Dieter arrived just before the cops. I only had to put up with a few minutes of his officious posturing, and it was mostly for the benefit of Norbert Wiggins and the little crowd that had grown a little larger outside the door of Post Production 73. I was just down the hall, standing a little apart from the rest of them with Beatty when Hans-Dieter burst upon us, shouting loudly that this was all wrong. "A terrible mistake" was what he kept saying. He pushed through and paused at the door and looked inside just long enough to see the body beneath the table, then yelled at Wiggins that he was to touch "absolutely nothing, nothing at all." Then he began browbeating and threatening all those around him, ordering them to get back to work. He waved his arms at them. "You think we are paying you to stand and look?" he demanded.

They shuffled a few steps backward.

"Get to work! I take this up with the union!"

One or two broke away from the group and headed down the hall. The rest stood their ground.

Then the cops arrived. No, there were no sirens. But there must have been a window open someplace because all at once we all became aware of that unmistakable squawk of static and the bored female voice of the radio dispatcher down on the studio street. Everyone heard it. Even Hans-Dieter knew what it meant. He looked around wildly, obviously angry that the decision, the choice of the moment, had been taken away from him.

Then his eyes settled on me. "You!" he yelled. "You called the police, didn't you?"

"I sure did," I yelled back.

Two uniformed cops appeared at the top of the stairs. They walked briskly and purposefully forward, like they knew just what they were doing.

"We talk about this later," said Hans-Dieter. There was a threat in what he said.

But all I did was nod in reply.

Eventually, of course, we did talk about it, but it was so long after the fact that it hardly mattered. Hans-Dieter and I never really had a lot to say to each other anyway. The thing was, I had already done Majestic Pictures a big favor by talking to Tom Beatty. By the time we finished there in Room 78, I had him settled down pretty well. He'd wept. He'd stifled a scream. He had even thrown out an unfounded accusation against Donny Emmett, the director of the film.

"Wait a minute," I had said in a nice, even, let's-be-reasonable tone. "You're saying you think Emmett killed Worley?"

Beatty had stuck out his chin then, suddenly certain. "Sure. Why not?"

"Well, he's the director. Why would he want to do that?"

"Because he's a goddamn homophobe."

"Then why did he hire Worley to do the picture? Why did he hire you?"

"Because Jimmy's the best, and well, I'm pretty good, too."

"But look," I said, "that doesn't make sense. He wouldn't sabotage his own picture that way. What's the point?"

"The point is," he said righteously, "that these macho types like Emmett have an irrational fear of the plague."

"The plague?"

"AIDS!" He threw up his hands like he was talking to a dunce. "They think they'll get infected just by touch or something. Maybe he thought he'd get it touching the work print Jimmy was handling."

34

"But did Emmett know Worley had AIDS? If he's as weird as that about it, he wouldn't have hired him. You think Worley told him?"

Beatty looked away then, suddenly silent. Then, eye contact at last: "No," he said, "I did."

It turned out that Emmett was putting a lot of pressure on the music editors. Not surprising from what I had heard a little while ago from Bill Schmidt. Majestic had a lot riding on this picture. But Emmett was pushing so hard that he had them editing source music and some Tommy Osborne stuff over montage sequences while they were still shooting hotel room interiors over on Sound Stage 5. That was pretty unusual, though maybe not unheard of on a music picture on a hurry-up schedule like this one. What this meant, Beatty explained, was that Emmett would come off the set and head straight for the Post Production Building to see what they'd done that day or half day or whatever. And he'd shout and scream at them that they had to go faster! faster! That's how it had been for the past ten days or so. It was hard enough for Beatty to take, but he could see that this routine of browbeating and sarcasm was wearing Worley down visibly.

"He was bad enough that he'd been on AZT for a month before he took this job," Beatty told me. "Then the end of last week he put in two twelve-hour days. Maybe longer, I don't know, I went home. He didn't. By Saturday Jimmy looked just terrible. I wondered if he'd make it in on Monday. But there he was yesterday morning, looking just as bad."

Emmett had come in at one o'clock, snarling and cursing his way up and down the hall, worse than ever before. But then, when he had run out of steam at last and left, Beatty had run after him and got to him on the studio street, just outside the building.

"I told him," he said. "I told him he had absolutely no right treating Jimmy that way because Jimmy was a sick man, and he was giving him a one-thousand-percent effort anyway. I really wasn't going to say any more than that, but Emmett was so snide. He started in with this fag-baiting routine. Like, 'Oh, has the little dear got a cold or something?' And I just looked

35

at him. I gave him the coldest look I could, and I said, 'No, he's got AIDS.'

"My God, you should have seen his face! First disbelief, then fear. The man looked absolutely crazy, like I'd told him *he* had AIDS. Then you know what he said? He said, 'Why, he could kill us all!' What I thought was, 'Not unless he gives it to you in the ass without a rubber, sweetie!' I mean, there is such a thing as safe sex! But I didn't say it, of course. I tried to explain things to him, but he wouldn't listen. He walked away from me, positively ranting. 'He's off the picture,' he said. 'He'll never work again in this town.' Well, if you ask me, he decided to make sure he wouldn't work again."

"That's pretty far out," I said. "Somebody in Emmett's position committing murder."

"Oh, he could have had it done. Oh, believe me, he could have. People like him always have things done for them."

I thought a moment. "Well, in fact, Worley wasn't fired, was he? He was on the job today."

"Yes. That's what makes me think Emmett decided to handle it this way."

"Did you tell Worley any of this?"

"No, I . . ." He hesitated. "I just didn't have the heart to worry him more. I didn't want him to think that I . . ." He left it unfinished.

And then I understood. Worley's death had shocked him, of course. He was his friend and maybe something more. No need to ask him about that now. But the reason he had reacted so strongly was that he blamed himself. The way Beatty had worked it out in his head, he had caused Worley's murder by letting it out that he had AIDS.

What a burden! I wanted to lift it from him, but I couldn't think what to say. I did persuade him not to pass on his suspicions about the director to the cops: "If they ask you about it, fine. Don't hold back. Just don't go volunteering anything. I promise I'll follow up on that myself."

He looked at me. "You really will? You're not just saying that?"

"I really will."

36

"Well . . . all right. But if it looks like you're just bullshitting to keep me quiet, I'm going straight to the police."

"Be my guest. One last thing. Could I have Worley's address?"

The cops came in waves, as they always do. The two early arrivals secured the crime scene, moving Norbert Wiggins and the guard out of Post Production 73, ignoring Hans-Dieter's urging that they get the body out of there as quickly as possible. The two of them consulted, then split up. One remained at the door. The other headed back downstairs to direct the next wave in. I knew the drill from my two years as a uniform cop.

Hans-Dieter at last managed to bully the rest of the crowd back into the offices and workrooms up and down the corridor. All except Tom Beatty. He came up to us, and ignoring me, spoke directly to Beatty: "So? You don't have a job, too? Go do it!"

Beatty threw me a questioning glance.

"Leave him alone," I said. "He's Exhibit A."

Hans-Dieter looked at me blankly. "I don't understand."

"He found the body. The cops will want to talk to him first thing."

His eyes widened. To Beatty: "You must tell them nothing harmful to the production. It's better you tell them nothing at all. Stand on your constitutional rights!"

Beatty was in a sudden panic. Hans-Dieter seemed determined to undo all the work I'd done in the past few minutes. I sighed, gave Beatty a pat on the shoulder, and said, "Excuse me a moment, Tom." Then I put a lock on Hans-Dieter's arm and all but dragged him out of earshot.

"Now, look," I whispered between clenched teeth, "you leave this guy alone. Studio administration is your job. Dealing with the cops is mine. I don't report to you. I report to the old man. If you mess around in my turf, I'm going to plead with him to send you back to Germany, which is probably where you belong anyway. Do I make myself clear?"

He didn't say a word, but he gave me a furious look. Then

37

he turned on his heel and stalked down the corridor. How to make enemies and alienate people. I was an expert.

It occurred to me as I watched him disappear down the stairs that I was acting a whole lot more confident than I had felt a half hour ago. Why? Maybe because it seemed like I had nothing to lose. Maybe because for the first time in about four months I wasn't bored.

I walked back over to Beatty. "Don't pay any attention to him," I said. "Just talk your way through it."

He nodded, apparently relieved. But then he said, "This is scary."

"Sure it is. It's always scary talking to cops. It's their job to make you nervous. Don't let them."

He sighed. "Okay."

And then they made their entrance, up the stairs and down the corridor, good cop and bad cop personified. The first one was blond and sort of slight in build. He wore an open-collar shirt with a blue blazer and slacks. The second was sweaty, big-bellied, and brawny. He was spilling out of a suit and had his tie pulled down at the neck. Guess which was which.

"Just remember one thing," I said to Beatty.

"What's that?"

"The little guy is *not* your friend."

Pausing at the door to Post Production 73, the two of them looked inside, had a few words with the uniform cop there, then spoke briefly to Wiggins, who nodded and pointed over in our direction. They split up, the good cop went into the room for a look around. The bad cop came over to us.

"This guy is going to come on strong," I whispered. "Just talk your way through it."

Beatty flashed me a faint smile.

The big guy already had his wallet out. He opened it just long enough for us to get a glimpse of his badge and police ID, then he snapped it shut and pocketed it.

"Detective Warnecky," he said, just in case we'd missed it. "Hollywood Division Homicide."

Beatty foolishly stuck out his hand. Warnecky ignored it.

"Which of you two found the body?"

Beatty pulled back his hand and self-consciously tucked it behind him. "I did."

"Where can we talk?"

"In my workroom, I guess." Beatty looked at me like he was asking permission to leave. I gave him a reassuring nod and a wink.

They started back toward Post Production 78, Beatty leading the way. But Warnecky looked back at me and called out to Beatty, "Hold it a minute. I'll be right with you." Then he came sauntering back to me. Or it was as close to a saunter as his thick, overburdened legs could manage. He stopped and looked me up and down. As he did, he dug into an inside pocket of his suit jacket and pulled out a cigar. "Who're you?" he asked. Then he bit off the back tip of the cigar.

"My name's Cervantes," I said. "I'm a, well, a security consultant here." It sounded pretty phony even to me. What *was* I doing here anyway?

"Private, huh?"

"That's right."

He lighted the cigar then, being careful to blow a little of the smoke into my face. Finished at last, he took a long drag from the cigar, then held it out for inspection like he was giving it the taste test or something.

"Why don't you do both of us a favor," he said, "and just take a walk. If we need you for anything, I'm sure we can get hold of you."

You know what? I took his advice.

Five

It was a pretty long walk, too—all the way back to the parking space with my name on it. The distance I had covered in Norbert Wiggins's Jeep Cherokee, with its dome light flashing, took almost ten minutes to backtrack on foot. I might have made it faster, but I didn't know my way around this corner of the lot and I took a wrong turn. All the buildings look alike. A guy on an old balloon-tired bicycle put me back on course.

With the Alfa in sight, I ran the last forty yards, jumped in, and revved the engine gradually up to speed. Then I pulled out and, careful of the speed bumps, made it to the gate and—with just a wave at Alta Jean—drove right through. I turned west and headed for the address Tom Beatty had given me—Worley's place in West Hollywood.

Any big city has its gay neighborhood these days. Castro Street in San Francisco and Christopher Street in New York are sort of famous, I guess. But militant and political as they are in the Castro, they haven't yet seceded from the city of San Francisco, which is more or less what the gays of West Hollywood managed to do a few years back. Since most of Los Angeles is made up of small towns that were once suburbs, there is always the legal possibility that since they opted into the city, they can opt out again. That's what West Hollywood did in 1984. It wasn't exactly that the gays were in the majority. After all, West Hollywood includes a lot of the old Jewish neighborhood around Fairfax, and lots and lots of assorted straights—I mean, *I* live in West Hollywood, after all. But the gays and their sisters had organized for it, and they wanted out. They were tired of being hassled by the cops up and down Santa Monica Boulevard. Anyway, they pulled it off, and every year now when they march on Gay Pride Day, you can bet that Santa Monica Boulevard belongs to them.

Well, it was my street now: I was buzzing along through a stream of traffic that as usual was moving pretty slowly, weaving in and out, pushing the yellow lights into red. I was in a hurry. Why? Well, I wanted to beat the cops there and have a little time to myself.

What I was planning to do wasn't really kosher. Well, sure, of course I know that breaking and entering is against the law. But I'd done it before, and anyway, I planned to be out the back door the moment the cops came in the front. If not before. That wasn't the part that made me nervous. See, no matter what you get from TV, cops basically don't like PIs. It's to my advantage to work my old contacts on the LAPD whenever I can, but I left the force over ten years ago, and in that length of time your contacts dwindle. So practically all the time now, I'm out there on my own, which is the way it's supposed to be. As a matter of fact, a PI isn't supposed to involve himself in any case under active investigation. That's okay. I've made a living off the other kind for a lot of years now. So the idea that I'm messing around the edge of a homicide investigation makes me nervous.

Then why was I doing it? I remember asking myself that as I turned south onto Worley's street. Well, I reasoned, I was doing it for the studio, wasn't I? It was part of my job. Maybe a private investigator had no business working a homicide, but the security consultant for Majestic Pictures had a responsibility to do what he could in his employer's interest. Why, I'd said as much to Wiggins just a little while ago.

Sure. Right. Of course. But that was just so much high-minded bullshit, wasn't it? Deep down, I knew that I had hopped into my car and headed for Worley's place for one reason. Because today, now, during the past hour or so, I was feeling really alive for the first time in about four months. Nothing like a good, messy murder to make your motor run faster.

I drove about three blocks south of Santa Monica Boulevard, beyond the rows of court apartments with their shaggy, sickly palms, onto a street of small houses. They were Spanish colonial most of them, with the kind of red-tile roofs you see all over Los Angeles, and there were little California bungalows mixed in among them. It was a block of well-kept houses and well-tended lawns, L.A.'s version of Hometown, U.S.A.

I pulled up in front of one of the bungalows, checked the address on the curb against the piece of paper in my hand, and got out of the car. The driveway was empty. There didn't seem to be anyone on the street, but you could never tell who was looking out from behind the curtains across the street. And so I hitched up my pants, straightened my jacket, and headed for the porch. After a good, firm knock on the door, I waited, then knocked again. No answer. I didn't expect any. Then, making a show of it, I went out to the middle of the walk, turned, and stared at the house for a moment, as though looking for signs of life inside. There were none. I didn't expect any. With a shrug, I walked across the lawn and headed briskly down the driveway to the back of the house. If anybody was watching, at least they couldn't say I was sneaking around.

The backyard was fenced, but the gate was unlocked, and there was no dog inside, thank God. I wasn't up to wrestling with a rottweiler. There was a little brick patio just in front of the back door with two old-fashioned lawn chairs stretched out across it and a table between them. As I made my way past, I noticed a half-eaten apple on a plate, together with a short, sharp-looking paring knife that had been used to slice chunks from it. The meat of the apple wasn't brown yet. Maybe there was somebody around. Just to make sure, I banged loudly on the back door, just as I had on the front. Nobody. Nothing.

I had a credit card out, ready to attack the lock before I noticed that it wasn't that kind. No, it was an old-fashioned

42

key job. Well, there was only one thing to do—break the glass pane just above the doorknob. I managed it pretty quietly with my elbow, knocking a round hole about four inches in diameter in the glass. There's a trick to it. I took off my jacket then and reached carefully through the hole and then down. That was the tough part. Although there were no jagged shards sticking out (I told you there was a trick to it), the smooth edge of the broken glass was sharp enough to slice deep if my wrist should come in contact with it. But it didn't. I was just able to reach down, find the key in the door, and twist it without springing a leak. I withdrew my hand and, covering it with my handkerchief, tried the knob. The door swung open.

There was a little entranceway that led directly into the kitchen. I closed the door after me and went inside. The kitchen was, well, nice. It was a lot bigger than my own, big enough to have a table and chairs off in one corner and a butcher-block table down the middle. There were little paintings, framed, stuck up in the right places—strong colors that stood out against the pale yellow walls. I stepped closer and looked at one of them—green and red, a watermelon. It seemed sort of Mexican, like a Tamayo—only it couldn't be because Tamayo never worked this small. I checked out the rest and saw they were fruit-and-vegetable pictures. Well, why not? This was the kitchen, wasn't it?

Dining room and living room were all one. There was a big grand piano near the window. That didn't surprise me. Worley had to be a musician. The furniture, the usual stuff, was sort of modern and in bright fabrics, but well-worn. Altogether the place had kind of a homey feeling to it. There were more paintings on the walls, all of them apparently by the Tamayo guy but all of them on the small side. The biggest was hung over the fireplace, and it was only about a foot and a half square. I stared at it for a moment, trying to draw some shape, some plan, from it. Was it just colors—browns, yellows, and a brilliant blue? And then I saw—the desert, Sonora, a village in brown off in the distance to one side. There was even a church with a tiny crucifix brushed in so lightly you could

43

hardly see it. If this guy wasn't Mexican, he'd sure been down there.

I wandered into Worley's workroom up in the front of the house. It was sort of bare but bright and friendly. It was more or less a duplicate of the editing room I'd seen at the studio, with a computer and all, except instead of the moviola there was a state-of-the-art VCR next to a TV monitor, and over in one corner stood a small electric piano. There were piles of video- and audiotapes on shelves around the room, a few books, and a stack of music, sheet music, not printed but penciled in. I remember thinking that all this might be important, but I had no idea how. I didn't have a handle on it.

Out of there and into the bedroom. It seemed like there was two of everything in there—two chests of drawers, two closets with two separate and complete wardrobes, two lamps on two tables—but only one bed. And above it, the big surprise, one crucifix, a weathered wooden cross with an iron Christ twisted in pain upon it. I frowned, concentrated, trying to put things together, then went to the two chests of drawers and began going through them. Not much to report there, except that in the bottom drawer of one of them I found some old family photographs tucked away under some clothes. Mexican—all women, except for one old Mustache Pete who looked like he'd posed for the picture around the time of the Revolution. But they were sort of hidden away, all of them. Why? And in the top drawer of the other chest I found about a year's supply of condoms.

It's funny, poking around somebody's house. You find out things, but you don't really know them. You draw conclusions, but you don't know if they're valid. Burglary must be a fascinating profession. Investigating a homicide, on the other hand, is brutal. And the brutality is directed not only at the murderer, or even the suspects, but also at the victim. Would you want somebody snooping around in your life just because you'd happened to meet a violent death? That comes under the heading of injury, adding insult to injury, doesn't it?

Walking around the living room–dining room area, I noticed at last what I hadn't before—a door that must open onto a small room next to the kitchen. There was no access from the kitchen to it, or at least I hadn't noticed any. The door was closed, an old-fashioned wooden one with paneling but no lock visible. Just a doorknob.

I went over and tried the door. It wouldn't open. Maybe there was a dead-bolt on the other side, and if there was, somebody was probably in there. I tried it again. No, not a dead bolt. There wasn't that clunk of resistance you get pushing up against a drawn bolt. It was, well, it was sort of squishy. It gave a little, then it came back almost as though there was somebody a couple of inches away pushing hard every time I pushed. In fact, yeah, I decided that was what it was all about. There was somebody there holding the door. I threw my shoulder into it this time. So did he. It was a draw. Then I went back as far as I could with the dining table standing in the way, got about two and a half good steps of a running start, and slammed into the door with my shoulder as hard as I could.

I flew right through it, airborne, landed on my face, almost lost consciousness, pulled out of it, looked around, saw the bottom half of a body, just a pair of trousers and bare feet, disappearing out of a window. I jumped off the floor, grabbed the feet, grappled up to the knees, and pulled. Pulled hard. My arms hugged them, working them right, left, as I tugged and hauled. I braced one foot against the wall and pulled some more.

Then all at once he was on top of me, all of him. We rolled around the floor, knocked something over, wrestling, slamming back and forth, him on top, then me, then him. In all this, I never exactly hit him, but I banged his head against the floor, and that, thank God, was enough. He was stunned—not long, no more than a few seconds, but long enough for me to wriggle out of his grasp, turn him around, and apply the notorious police choke hold.

He came out of it and tried to pull away. I pulled back tight on him, and he began gasping. I eased off a little, and he began to curse: "Jesus, María, y José! Chinga! Chinga! Chinga! Dios ayudame!"

Was he cursing or praying? A little of both, as men do in

extreme situations, when angels and devils hover to grab them. I struggled up to my feet, pulling him up with me. He had no choice but to come. Glancing around the room for the first time, I saw that it was a kind of small artist's studio. Paints, brushes. We'd knocked over an easel with a half-painted canvas. I had my Tamayo look-alike.

Pushing him at the knees, step by step, one wrist behind him in a lock, I marched him out of the room. And all the while, he kept up a steady, gasping, whispered monologue: "Dejame, dejame. No es necesario a matarme. Bueno, bueno. I geeve op. Please, okay?"

Well, at least he was saying what I wanted to hear. I pushed him down on the sofa next to the piano, and stood over him, looking tough, daring him to make a move. I wouldn't scare me, but I guess I intimidated him because he didn't make a move. He just sat there, panting, evidently glad just to be breathing normally again.

I studied him. He was about my size—Mexican, I was sure—small-boned but running to fat at his middle. His face was round, too, more Indian than Spanish, a campesino, the kind of kid who had probably come up from a little brown village in the Sonora like the one he had painted. He seemed like a pretty good kid, not mean, just scared.

We must have passed a full minute without a word. At last he broke the silence: "Migra?" He was asking if I was from Immigration.

I shook my head no. "I have nothing to do with them," I told him in Spanish. "I'm not from the police either."

He relaxed noticeably. He nodded. His shoulders went down. His hands unclenched, and his fingers flattened out on his thighs. Then he frowned, realizing that things didn't quite add up. "Then . . . who are you?" In Spanish. "Why are you here?"

This was going to be tricky. I wanted to find out what I could from him before hitting him with the ugly fact of Worley's death. Taking a deep breath, I plunged in, hoping for the best. "I'm from the studio," I said.

"Where Jimmy works?" He said it *Gee-mee.*

"Sí. Claro."

"Is something wrong? Has something happened to him?"

I ignored his questions and pressed on: "We need information."

"Of what manner?"

"About Worley."

He folded his arms across his chest. "I tell you nothing. Jimmy is my friend."

"Has anyone threatened him?"

He looked confused, perplexed, concerned. "I know nothing of that," he said. "What has happened?"

I answered his question with a question: "Has he been worried?"

"No. Just sick. You know he's sick?"

"I know. Beatty told me."

"You know Tom?"

I nodded.

He looked me over, frowning, like he was sizing me up, trying to figure out if I was okay. At last he volunteered, "Maybe the last couple of days there was something. He was not worried, but I think he was trying to figure something out. He had that guy over to listen to the tape."

"Momentito!" I jumped in. "What guy? What tape?"

"Oh, I don't know, the guy—Clay, Cray, something like that, a real gringo. Cómo se dice—'redneck.' " The last word in English, of course, and continuing: "not on the bus."

"Qué quiere decir 'not on the bus?' "

He looked at me slyly, like he had something over me. "It means something," he said.

We'd get to that later. Let him have his little joke. "Okay. This guy, he came over, and listened to a tape with Worley. What was on the tape?"

He shrugged. "Nothing. Just music, you know, for the movie."

"And what did they say about it?"

"I don't know. They were in the other room where Jimmy works. I was trying to paint. They play it over and over. They make it hard to work. But I don't complain. Jimmy is my friend."

"Look," I said, "there's something I have to tell you . . ."

He studied my face a moment, "Jimmy is dead," he said.

"Yes, he is."

I waited for a reaction. I didn't get much. "I thought so before," he said. "You wouldn't tell me before because you wanted to ask me questions." He seemed pretty cool about it, but he sure had me figured. Then he turned away, not to hide anything—no tears, no trembling lip. He had put on that Indian face that masks emotion. He seemed only to be thinking. At last, he turned back to me: "It wasn't the sickness?"

"No," I said, "he was killed, murdered—a homicide."

Again, his reaction was no reaction.

"You have any idea who would do this thing?" I asked him.

He thought a moment. "No," he said at last.

"The visitor, Clay, whatever his name was, did they fight? Did they argue?"

"No."

"What did he look like?"

He thought about that a moment. "Old-time sixties guy. Tall and thin with his hair in a ponytail and a big mustache."

"Anything else?"

"His hand." He held up his left hand. "He had bent fingers."

"Bent?"

"Very bad-looking." He shrugged. "I don't know."

I must have sighed then, sort of deflated. Anyway, there didn't seem much point in trying to bully him, so I sat down beside him on the couch. He made no move to get away. I wouldn't have stopped him if he had. He just sat there quietly, looking thoughtful. I touched him lightly on the arm then, interrupting him. "How are you called?" I asked him.

"Eduardo," he said. "Eduardo Calares y Ochoa." He made it sound like a grand name, like there was some hacendado to which he could claim direct lineal descent. Who knows? Maybe there was. But looking at that brown, round face, I doubted it.

48

"How long were you living here?"

"With Jimmy? Six months."

And then he told me a story, their story, of a meeting down in Mexico, one of those chance events that changed lives. It was, of course, a love story.

Eduardo was, as I had guessed, from a corner of the Sonora, a western corner. He had grown up drawing pictures, then painting them in watercolors, then doing little pious carvings in wood for the priest in their village. There was no one to teach him, so he taught himself. Of the seven brothers and sisters in his family, he was the only one who showed such a talent, the only one in the village who could do such things. His mother said he was blessed by God and did what she could to keep him from the hard work in the fields. The priest agreed and bought Eduardo a set of oil paints. Eduardo tried them out with great success and, at the age of fifteen, took them and ran away to the city.

He was lucky in the place he chose—Guaymas on the west coast of Mexico, just a town really, but its location on the Gulf of California made it a favorite spot for American sportfishermen and for tourists looking for quiet. He got a job in the big hotel in town, painted, probably turned a couple of tricks on the side, and even managed to send a little money home to his mother. He had had a pretty good life there for two or three years, and then he met Worley and everything changed—for the better. For the best, to hear him tell it.

He was in the habit of showing his work on Sundays just outside a restaurant frequented by Americans down on the marina. Worley—Jimmy—came by on one of those Sundays and looked at Eduardo's paintings.

"There is a way of looking that shows understanding," said Eduardo. "Others came. They nodded. They bought sometimes. But Jimmy looked, and he understood. He wanted to know who had painted the pictures." Eduardo smiled, remembering, even chuckled a little: "Jimmy could not believe that I, un joven, could do such work, that I had such a talent. You see, he *recognized* me as an artist. We fell in love immediately."

During the next few days they were together constantly—on the beach, at the house Worley had rented, in town. But Eduardo was puzzled. Perhaps Jimmy loved only his talent. He wouldn't, couldn't, touch him as men had touched him before. And there was about him, too, a sadness that Eduardo, who was so exuberantly happy, couldn't understand. Then, on what was to be their last night together, Worley told him why he had held back. Eduardo knew all about AIDS, of course, but he was sure it couldn't happen to him; he was too young, too full of life. And so he told Worley he didn't care, that he wanted to be with him, to go with him, no matter what.

"We make love then for the first time. It is beautiful. Jimmy is very careful. He use the rubber thing then and always. To this day I got no HIV from him. Then he ask me to come with him to Hollywood. I said yes right away—sí, sí, sí! And so the next day we leave together. All I take with me was my paints and pictures."

"Where did you cross over?" I asked. I was curious about that.

"Mano, we went in style. Jimmy had the connections. We flew in on a little airplane at night. My first time ever in the air. I would have been scared to death, but Jimmy was along, and it was okay. He held my hand. You got the money and the connections, you can do it."

"Yeah," I said, "I suppose that's true."

He was a pretty smart kid. The last part of the story, the part about Worley, he had told in English. And it was true, he was talented, but I couldn't help wondering how he would survive. So I asked him, "What are you going to do now?"

"That's what I'm trying to think." He was silent for a moment. Then: "I got some friends here, Jimmy's friends, maybe I go and stay with them."

"You have any money?"

"A little. I sell some pictures here. Jimmy give me some. He was good man."

I nodded. "Okay, look," I said. "I'm not the police, and I'm not the migra. But the police are going to come, and they'll ask you questions, and say they'll turn you over to the migra if you don't give the right answers, and maybe they will turn you over. Who knows? Anyway, I think you'd better pack up and get out of here."

He thought that over a moment. "I think so. Yes."

"But look," I went on, "I want to find out who killed Jimmy as much as the police—no, more than the police. I want you to help me. Will you do that?"

"Sure. I help you."

"Okay, here—" I pulled out my wallet and fished out a card. "Here," I said, handing it over, "if you can think of anything you haven't told me, just give me a call—okay?"

"Okay." He took the card and tucked it into his shirt pocket without even looking at it. That wasn't reassuring.

"One more thing. Did Worley have an address book? I didn't see one lying around. You know where it is?"

His eyes shifted. He was thinking fast. So when he shook his head and said, "No," I knew he was lying.

I turned on the tough act again. "Bullshit!" I said, "Entiende bullshit? Get the address book!"

I pushed my face up close to his and saw him crumple. He looked hurt, betrayed. The problem was, he felt he needed the address book to resettle. I could understand that. We negotiated. He went into Worley's workroom and brought it to me, leather-bound and neatly notated. Then we took about ten minutes copying out names, addresses, and phone numbers of some of the more likely prospects. Anyway, we did it. He got what he wanted, and I got the address book.

Six

Here I was, sitting at one end of the long bar in Barney's Beanery, a bottle of Dos Equis in front of me, trying to decide how I really felt about all this. I had come here from Worley's place, just a few blocks away, after dropping Eduardo off along the way at a little bungalow in the next block over. All he had with him was a suitcase of Worley's into which he had thrown enough clothes for a week, and under his arm a sketch pad and a box of watercolors. He ran up the walk, knocked on the door, and gave me a wave from the porch. The door opened, and I drove away. Well, I had the address, anyway. Theoretically, at least, I knew where I could get hold of him.

I had claimed what the regulars at Barney's call the Janis Joplin Memorial Bar Stool. It's right under the window and about the only place the daylight filters in even during the bright afternoon. According to local legend, this was the one she sat on every night during that last recording session, the one that ended when she overdosed in that motel on Franklin. I never saw her here. All that happened about fifteen years before I moved in around the corner and made Barney's my local.

But this is one bar, one of the few in Los Angeles, with a history—an infamous history, some would say, for Barney's is notorious as the last bastion of the "breeders' in gay West Hollywood. Back in the sixties and seventies when there were

52

gay bars on nearly every block of Santa Monica Boulevard, the management at Barney's posted signs that said FAGS KEEP OUT. That made it pretty plain, didn't it? Of course, when West Hollywood went independent, the signs had to come down. There were a few halfhearted attempts to "liberate" the place, but stony silences and surly remarks proved to be just about as effective as the posted notices had been. Nobody really likes to go where they're not welcome.

And this was the place I had chosen to spend numberless hours of my time. That said something about me, didn't it? Like a lot of men, I feel a couple of different ways about the whole gay thing. On the one hand, I don't much care what people do for fun if it isn't dangerous. AIDS? Well, it's dangerous, but I didn't think it was the judgment of the Lord upon them or anything. I thought it was a disease. If they wanted to take the risk, it was up to them. I'd taken a similar risk with Alicia.

On the other hand, getting real with myself, I had to admit that I was put off by the very idea of homosexuality—threatened, I guess. A lot of men feel that way, maybe most, and it doesn't have much to do with whether you were brought up macho or not. For a Latino kid, I was practically a wimp. But my father, by his example, and the other guys in Boyle Heights, by their horror stories and jibes, managed to communicate to me that there were certain acts which, for a real man, were absolutely unthinkable. They stayed unthinkable until I became a cop, and then they soon became just another element in the urban pattern. It came with the territory. A domestic beef might turn out to be a man and a woman, two men, or rarer, two women. Any way it came up, domestic beefs could turn out nasty. Cops get caught in the middle all the time.

So here I was on the edge of a case where sexual preference, if you wanted to call it that, might turn out to be pretty important—maybe the most important aspect of all. And I felt, well, squeamish about it. I found that out during my session with Eduardo. I had the feeling this was a case for Dave Branstetter and not for Chico Cervantes.

Dorrie, the barmaid, came over and asked me if I needed another beer. I weighed the bottle in my hand and said no. She started away, and then I called her back.

"Hey, Dorrie," I asked her, "what does it mean when somebody is on the bus?' "

She looked at me and shrugged. "That depends."

"On what?"

"Well, when somebody's on the bus, it just means they're 'one of us.' You hear it in this neighborhood, it usually means they're gay. If they're not on the bus, they're straight."

"Oh."

"Just keep your ears open, Chico. You'd be surprised what you can pick up."

"Uh, yeah. Thanks."

She walked away. She'd one-upped me, and she knew it.

I wasn't sitting on the Janis Joplin Memorial Bar Stool because it was such a big thrill to plant my ass where hers had once been. (Though I admit the woman moved me.) No, it was because it was the only place in the joint where I could see well enough to page through Worley's address book. It was thick with names, connections, and annotations—business and social. Judging from some of the comments penciled in the margins, Worley had led a pretty active sex life. There were a few big names scattered in among the rest. One of them belonged to a ball player who was performing in the game they had tuned in at the end of the bar. A little cluster of afternoon drinkers were down there taking it in. Was I shocked to find a famous right-hand batter was really a switch-hitter? Not really. Surprised? A little. The appearance of four or five show business names in the book didn't shock or surprise me. After Rock Hudson, you sort of expected it.

But no Clay and no Cray, not even a Clayton or a Creighton. I'd been through the book once and had started through it again. Nothing. But wait a minute. Here, under *C*—how could I have missed that? Henry Claessens. That would work out to Clay, wouldn't it? Well, of course it *could*. I hurriedly copied down the name and phone number into my notebook and continued on through the entries, a little encouraged at last.

At the end of my second trip through Worley's book, I had only one other name—Jack Kayman—and that was a real stretch. But I felt I'd gotten about all the book could yield. The question was, what should I do with it now? It belonged to the cops, no doubt about that. They would say it was a source of leads in an ongoing investigation. They had the resources to check every name in the book. I was pretty sure they wouldn't, but if this turned out to be a headline homicide, they might be forced to do just that. So I really couldn't hold it back from them, could I?

But I hesitated. Why? I guess it was because of the ball player's name in the book and the notations after it that made it clear Worley's relation to him was not strictly social. Information like that often found its way into the tabloids. They paid for it. I'd known that to happen before. Or worse: an athlete could be blackmailed; I'd heard rumors of that happening, too.

So I decided to hold on to the address book for a while. If it looked like they really needed it, I'd cough it up with some story about how I found it by accident—or maybe I'd just mail it to Hollywood Division Homicide and let them take it from there. In the meantime, I'd see how the investigation went, theirs and mine.

It occurred to me then that I'd better get back to the studio and check on that. I looked at my watch and saw that it was almost four o'clock. This time of day I ought to be able to make it there by—

Alicia!

I had forgotten about her completely. I was supposed to pick her up at Ursula's office at two o'clock. Maybe she was still there, waiting.

Did I feel guilty? You bet I felt guilty. I jumped up and hopped over to the pay phone nearby, pumped a couple of dimes into it, and dialed through to Ursula's office. Her secretary answered—a man, of course.

"Uh, yeah, well . . ." I was flustered. "This is Antonio

55

Cervantes. There was a lady with a baby. I was supposed to pick her up a while ago. Uh . . . is she still there?"

"No, Mr. Cervantes. She left for home just a few minutes ago. Hold on. I'll put you through to Miss Toller."

"No! Hey! I—" But it was too late. I was talking to dead air. Should I hang up? No, I couldn't do that. But the last thing I wanted was to get a lecture from Ursula. Yeah, but I was busy on their behalf. This was what they were paying me for, wasn't it? I'd just tell her that I—

"Sooo—" Very cool. The lady in charge. "At last you call, uh?"

"Now, wait a minute," I said. "Maybe you haven't gotten the word yet, but there was a murder committed there on the lot today. The cops are probably crawling all over the place right now."

"I hear about that, yes. So?"

"That's where I was. Taking part in the investigation." Breaking and entering, withholding evidence, suborning witnesses—yeah, I guess they could be broadly defined as "taking part."

"And so now what do you do? Where are you now?"

"I'm still working on it."

"I hear how hard you work." I hadn't really thought about it before, but the jukebox had the Allman Brothers cranked up loud enough for Ursula to hear at the other end of the line. She must have had the idea I was calling from a bar or something. "But listen to me," she continued, "Alicia can get along without you. You'll see."

And then she hung up on me. People are always hanging up on me.

I tossed some bucks down on the bar and headed out the door. Running around the corner to my place, it suddenly hit me that Ursula had threatened me. What was it she said? I'd see that Alicia could get along without me. Was this some kind of vendetta? I'd never understand Germans. Or maybe it was women I'd never understand.

Just as I chugged up to the entrance of the building, a Mercedes sedan pulled up. The driver hopped out and opened the rear door. Then, by stages, shifting, feeling for the pavement beneath her feet, Alicia emerged with the baby. Balancing awkwardly, she reached inside for her purse and a sheaf of papers, then turned back to find me hovering there behind the driver.

"Chico!" Her face lit up like Cinco de Mayo, and she sort of pushed the driver aside and handed Marilyn over to me. I took the kid gingerly. She was evidently asleep, and I wanted to keep her that way.

The driver, in his fifties and big around the middle, gave me a big grin. "I had 'em like that," he said in a loud whisper. "You think they're gonna break."

"Not her," I said, "this one's tough. You ought to hear her yell."

I heard her," he said. Then, to Alicia: "Everything okay then, Seen-yo-reeta?"

"Oh, sure, Al. His name is Al," she explained to me. "He is a teamster. Debemos pagarle?"

"No," I said firmly. I thanked him. Alicia stood on her tiptoes and gave him a kiss on the cheek. And Al, beaming, demonstrated how quietly a Mercedes door can be closed. The baby didn't so much as stir in my arms. A moment later the car was gone.

"You sure we don' pay him?"

"I'm sure." Al probably cleared more in a bad year than I did in a good one.

"Not like a taxi?"

"Not like a taxi."

She nodded seriously, fixing that in her memory. Then she brightened suddenly: "Oh, Chico, I got the big news for you! I went to—oh, but let me say first I'm very *sorry* I was late. Lo siento mucho—mucho, mucho, mucho! But what make me late is the big news."

"Hey, wait a minute," I said. *"I* was late. I wasn't there."

"No? Well, it doesn' matter. Listen!"

And all the way upstairs and into the apartment she told me about her afternoon. When I'd left her at the commissary, Ursula had taken her over to meet a television producer—

"Arnie Gresham, real young, jus' a keed" (I guess that was meant to reassure me). What I got from Alicia was that this guy Gresham had a sitcom in development, working title, "Lupe," about a girl up from Mexico, on a merry-go-round of hilarious adventures in Beverly Hills and East L.A., as she ducks the migra and tries to grab the gold ring that keeps eluding her. The gold ring, of course, being the green card. Knowing more than a little about the realities of that situation. I thought it seemed like a pretty faulty premise. But sitcoms have been built on faultier ones—talking horses, talking cars, visiting Martians—so I didn't argue with her. It wouldn't have done any good anyway.

Ursula had left her with the guy, and the two of them talked a long time about his plans for the show, how he really wanted to make a statement about the problems of immigrants in "El Norte" (he'd seen the movie, of course), and how—if it was a hit—it could really make things better. "Chico, he's *real* serious," she said. Then he asked her about her own experiences. "I tell him adventures, all boolsheet, natur'ly. Then he want to know how I got my green card."

That would take some explaining. "What did you tell him?" I asked, a little afraid of the answer.

"I tell him, 'In service to the United States gover'ment—DEA.' He's very impressed by that. He say, 'Undercover?' I say, 'Sí, under the covers.' And he laugh and say I got real comedian talent. Is that right? How do you say that?"

"Comedic talent?"

"That's what he said, sí. So then I give him my résumé and he's very impressed by that, too. 'Oh, you're trained,' he say, 'a real artist!' And I say, 'Natur'ly.' "

Well, Arnie Gresham took Alicia Ramirez y Sandoval very seriously indeed. He gave her a copy of the pilot script and asked her to look it over and be ready for a reading in a few days. He also asked her to check it for accuracy. *Accuracy?* Jesus, Mary, and Joseph! I could give him a reading on that.

Anyway, that was the sheaf of papers she'd gathered up from the backseat of the Mercedes. She had her big chance at last, and I didn't have the heart to remind her that she wasn't trained and that she had no experience as an actress, and to warn her not to get her hopes up. It wouldn't have done any good anyway. Let her try.

So by this time the baby was tucked away. Alicia was pacing around the room, gesticulating, right over the top. She's telling me this is her destiny, this is why God put her in purgatory there in Culiacán, this is why he brought her here to Hollywood.

"West Hollywood," I said.

And then she said—I swear she said it—"Whatever."

At that moment, thank God, the phone rang. It was Norbert Wiggins.

"Cervantes, where the hell did you go?"

"Well, I had some things to check on. The cops seemed to have things under control."

"Well, I don't! You get down here right now!"

"Fifteen minutes," I said.

"Make it ten."

I hung up.

"Listen, chiquita," I said, "I gotta go back to the studio. There's been a murder right there on the lot, and I have to help out the security people. I'm sorry."

"Oh," Alicia said, "don' be sorry. A murder? Tha's tereefic! Now we both got work to do!"

Seven

All I can say is, the lights weren't nearly as bright as I expected they'd be. There were four of them, one each attached to Minicams belonging to the three network stations and the one independent that really made the effort at local news coverage. Two papers, the *Trib* and the competing *Chronicle* had reporters out there, too. There were just three of us up there on the stage of the screening room—Wiggins, Donny Emmett, the director of *Cold Wind,* and me. The burgundy velvet curtain had been pulled over the screen to provide some sort of backdrop, but in a way that was unfortunate. I was pretty sure it would be described as bloodred in the newspaper reports. TV viewers would be free to draw their own conclusions.

It had been Hans-Dieter's idea to handle the media all at once with a press conference. Reporters and camera crews were swarming at the gate, demanding entrance only minutes after I left. I should have expected it and hung around, I guess, but I'd never been involved in a murder at a movie studio before. Who had? They'd interviewed the cops in front of the Post Production Building and got nothing, of course—they never do—and now it was up to us to speak in turn for the studio and the production. That was why Hans-Dieter had gathered the three of us there in front of the lights. All in all, I had to admit that it was probably the best way to handle it.

Except for Norbert Wiggins. The guy was absolutely tongue-tied. It was his idea to bring me in on it. That's why he'd called me up in a panic and told me to get over in ten minutes. He must have had some sense that he might need help. But how could he know in advance that he would be struck catatonic at the first question?

TV reporter: "Are you assuming, Chief Wiggins, that this is an isolated incident, or is there a possibility there's a serial killer at large here at the studio?"

Wiggins: "Uh, uh, well, uh . . ."

More than his failure to speak, it was the look of absolute desperation in his eyes that alerted me to imminent disaster. So when he suddenly thrust the microphone to me, I was almost ready for it. Anyway, I started talking fast.

"What the chief is getting at," I said, "is that we're not assuming anything. The actual investigation of the homicide is, of course, in the hands of the police. It's up to us in the meantime to keep things running smoothly and safely—I emphasize *safely*—here at the studio."

Trib reporter: "Will you be adding to the security force?"

I glanced over at Wiggins and half offered the microphone back to him in a kind of furtive gesture. But he still had that look in his eye. I could tell I was on my own.

"That shouldn't be necessary." I said it just as firmly as I might have if I had known what I was talking about. "We've got a completely professional force here. Numbers matter less than quality."

Then there were about three or four questions tossed out at once from various sources. I seized upon one I thought I understood. "Will the security force be armed? Is that the question?" There was a grunt of assent from beyond the lights, so I continued: "That's Chief Wiggins option. All of them are licensed for weapons and trained in their use." I hoped that was true. It sounded pretty good, anyway.

And that was how it went. They asked the questions, and I manufactured answers right on the spot. I knew from watching "Eyewitness News" that it wasn't so much what you said that was important, just that you said it smoothly and with an air of confidence. Style over substance, form over content. A man could get to be president that way.

Finally there was a pause, and a female reporter—she turned out to be from Channel 7—stepped up in front of her Minicam and spoke into her microphone.

"Was that a question?" I asked.

"That was a question," she said.

"What was it?"

"I asked if there were any plans to shut down the production."

"That's not something that either I or Chief Wiggins can answer. That's up to Donny Emmett here. Donny?" I'd never met the man, but naturally we were on first-name basis. This was Hollywood, after all.

I handed over the microphone to him. He took it and cradled it for a moment in his two big hands, and at last began speaking in a deep, commanding voice. "You know," he began, "there's something ironic, *suitably* ironic, in the fact that that violence should visit us during the shooting of this motion picture, this picture that seeks to re-create that terribly violent era of our recent past. We thought we'd left it all behind us, didn't we? But no. It's come back to haunt us, hasn't it?"

He paused dramatically and swept the cameras slowly with his eyes. I had to hand it to him. It was a real performance, dramatic in the best sense, almost charismatic.

Then he continued: "It looks like a lot of that old hate is still around. The vicious, virulent hate that was directed against the Woodstock generation, the hate that kept that awful war going, the hate that ultimately killed Tommy Osborne—that hate has now revisited us two decades later.

"Someone—or some crazy extremist group—doesn't want this picture about Tommy Osborne and his generation to be made. But I promise you, this picture *will* be made. If I'm the next one to go, well, I've already designated my successor. And he's just as determined as I am that *Cold Wind* will be in theaters across the nation by Christmas."

Emmett sent a hard look into the cameras. "That's all," he

said. Then, with just a glance, he tossed the microphone to me. Lucky thing I happened to be looking his way. He jumped off the stage, shouldered his way through the cameras, and strode off down the center aisle of the screening room. Nobody pursued him. They just stood and stared.

Holy shit! Emmett had just as good as accused some nameless neo-Nazi terrorist group of murdering a sound editor in order to shut down the picture. Film at eleven!

The lights shut off. The camera crews were rushing to pack up. The reporters were talking among themselves. I turned and handed the microphone to Wiggins.

"Oh, hey, thanks, Cervantes. I don't know what happened to me. I just—"

"I gotta run," I called to him, moving away. "I'll talk to you later."

I jumped off the stage but found it a lot tougher getting through the twisting knot of technicians than Emmett had a minute before.

"How do you spell your name?" a reporter asked as I pushed past.

"Like *Don Quixote.*"

"Huh?"

Another one: "You're a private detective. Are you on the case, too?"

"I'm a security consultant for the studio."

Finally, I managed to work my way through the bunch and hurried down the aisle in pursuit of Emmett. He was nowhere in sight, of course. I rushed through the little anteroom that served as a lobby. Then I was out the door and looking up and down the studio street. No sign of Emmett. He had to be heading back to the soundstage, so I took off that way at a run, turned a corner, and spotted him moving along at a pretty good pace fifty yards ahead.

"Emmett!" I called. "Hey, Emmett, wait!"

He turned, looked back, not much more than a glance, and kept on. So I started running again. Then he surprised me by stopping and taking another look. Standing with hands on hips, he stood and waited for me.

When I reached him at last, puffing a little, he gave me a grin and said, "Hey, sorry. I didn't recognize you at first."

"I just wanted to talk to you for a minute."

"Sure," he said, "I just didn't want to talk to any of those reporters." I could understand that. What did seem funny to me was that his attitude seemed to have altered drastically during the hundred yards or so he had walked from the screening room. He seemed oddly relaxed. As he started walking again, he moved along at not much more than an amble. "You were pretty good up there," he said to me. "Great cool. You've got a future in public relations."

"Yeah, well, thanks, I guess. What I wanted to talk to you about was what you said back there about somebody, maybe some group, killing Worley to stop the production."

"You want to talk about that? Sure, I'll talk about it."

"Well . . ." For a moment I didn't know quite what to ask. But I plunged in: "Do you have something to base that on? Were there any threats? Anonymous letters? Or . . ." I hesitated again. "Is it just a theory?"

"Just a theory."

"Well, you sounded pretty sure up there. Have you passed this on to the cops?"

He smiled, something between amusement and sympathetic indulgence, I guess you'd say. "The cops have their own theory. And to tell you the truth, I happen to think it's a pretty good one."

"Wait a minute. You came out with this idea about a right-wing plot, and you don't even believe it yourself?"

"I think it's a possibility, don't you?"

"Well, sure. It's a possibility. These days anything is."

He stopped then and looked at me seriously. "Cervantes— that's your name, isn't it? Cervantes?"

"Yeah, that's right."

"Let me ask you, just how much have you had to do with the picture business?"

"Not a whole lot."

"Well, you work for the studio, so I'll put it plain to you. I've got a problem because I have to get a new music editor.

64

But you know what I did just now? I turned that problem into an advantage. I sold tickets up there. When that film goes on the air tonight people are going to be pissing in their pants to see this movie somebody got killed for. We've got controversy now. And I personally believe there's nothing that sells tickets like controversy."

"But," I said, "but the guy who was killed—"

"The guy who was killed," he said, speaking slowly, giving instruction, "was a music editor. If you wanted to stop, or at least slow down, a production like this, that's one of the places you'd hit. Worley was a key player."

"But you don't believe that was the plan? You personally don't believe that's why Worley was killed?"

"Fuck, no!" We'd started walking again. He began gesturing—short, choppy moves that made it look like he was hitting the air. "Listen, Cervantes, the guy who was killed was a fag. What do you do when a fag gets killed?"

"I don't know. You tell me."

"You look around for the nearest fag. Come on, you used to be a cop, right?"

"Right."

"Well, then you know how they kill each other off. *Crime passionnel.*" He drawled that last two words like they tasted good on his tongue.

"Huh?"

"French. Crime of passion."

"I figured."

"So who's the nearest fag? That creep Beatty. He had access. He 'found' the body." You could hear the quotation marks in Emmett's voice. "Nice coincidence, huh?"

From my talk with Beatty I figured it was just that—a coincidence. "Well, uh, did you tell the cops about this? Is there any motive? Any—"

"I didn't have to tell them. I talked to them. And it was pretty obvious to me they had him fingered for it. You know. You can tell. They give little hints."

"Like what?"

"Nothing specific. You read between the lines. They asked

me about him. Well, they asked me about Worley, too. How I happened to hire them. Stuff like that."

"Well, how *did* you happen to hire them?"

"They came recommended. But listen, you know what Beatty tried to do? He tried to put the cops on me. He tried to tell them that I killed Worley, or had it done. Now, why would I do a stupid thing like that? The guy was a key player."

"Because he had AIDS? Because you were afraid he might infect the company?"

"Oh, you talked to the cops too, huh?"

We had reached the door to the soundstage. Emmett stood facing me, hands on hips again, talking down at me from a height about six inches above mine. I hesitated, not because I didn't know what to say but because, as we were talking, a Maserati Quattroporte had appeared and was now inching up, playfully close. It came to a full halt less than a foot from my knee. I could see the driver, a big, ugly guy, was grinning. I looked back at Emmett and noted that he had managed to ignore the car completely. Good trick. The way we were standing, it was just as close to him as it was to me.

Well, if that was the drill, I'd try, too. "No," I said to Emmett, "I didn't talk to the cops, I talked to Beatty."

I heard the door of the Maserati open.

'And he told you that, too, huh? Just as soon as I can find a replacement, he's off the picture."

"Donny, oh, Donny love, we must talk." It came from the car. I glanced over and saw that it wasn't the driver but a tall, lanky guy who had emerged from the back seat, English in dress and accent.

I turned back to Emmett. "But did you say that? Did you think it? I mean, that Worley could infect everybody?"

In just an instant a change came over Emmett's face. It suddenly tightened up. But it was his eyes: they went cold and hard and opaque. I was now the enemy. He turned away from me abruptly and strode over to the English guy, his hand outstretched.

"Alex! You've heard about our tragedy on the set." I couldn't see his face, but Emmett's voice was grave.

66

"I have heard," said Alex, "and that's what we must talk about."

"Certainly, certainly. I'd just finished up here with Mr. Cervantes. He's handling the case for the studio."

"Is that so?" Alex looked over in my direction and gave me a nod. "Then I must apologize to you for the little trick we played with the car," he called over to me. "We were just trying to get Donny's attention. That's usually awfully difficult to do." He flashed a smile that was meant to dazzle.

"Apology accepted," I said. "Only, who're you?"

Emmett turned and gave me a cold look. "Mr. Wakefield is the executive producer of the picture."

"Sort of ex officio, you might say, being Tommy Osborne's manager and the executor of his estate in perpetuity. Nice phrase that, in perpetuity. Means forever, more or less."

"I know what it means. I'd like to talk to you."

"In due course, in due course." He gave me a wave. "Right now, I have Donny, and I'm not going to let him go."

With that, Alex Wakefield took Emmett by the shoulder and led him off for a little stroll and a bit of talk that was to be strictly confidential. I watched them go.

The left front door of the Maserati opened, and the driver got out. He wasn't as tall as I'd expected. His legs were short, shorter than mine. But they supported a massive trunk with sloping shoulders, a big chest, and an even bigger belly. The loose jacket he wore disguised none of this. His face was big and blotchy. He wore a drooping mustache and a sour look.

"Hey," the driver said to me, "you heard what he said. Later." He gestured with his head, just a short jerk to the right.

I wasn't in a position to argue the point, especially not with him.

Casimir was on the telephone. He spent a lot of time on the telephone these days. This was about the third call he'd had to take since I'd sat down in his office ten minutes before. Just when we'd start to talk, his secretary would call out the name of the caller. Once when he said, "Tell him I'll call back," she replied, "You better take this one. Trust me." So he trusted her and took it. He seemed to be talking to agents all the time. Most of the time it was just, "Yes. Yes. Sure. Sure. Just send it by messenger over." Which was the way they taught him to say it in Hamtramck. But once he cut a guy off: "No auctions. Majestic Pitchers is not in the business to do auctions." He got off the line then, shook his head and said, "Jeez, it never stops." And then the phone rang again in the outer office.

When I had left Donny Emmett—or rather, when he left me—I walked over to the Post Production Building to see what I could find out there. Not much. There were a couple of uniform cops still in front. I showed them my studio security card and talked my way past. Climbing the stairs, I tried to decide which questions to ask, which questions I was allowed to ask. Working this end of an investigation was new to me.

There was another uniform cop in front of Post Production 73. I didn't try to get past him. I just held up my studio security ID and looked over his shoulder inside the room. The body had been removed, its position marked out in chalk on the floor. The crime-scene squad, three of them, were still there, getting in each other's way as they went over the room inch by inch. That couldn't be much fun.

Nobody around. Detective Warnecky was probably off someplace still asking questions. As for the other guy . . . I shrugged and started back for the stairs.

"Hey, you. Come here."

I turned and looked down the hall. It was the other guy. The good cop. Only by now he looked frazzled and disheveled and not that much different from the bad cop. His blazer was off. His shirt was wrinkled. His blond hair was matted with sweat. That's what four hours of questioning will do to you. He swung his arm in my direction and, just so there'd be no mistake, said, "Yeah. You."

I walked back to him. He was standing outside an empty office, his arms folded, waiting.

"I thought Warnecky told you to take a walk."

"I took a walk."

"But now you're back."

"That's right."

"Why?"

I sighed. "Look," I said, "I came back to find out what I could about how the investigation's going. From what you're showing me, I don't think I'm going to find out shit about that. But I just want you to know one thing. I represent the studio in this. And the studio has got a right to know what's going on. If I have to go behind your back, I'll go behind your back, but I'm going to keep my people informed."

"We can pull your license," he said, not loud, not a threat, just a reminder.

"Probably not. But maybe. But anyway, I'd still be working for the studio, and it's still my job to keep them informed." I sighed. This was such a lot of shit to get through, wasn't it? "So, here we are," I said to him, starting over again. "Have you anything to report about the progress of your investigation, Detective—Detective—?"

"Pell. Detective Pell. No, I have not, Mr.—Mr.—?"

"Cervantes. Antonio Cervantes. Su servidor. Well, then, thank you. I believe our interview is at an end." I nodded with exaggerated politeness, turned, and headed back for the stairs.

But I'd only gone a little way when he called after me, "Hey, Cervantes." I turned and looked back but kept right on walking. "Be cool, Cervantes." And he gave me a grin. It was probably the most fun he'd had all day.

But that was then and this was now, and here I was, sitting across from Casimir, just waiting for him to get off the phone. At last he managed to do just that. He banged the receiver down in the cradle and yelled, "No more calls, Lorraine. I don't give a shit. No more calls!"

Lorraine appeared at the door, purse in hand. "I'm going home, Caz. Just don't pick up. Let it ring." She smiled at both of us. She had buckteeth but looked pretty good anyway. "Good night," she said, then disappeared.

For a moment we listened to her stiletto heels, click-click-clicking down the hall. Then Casimir sighed and said, "Where were we at?"

"I was telling you about the homicide over in postproduction."

"Oh, yeah. A disaster, huh? The only picture we got in production. Now this."

"Not a disaster," I said, trying to sound confident for his sake. "This guy, the director, Donny Emmett, he seems to have things pretty well under control. What he doesn't have under control is himself."

Then I told Casimir about the bombshell Emmett had dropped just a little while ago at the press conference, his conspiracy theory, and how he didn't even believe it himself. When I'd finished on the facts, I didn't know what to add as commentary, so I just said, "I think you'd better tell Ursula to take a look at the eleven o'clock news."

"Yeah, I will," he said, "if I see her before then." He sounded pretty unhappy.

"Not much time together, huh?"

"No."

"Well, she's got a lot of responsibility. This is the big time."

"Yeah, and I'm pretty busy, too. But it's all this bullshit on the telephone. I'm supposed to read scripts, but I don't even have time for that. I didn't know it would be like this."

"Second thoughts, huh?"

"No. Not yet. It just takes getting used to, I guess."

"I guess."

The phone rang in the outer office. Both of us looked at the row of lights on his phone and saw that the first of them had lit up.

It rang again. Casimir said, "Oh, shit," and picked it up, disgusted with himself for doing so. He gave a gruff hello and listened for a moment. Then he handed it over to me without a word.

"Yeah? This is Cervantes."

"This is Warnecky. You remember me? Wiggins thought you might be at this office, this guy Urbanski—used to be LAPD. Right? So now I know where you are. You know where I am?"

"No, Detective Warnecky. Where, are, you?" I wasn't in the mood to play games just then.

"I'm at the domicile of the deceased," he said. "Worley's, over in West Hollywood. I just came to take a look around. And you know what? Two things strike me as very interesting here."

"Yeah? What two things?"

"Okay. Number one, the place has been broken into. Number two, the house was obviously occupied by two people, and the second party isn't here anymore. Just fucking vanished. You know anything about this?"

"Not a thing, Detective."

"You better be straight with me, Cervantes. I'm going to ask around the area, and if anybody's seen anybody who looked like you around today, then I'll jerk you in to Hollywood Division faster than you can fly. You got that?"

"I've got that."

Neither one of us said good-bye. I think we hung up on each other.

Was I worried? Uneasy that Warnecky might locate somebody who had spotted me there a couple of hours ago? Of course I was.

Eight

"Chico?"

"Yes, Chiquita?" I was sitting by the telephone, drumming the table in frustration, wondering what to do next. I had tried the two names I'd copied out from Worley's address book. Jack Kayman was a complete washout. A woman answered. I asked for Kayman. Nobody by that name there. I checked the number with her. I'd dialed it right. It was obviously out of date. Kayman had moved, and the number had been reassigned. Something like that. I had thanked her and hung up.

"I think you like to help me a little bit with this script?" Alicia was smiling at me from across the room. She was giving me her most persuasive smile. Then she patted the seat on the sofa next to her. Who could resist?

Well, I could try. "I need to think about things for a minute," I told her.

"A minute, eh?"

"Well, maybe two." Henry Claessens was a possibility. The number I dialed to reach him put me through to a gay bar on Santa Monica Boulevard, Rico's. It was evidently the bartender who had answered the phone. Like bartenders everywhere, he was rushed, and he tried to get off the phone just as quickly as he could. All I managed to do was get in a question about Claessens—was he there. "Maybe later on," said the bartender and hung up.

I glanced at my watch. It was nearly ten o'clock. The independent station that had sent a camera crew to the studio would be coming on soon. Their coverage would duplicate the others, and I could catch it an hour earlier. Then maybe I'd go out and see if I was able to locate Claessens. I could only hope he was the mysterious Clay, ponytail and all.

"No more two minutes," said Alicia. "It's gone."

"Okay," I said, "but just until the news comes on—agreed?" I got up and walked over. I sat down next to her on the sofa.

She nodded. "Okay."

"What have you got in mind?"

"I have in mind we read the script. I play Lupe—tha's my character. And you play everybody else. Okay?"

"I guess so. Let's try it."

She snuggled up close, making the situation sort of pleasant . . . for the moment. But listen, if you think television looks bad on that glass screen, you ought to see it on the printed page. Or the Xeroxed page.

But I'm getting ahead of myself. Actually, I gave it a good shot, even made up a little intro music for the show. You know, the usual Pat Williams stuff—"Lupe! Bopadah—Bopadah! Beep—beep! Lupe. Bopadah—bopadah! Beep—beep!" This broke her up. She laughed until tears filled her big eyes, then she wiped them dry and punched me on the arm less than playfully.

"Come on, Chico," she scolded. "Thees is serious beezness."

"Oh! Serious sitcom—a new form. You think America is ready for it?"

"Come on."

"Okay, okay."

So we got started, more or less. I tried doing funny voices, but a fierce look from her made it plain I'd better play it straight. I could see she needed some work with the script: she had to have help with some words. But after we repeated a line a couple of times and she had it down, she could put real energy into it. She was doing it all with her ear, listening to herself, changing inflections, then—wham!—she delivered.

All I can say is, she was doing pretty well, a lot better than I expected, but the script was going from bad to worse. Oh, there were some laughs in it. This guy Arnie Gresham knew his trade. But the situation was simply ridiculous. Get this: here she is, Lupe, water still dripping from her back, and she shows up at a branch of the State of California Employment Development Department. Well, she talks with the people in line, and this is okay, I guess, some funny stuff, but nobody, not even the mamacita who's there just to pick up her unemployment check, even hints she might be in the wrong place.

But then we came to the part where Lupe talks to the counselor, and I started arguing with Alicia. The counselor, Anglo, has a tough exterior but a heart of gold—well, high-grade silver, anyway. She decides that even though Lupe is obviously an illegal immigrant—has no documentation, no green card, no nothing—that even so, maybe just this once she'll bend the rules a little. Hijo la! Come *on!* "This could never happen," I tell her.

"Maybe it could."

"No way! Forget it!"

We go back and forth like this a couple of times, and finally Alicia folds her arms and says very coldly, "Chico, it don' matter if it could happen or it couldn'. Eees in the scrip'!" Which is probably what Arnie Gresham himself would have told me if he was sitting here on the sofa beside us.

I threw up my hands in exasperation at that and as they dropped back down on my knees, I happened to glance at my watch. We were ten minutes into the news. I jumped over to the television without a word and switched it on. Even before an image filled the screen, what should I hear but my own voice, a little thicker and deeper than I thought it was, coming out of the speaker. And suddenly there I was in living color, telling all of Los Angeles that members of the Majestic Pictures security force were licensed for firearms and trained in their use.

74

"Chico," said Alicia in a hushed voice, "that's you." I turned and found her staring awestruck at the screen.

They cut the rest of my Q and A. There was an awkward jump in which I was saying something but nothing was heard. Instead we got the voice of the reporter—squeaky female—preparing us for what was to come: "Then studio spokesman Cervantes handed over the microphone to director Donny Emmett, who stunned reporters with a startling revelation."

And there was Emmett, cupping the mike meditatively, adding to the drama of the moment.

"I heard of him," Alicia whispered behind me. "He's beeg director. You know him?"

"I talked to him. Shhh."

And then Emmett went into his act. I have to hand it to him. Even knowing it was all bullshit, I was pretty impressed. The pauses were dramatic. The rising intensity of his indignation was totally believable. It was a real performance, all right—Academy all the way.

Then we saw him jump off the stage, and there was a quick cut to the news set and the reporter speaking into the camera: "And then he walked out, leaving us all to wonder."

"A lot to wonder about, Lucy," said the male anchor. "Murder at the film studio . . . and the ghost of decades past."

"Sounds like it would make a heck of a movie," the female anchor agreed. Then, into the camera: "Next up, Olvera Street prepares for the Day of the Dead . . . after these messages." A commercial came on. I went over and switched off the set.

"Oh, no, Chico, leave it on," Alicia cried. "Maybe they'll have you on again."

"Nope. That's all. If you want to see it again, they'll have it on the network channels at eleven."

"Thees eez really exciting, Chico. That's a pretty big murder you got, huh?"

"Pretty big."

"Well, who dunned it?"

"Did it," I corrected her.

"Okay, did it. Who did?"

"Who knows? Maybe that guy you just saw."

"You think so?"

"He's as good a bet as anybody right now," I said. And even though I didn't for a minute buy Beatty's theory, what I said was true: Emmett was as likely a suspect as the mysterious Clay, or even Beatty himself right now. Which meant, of course, that there were no suspects. I had to go out and find one.

What hit me with a big *swack* when I started into the place was a solid wall of sound—dance music, I guess, only nobody was dancing. You could hear some shouted lyrics and once in a while a guitar lick, but mostly it was just rhythm—a fast chuck-uh-chuck-uh-chuck-uh with an even faster counter-rhythm beating over it, under it, and all around. The kind of stuff they do with programmed drum machines today.

I didn't walk through the wall, but plunged into it, a dark, thick viscous sort of atmosphere, smoke-filled, crowded with bodies along the bar, swaying to that driving chuck-uh-chuck-uh-chuck-uh beat. I worked my way through them, pushing farther, looking for an empty bar stool without ever finding one. There was an empty space at the bar, though. I grabbed it and waved the bartender over.

Right away I had an argument with him because they didn't have Dos Equis and he tried to sell me Corona, like where it came from was all that mattered. I settled for Heineken, and as he went off to get it. I turned around and took the place in.

It was split in two by a half-wall. Beyond it there were tables and in the far corner a couple of big industrial-strength speakers on a little platform where all that chuck-uh-chuck-uh was coming from. And there was a pool table pretty close by, top-lit, the single strong source of light in the whole interior. Even so, the place didn't seem sinister. Murky, yes. Sinister, no. There were a couple of guys standing behind me against the half-wall who smiled automatically as my eyes grazed them. They were available. But practically everybody along the bar and at the tables seemed to be clustered in groups of three or four or more, shouting loud to be heard above the rhythmic din. There was a little cheek-kissing, some shoulder-squeezing, but nothing heavier. You might say it was like any other bar in town, except it was more crowded than most, and it was, well, a little friendlier. And, oh, yeah—there wasn't a female face or form in sight.

The bartender came back and slammed the bottle of Heineken down on the bar. I laid down a twenty and said, "You can keep the change if you'll point out Henry Claessens to me.

"Hank?"

"I guess so. Yeah."

"You a cop?"

"No." Not the way he meant, anyway.

He looked at me for a moment, sizing me up. I guessed I passed muster, because he nodded and pointed behind me into the next room. "Over there," he said.

I turned and looked into the far corner, but I couldn't see anybody. Turning back to the bartender, I saw him starting away. "Where?" I called after him.

"Behind the speakers," he yelled back.

With a shrug, I picked up the Heineken, socked back a gulp, and wandered over past the pool table just in time to see a golden-haired beachboy lay the cue ball into the corner pocket, worked my way through the tables, and headed for the speakers. The closer I got, the louder the din. But then, too, the closer I got, the more it seemed like music. The basic beat had changed to a kind of chuck-uh-chuch-chuck-uh-chuh with counterrhythm on top of that. But I could actually make out some phrases from the shouted lyrics "Hey, baby . . . dancing with you," and so on, what passes for Ira Gershwin these days.

I stepped up onto the platform where the speakers were mounted and finally caught sight of Henry Claessens behind them. He was the house deejay, the man who kept the joint jumping with a continuous beat. Claessens was rocking to it himself there behind the turntables, in a kind of a dance trance. He paid no attention to me; that gave me a chance to pay some to him.

I decided he couldn't be the guy Eduardo had described— not unless Claessen had got a haircut, shaved off his mustache, and had his fingers straightened in the past couple of days. This guy also looked like he would have been about five years old in the sixties. But gays fool you that way: they stay younger longer; if they've got a secret, I don't want to know it.

He caught me staring at him. The look he returned was downright suspicious. He yelled something at me.

I couldn't get it because of the music, so I pointed at my ears and shrugged.

He leaned forward from the control board and yelled again, even louder this time: "No requests. This is my show!" He was still dancing.

In answer to that—some kind of shorthand, I guess—I just hollered out to him, "Jimmy Worley!"

Claessens looked at me strangely. I guess he hadn't seen anything about it on the news.

So I yelled, "He's dead. Murdered."

I could see the shock in his eyes—and then some sort of comprehension: he understood why I was there. All he said in answer was, "He gave me tapes."

That was their relationship. I could buy that. I shrugged and nodded. Then I waved my thanks and started away. Glancing back as I stepped off the platform. I saw that Claessens had stopped dancing. Well, what the hell. It was probably the shortest interview I'd ever conducted, but I found out—well, I found out zip, zero, nothing, but at least I'd gone through the motions. I'd have to be satisfied with that. I took another swig of beer and picked my way through the crowd to my place at the bar. It had been taken. So I reached over somebody's shoulder and put the bottle of Heineken back on the bar, still half full. Then I pushed away and started working my way toward the door.

About halfway there a hand gripped my arm, and a voice shouted my name in my ear.

It was Tom Beatty. He seemed to be alone there, and he looked pretty unhappy.

"I should have taken your advice," he said right into my ear.

"I heard something about it—from Emmett," I said.

"That cunt. I was going to do it just like you said, you know, and keep my theory to myself. But this big detective— oh, he was disgusting—he began making a big thing of the fact that I'd found Jimmy's body. Like *I'd* killed him. So when this other detective came in, and he seemed pretty reasonable, I told him about Jimmy and Emmett, and what Emmett had said and all. Well, the big one, the one who smoked those nasty cigars, he was right there, and he seemed to think I'd just told this about Emmett to, you know, divert suspicion, and he began asking me these terrible questions about me and Jimmy, like we'd had a lovers' quarrel or something. Jimmy and I were *never* like that, friends but never that. It just wasn't there. And then the other detective—"

I turned my ear away and stopped him. "Look," I told him, "you've just had bad cop–good cop played on you. It's the oldest dodge there is. Probably perfected by the Romans."

He nodded and looked down, and then he said something like, "I suppose so." Or I think that's what he said. It was pretty hard to hear in there.

"Don't worry. They didn't book you. They didn't even take you down to the station."

"But I'm a suspect!" He fairly shouted it. The guy next to Beatty turned around and looked at him curiously. "I believe I'm actually a suspect."

I signaled for him to keep his voice down. Then I leaned into his ear and said, "At this point everybody is. But listen, who recommended Worley for this job? For that matter, who recommended you?"

He pulled away and looked at me like he was annoyed. Was it annoyance or was he uneasy? "I told you," he said, "Jimmy was the best in the business, and I'm pretty good myself. We're known in the industry."

I spoke into his ear again: "Right, right, got you. But one more thing. Do you know—or did Worley ever speak of a guy named Clay, or maybe Cray?"

"No," he said. But he said it a little too quick. I looked at him, wasn't convinced by what I saw, and decided we'd better go over this again. But not here.

I nodded and gave him a touch on the arm. "Later," I said. Then I started for the door again. It was interesting that he hadn't asked me what I was doing there. For all he knew, I could be following him. Or maybe he just assumed that . . . Well, never mind.

It was a relief to get out on the street and away from that driving rhythm. Oh, you could still hear it, but at least you weren't breathing it, swallowing it with your beer. At least you could hear other things, too.

Like that car that pulled up at the curb behind me. What did I hear? Not that whispering engine but the tires crackling against refuse in the gutter.

I turned and saw that it was a Maserati Quattroporte. Well, there aren't very many of those around, even in Los Angeles, so I wasn't a bit surprised when Alex Wakefield popped out of the backseat. He didn't see me at first, and I didn't step forward. I expected him to go inside, and I thought I might follow him in to see if this was just a night on the town, or if maybe he had come to meet Tom Beatty.

Then I made my mistake. I started to turn around, so as not to show my face. The movement I made must have drawn his attention to me.

"Mr. Cervantes! Well, well, well. The proverbial bad penny."

"Oh . . . uh . . . yeah," fumbling, caught out, "the executive producer."

"Wakefield. Alex Wakefield."

"Sure. Sorry."

"Think nothing of it." Then he stretched his lips and gave me another one of those dazzlers. "Imagine meeting you here of all places."

"I just stopped in for a beer. I live in the neighborhood." When would I learn to keep my mouth shut? I noticed that the Incredible Hulk had just squeezed out from behind the wheel and was rocking over in our direction.

80

"My," said Wakefield, "in the neighborhood. Isn't that convenient?"

"You said we might talk."

"Not now. Sorry."

"When?"

"You *are* persistent, aren't you? Well, why not? Come to my office nine-forty-five tomorrow. At nine-forty-five sharp, mind. I've a busy day tomorrow."

"Okay, but where?"

"Nine thousand Sunset."

"I know the building."

"Everybody does. Till then." With that, he turned away and headed into the bar.

I made just the slightest move to follow and immediately found my way blocked by the Incredible Hulk, droopy mustache, big belly, and all. He had bad breath, like he had a lot of cavities and each one was filled with a bit of rotting beef.

"You heard what the man said." He tried to smile, but it didn't quite work. The corners of his mouth went up, but nothing happened to the rest of his face.

"Yeah, nine-forty-five."

"Be there."

There was no getting around him, even if I wanted to. And at this point, I didn't need to see Wakefield actually talking to Beatty. I was pretty sure that was why he was there. So I just shrugged and walked away.

But when I got home I went straight to the place I'd tucked away Worley's address book. I looked in the *W*s, and there he was—Alex Wakefield, the 9000 Sunset address, and below that, one in Bel Air. In the margin there were also some interesting notes. I'd have to ask Dorrie, the barmaid at Barney's, to interpret them for me. She seemed to be a lot better informed than I was.

Nine

Nine thousand Sunset is a monolith of cement and black-tinted glass standing out near the end of the strip. There really isn't much to say about it, except that it's there, dwarfing the one-, two-, and three-story buildings around it by ten stories or so, a standing provocation to the big earthquake that all the seismologists predict for Los Angeles. It's built on a hill, as are all the buildings on that side of Sunset. If it toppled down, the wreck of it would cover a city block and leave agents and independent producers scattered all over the hillside. And maybe an artists' manager or two.

I had no trouble finding Alex Wakefield's listing on the building directory. It was there, cross-referenced to Marl-borough Management. I took the elevator up, found the right door, and glanced at my watch. It was 9:43. Satisfied, I walked right in and up to the receptionist's desk.

She was a black-rooted blonde, also a Brit—pretty enough, but judging by the way she brayed out her "G'mawning," I placed her a couple of rungs down from Wakefield on their social ladder.

I told her I had an appointment with her boss at 9:45. She told me to take a seat. I took a seat.

It was a good-sized reception area with chairs, a sofa, and the inevitable coffee table piled high with industry trade papers and copies of *Rolling Stone*. I picked up a *Stone* and began thumbing through it. Before I was more than a few pages into it, something struck me about the cover. Looking back, I saw that yes, it was the latest issue, all right, but what was interesting about it was the face on the cover. It was a big composite photo. The right side was Tommy Osborne's and the picture must have been taken about 1968; the left side belonged to Ted McCoy, the guy who was playing Osborne in *Cold Wind*. I guess it was meant to show how much the two resembled each other. And, yes, I guess their features were pretty similar. There was a kind of basic family look there, but if you looked at the two eyes, you saw that there could really be no mistaking these two for one. McCoy looked angry. Osborne looked crazy.

There was a big package inside on the movie in production—with lots of pictures of Donny Emmett looking serious on the set—an interview with the young star, and a long article on what they headlined "The Tommy Osborne Phenomenon." For some reason, maybe because I remembered Osborne pretty well for the sixties, I was interested enough to read about him. And as I read, I realized how little I knew about the guy.

What I remembered was the voice—deep, resonant, and fully adult at a time when adolescent tenors were in style. There was something irrational, threatening, almost dangerous in that voice, and that was the Osborne image: *The cocksman from hell! Hide your daughters, or I'll rape them all!* That was his message to the world, at least as interpreted by the media. He dressed in black leather, sometimes wore a black cape, and never, never smiled. At a time when every rock group in America was preaching revolution, Osborne's brand of revolt was strictly Freudian.

He was a phenomenon, all right, but what they were talking about in *Rolling Stone* was his posthumous revival. Big before he died, he was even bigger today. There were die-hard fans who kept his memory alive, deejays who played the "classic Osborne" sides, but when previously unreleased material began to pour out a few years back, he suddenly became Top 40 material again. The generation that had grown up since his

83

death discovered him, and they liked what they heard. The *Garage Tapes* album had gone gold and had received a Grammy, and now, with the making of *Cold Wind* (the title of his biggest hit, of course), he seemed to be headed for that celebrity Valhalla where he would rub elbows with Marilyn Monroe and James Dean.

And who should be given major credit for pulling all this off? Why, none other than Alex Wakefield. I struggled through a few paragraphs of self-congratulation quoted from the man himself. Then I got on to the part I was interested in—a quick trip through the short life of Tommy Osborne. Basically, he was a kid from Detroit who'd had a bad childhood. (Sound familiar?) The writer managed to get it across that his mother was a hooker without actually saying so. She wound up in a state mental institution. But his unknown father must have had some sort of musical talent in the DNA he passed on to the kid, because something sure happened to Tommy Osborne when his voice changed. He began singing and writing—without ever really knowing music at all. He was a natural. And a natural poet, too. The writer quoted a couple of verses of a lyric he had written at seventeen. It was kind of a surrealiastic jumble, but it was the real thing, you could tell, and not too much different from the wild verses he chanted before the cheering few hundred thousand at Woodstock. By that time the group he had formed in Detroit, the DMZ, had become Tommy Osborne and the DMZ. Finally, just an album before his death, it was simply Tommy Osborne—with who? a bunch of studio musicians? I wondered what had happened to the original group.

Most of the conflict in his young life had been with authority—starting with teachers and disciplinarians in high school, leading inevitably to arrests afterward, most of them for assault, including sexual. There were rumors of rape charges that had been hushed up and probably bought off, once he made it big. When he toured, the local cops crowded him. And he did all he could to provoke them, including exposing himself and masturbating onstage. He was dragged off by the cops, as the writer put it, "still waving in the wind." That

84

became, for a lot of kids, the ultimate act of rebellion. It happened in Cincinnati. If it had happened, say, in Houston, it would have been the ultimate act of suicide. Out on bail, he went into seclusion in some secret retreat in northern California with just his true love Rachel for company. He quit touring, recorded that last album, then nearly a year later died in a spectacular flaming wreck on a steep mountain road high up in the Cascades, his car plunging four hundred feet to total destruction. That was in 1971. He was twenty-five years old.

I was just getting to the end of the article—"It's time to ask not just who Tommy Osborne was but what he meant to his generation . . ." etc.—when I realized that it must be getting pretty late. I looked at my watch. It was nearly five to ten. Tossing the magazine aside, I went back to the receptionist. "Look," I said, "Mr. Wakefield was pretty emphatic that I be here at a quarter to ten. At least let him know I'm here, will you?"

"Can't do that, love."

"Why not?"

"He's not in yet."

I threw up my hands in annoyance and turned back to my station on the sofa. But before I'd quite gotten settled, Alex Wakefield came bustling through the door, shouting orders to the receptionist: "Try to get Donny Emmett at the studio! Don't let them put you off this time! Tell them—" That's when he became aware of me standing there. He stopped and looked, unable for a moment to remember why I was there. Finally: "You! My God, I'd forgotten completely about you."

"You said nine-forty-five."

"Yes, yes, of course." He looked at his watch. "Well, we've a few minutes. Come along." He gave me a quick wave and led the way past the receptionist, through what turned out to be a rather small outer office decorated with event posters and album covers going all the way back to the sixties. Just outside an open door with his name on it sat a young man with his booted feet propped up on a desk. He was slender and sharp-featured, and had the blondest hair I'd ever seen, darned near white. Sipping coffee thoughtfully from a mug, he barely looked up as Wakefield approached. "Hi, Alex." He smiled distantly.

Wakefield slapped at the blond guy's boots as he went by. "Get your feet down and at least try to look busy, won't you?"

The only signs of real activity in the place came from a partitioned space at the far corner where two women worked, one at a typewriter and the other at a computer. Both of them were frowning in concentration, looking sort of unhappy.

Wakefield led the way into his office, far wider than it was deep, with a long view south through the smoked glass as far as LAX. He waved to a chair and collapsed into his own behind a big, wide cherrywood desk.

"Would you believe it? That *clown* out there is *supposed* to be my personal secretary." He spoke loud enough for the blond guy to hear. I figured it was for his benefit.

But what the hell. "Would I believe it?" I raised my eyes and put a hand to my chin like I was thinking it over. Then I said, "No, I wouldn't."

He looked at me sharply, then his face relaxed into a crooked smile. "No, of course not, Mr. . . . Mr. . . . ."

"Cervantes."

"Yes, of course. Very literary, eh? Excuse me a moment, won't you?" He picked up the phone and pushed a button. "Gertie," he said, "make us some tea like a good girl, and let me know the moment those young hoodlums arrive." He hung up and gave me the dazzler. "Now, I'm yours for a minimum of five minutes—though I must say I don't understand your part in all this. This is a police matter, isn't it? Currently under investigation?"

"Yes," I said, a little uncomfortably, "it is."

"And I understand you're a private detective. Now, I can't vouch for my source, but I have heard that you fellas aren't supposed to touch anything until the police drop it."

"Well, that's . . . correct, yes, but I'm also security consultant for the studio. Let's say I'm representing their interest in this."

He held back, then nodded. "All right, we'll say that. Go on. Please."

86

I didn't like how this had started out, so I decided to feed his ego a little: *"Rolling Stone* seems to think nobody's ever done a better job of posthumous career management."

"Nicely put. Yes, I daresay that's true. They said it. You said it. So I suppose it's permitted for me to agree. Tommy Osborne is much—oh, *much* bigger today than he was when he was alive. And a good deal less trouble, too, I might add. No, this country is amazing, really, the way they worship the dead. In America, you absolutely can't beat death as a career move."

This wasn't what he'd told *Rolling Stone.* "Did you plan all this? When did you start?"

"When did I start? Why, the moment Tommy fell off that mountain in his Corvette. Look, I'd seen the James Dean thing take shape. I was fascinated by that. I thought, Why couldn't I just go on managing his career, planning publicity and so on, instead of just hoping he might be remembered for a few years? And I knew I had the material to do it."

"Unreleased stuff?"

"Scads of it. I knew that Audiotone was sitting on a ton. I had a good store of my own. And when I went looking, I found even more, a regular treasure trove. So I just kept it coming and built up the legend with each release—articles, the book . . ."

"And now the movie."

"Exactly. Just as I'd planned." He paused then and looked at me curiously. "But I'm sure you didn't come here to talk about this."

"Not really. I am interested, though. I'm also interested in how long you'd known Jimmy Worley."

"Who said I did?"

"Me. I just said it."

"Well." He wiggled his eyebrows at me twice as some sort of signal. "All right, Cervantes, you got me," he said in bad imitation of a B-movie line. "It's true I did know Worley, but not well and not for very long. Less than year, I'd say."

"Did you recommend him to Emmett?"

"As a matter of fact, I did. But only because he's the best in the business. Or was."

"I hear that a lot."

"Because it's true."

"When you recommended him, did you know he had AIDS?"

"Good God!" he exploded. "You've been talking to that little queer Beatty, haven't you? His theory that Emmett had him killed because he was afraid Jimmy might spread it like the measles? Surely you don't believe that."

"Probably not. I was curious whether or not you knew, though."

"All right, all right. No, I did *not* know." He took a moment to cool down, and gave me a long, hard stare. I think this was his version of the look that makes strong men weak. "I fail to see, however," he said, "how any of this should be of any interest to the studio."

I shrugged. "It may not be. But it's of interest to me."

"Well," he said, "then I think—" He was interrupted by a buzz from the telephone. He picked up the receiver almost eagerly and listened a moment. Then he said, "Okay, good. I'll be right out. Just make sure they don't pull out knives and begin cutting up the furniture." He hung up and then jumped up to let me know my time was up.

Reluctantly, I got to my feet. "I don't believe I got that five minutes you guaranteed me."

His shoulders went up and his hands came out in an exaggerated shrug. "As they often say in Hollywood, 'So I lied!'"

Before checking in at the studio, I headed down Hollywood Boulevard for my office. I wanted to see what the mail had brought—that's right, I was looking for a check—and use the telephone. But just on an impulse I took a quick turn down Las Palmas, pulled up at the newsstand there, and bought a copy of the *Rolling Stone* I'd been reading in Wakefield's office. It seemed to me that I might have missed something in that article on Tommy Osborne. Wakefield mentioned a book, too. Maybe I could get hold of that. The more I thought about it, the more I felt that if I knew more about Osborne I might have some of the answers. Like Worley, for instance—maybe

88

he had some earlier connection with Osborne. But if he did, so what? Well, I just had to know more. That was all.

I swung open the door to my office and scooped the mail off the floor. Going through it quickly, I saw that it was just bills and junk. No check. That was another bad thing about divorce clients: they usually pay late, or not at all. By the time they get around to you, the lawyers have had at them, and they're looking to save money any way they can. This guy I'd helped had a prenuptial agreement, so it was worth his while to get the goods on his wife. Well, I should have asked for more money up front. I'm always shy about retainers.

I picked up the telephone and dialed Casimir at the studio. Lorraine put me right through to him.

"Yeah, Chico, what is it? I'm kind of busy right now."

"Okay, okay. But look, Casimir, see if you can get a copy of the madical examiner's report on Worley, will you?"

"Who's he?"

"James Worley. You know. The homicide over in postproduction."

"Oh. Sure."

"I figured you might still have some contacts at the county morgue."

"I know somebody who knows somebody by the morgue. I'll see what I can do."

"That's all I ask."

Next, I dialed Dee Dee's number. There it was in my telephone book. It stood open before me at the *L*s. Dee Dee Lazarus. It was pretty late in the day to reach her if she was working, and I fully expected to have another conversation with her answering machine. I'd spent months talking to her answering machine, months ago. But surprise! She picked up on the second ring. Not, "Hi, this is Dee Dee. If you'll leave your name and number and blah-blah-blah," but a simple, "Hello?" And it was her.

"Hi," I said, "this is Chico."

"Well," she drawled, *"this* is a surprise."

"How've you been?" I did my best to sound casual and

conversational You know—just an old friend calling to catch up.

"Oh, one way and another. I guess you heard."

"Heard? What?"

"The series was canceled. I'm on permanent hiatus."

"Permanent?"

"Well, until I can hook up with another show. Oh, Chico, this damned business! I *fought* my way up on this series. I *pleaded* to be let in on their damned script conferences. Now, just because I kept telling them they had to get relevant material into their stupid bang-bang scripts, just because I got them to *listen* to me once or twice—*now* they're blaming me for the cancellation. Ronnie—you remember Ronnie? the executive producer—he says it's all my fault. 'We had a formula, Dee Dee, we shoulda stuck to it,' he says. *I* changed it, he says. Just like *I*, a measly little *associate producer,* had the power to change anything." She paused, faltered, or maybe she was just catching her breath. Then she sighed and repeated, "Oh, Chico, this damned business. I'll never got another job."

"Sure you will." I meant it to sound encouraging. Maybe I said it a little too fast.

"Maybe as a script girl. Start all over again."

"Well, if you do that, you'll be producing before you know it."

"No I won't," she said glumly. "I can't write. Writers get to be producers."

That was the opening I was looking for. "Oh, yeah, Dee Dee, that reminds me—"

"Chico!" she interrupted. "You remember that idea we used to knock back and forth? A series about *you?* I know I could sell that—even to stupid Ronnie!"

"Oh," I said. "Yeah. Like I always used to say, Dee Dee, I don't have too many adventures."

"That's not what I've been hearing."

"No?" What had she been hearing?

"No. When you went down to Mexico that time, and I didn't hear from you, I started asking around, and the story I got was that you got in some pretty hot stuff down there—

and up here, too. I heard you almost got in big trouble with the DEA."

"Wait a minute," I said. "Where'd you hear all this?"

"Oh, I've got contacts. I also heard you came back with somebody, and that's why I hadn't heard from you. Is that true, Chico?"

Why deny it? "Yeah, that's true. But really, Dee Dee, where'd you hear?"

"You remember a guy named Rossi?"

"You know him?" I liked Rossi, but I didn't like him spreading stories about me, even if they were true. Especially not if they were true.

"I do now."

Well, then, why didn't she hustle him for a series? And then it occurred to me that that's probably what she was doing. That was when I decided this had gone on long enough. No more of this subtle, casual, look-for-an-opening stuff. I'd just hit her over the head with it: "Look, Dee Dee, you know somebody in television named Arnie Gresham?"

"I know *of* him," she said. "He's sitcom. That's a different world entirely."

"But what've you heard about him?"

"Ohhh." She seemed to be reaching back in her memory. "Good writer, if you can stand to watch that stuff. Got his start with Lear, which makes him not so young, but I hear he's not so old either."

And then suddenly she stopped, waited, as though she expected me to say something. But I didn't have anything to say. I wanted her to keep talking.

Then at last she spoke up again: "Why?"

"Come on, Dee Dee, this is just an ordinary inquiry."

"I know you, Chico. You don't make ordinary inquiries. This has got something to do with some case you're working on, hasn't it?"

"More or less." That was really stretching it.

"Really! Arnie Gresham! What do you want to know?"

"I guess basically I want to know if he's on the up-and-up. What's his reputation?"

"Well, I don't know. Pretty good, I guess. He had one series as a producer—'Millie,' about a black maid who really runs the family. It kind of ran out of gas after a couple of seasons."

Uh-huh, I thought, a minority specialist.

"I understand he's got a contract with Majestic Television. Is this the kind of thing you wanted to know? It's all from the trades—but you don't read the trades, do you?"

"Maybe I ought to start." I hesitated, then I went ahead and asked it anyway: "Is he married?"

"I don't know. Look, Chico, I said I didn't know the guy. But maybe I could find out. You know, get a whole file on him. It might be fun."

I didn't like the sound of that. "No, I don't know if that would be such a good idea. Maybe you shouldn't—"

"Sure! It's not like I have anything better to do. Why not? And look, when I find out some stuff, some *real* stuff, we can get together, and we can also talk about *your* series."

Is that what it was going to cost me? "Well," I sighed, "if you start asking questions, don't be too obvious about it."

"Questions like what?"

"Well, is he a womanizer?"

Silence. Then: "Oh, Chico, is this a divorce case?" She sounded terribly disappointed.

"Never mind," I said. "Forget all about it." I meant it. All of a sudden this seemed like a terrible idea. I wished I hadn't called her.

But it was too late: "No, no, it doesn't matter. I'll get right on it. This should be fun."

Reluctantly, I gave her my office number and told her to use that. "Leave a message with the answering service, and I'll get right back to you." She said it shouldn't take more than a day or two, and then, with a short speech about how great it was to hear from me again, she hung up.

And not a moment too soon. After replacing the receiver, I sat for a moment, drumming my fingers on the desk, annoyed at myself. Was I jealous or what? No, I assured myself, I just wanted to make sure this guy Gresham was okay. I didn't want Alicia to get hurt, that was all. Not that I thought there was a chance she'd get the part. I just didn't want him leading her on, getting her hopes up. But what was this all about, anyway? She and I weren't married, hadn't talked about it seriously. When you came down to it, we were just sharing space—she and me and the kid. Alicia was free to go anytime she wanted. With anyone she wanted.

Well, that was enough of that. I rose out of the chair and started around the desk for the door. Then, just as an afterthought, I stepped back and dialed my answering service and asked Evelyn if there were any messages.

"Just one," she said, "around nine-fifty, I've got it, here. Somebody named Eduardo. I could hardly understand him. He was pretty upset and his English wasn't too good either."

"What'd he say?"

"Well, as near as I could tell, he wanted you to come over to the house. You know where that would be?"

"Yeah. He didn't want me to telephone first?"

"No, just come quick."

I glanced at my watch. He'd called almost an hour ago. "Okay, Evelyn, thanks."

I don't know why, but I half expected Detective Warnecky to be waiting for me, chewing on his cigar, when I pulled up in front of Worley's little bungalow in West Hollywood. Guilty conscience, I guess. I knew I shouldn't have gone in there and taken that address book, and he knew I knew.

But no, there it was just about the way I had first seen it the day before, except now there was a police seal across the front door and a notice posted that said the premises were closed pending police investigation. I didn't read it. I knew what it said. I didn't even go up on the porch. If Eduardo was inside, you couldn't tell. The drapes were drawn, and in the windows along the side of the house all the shades had been pulled. I trailed along to the rear, hoping I might find him there.

I didn't see him, but the seal on the back door was torn aside, and the door stood half-open. The panel of glass I had broken had been replaced by a piece of plywood. But another panel had been knocked out. I gave the door a push with my knuckles, and it swung open the rest of the way. Had I been set up? Now I half expected Warnecky to be waiting for me inside. But as I entered the kitchen, I knew I wouldn't find him there or anywhere else in the house.

The place was a mess, a total shambles. It was like a bomb had exploded in the middle of the room, some kind of clean blast that destroyed nothing but tossed the contents of the whole room out onto the floor. Knives, forks, spoons, canned goods, pots, pans littered the linoleum tile. Cups and plates, some of them broken, were down there, too. Drawers of cooking utensils had been upended and then tossed aside. The refrigerator had been pulled out, and its door hung open. Even Eduardo's Tamayo-style miniatures had been ripped from the wall and thrown on the floor.

I waded through and over the shifting clutter and into the dining area that connected onto the living room. The dining area wasn't so bad. There wasn't that much to turn over there. But the living room was the worst yet. The stereo had been ripped apart. The television and VCR had been opened up, and parts were scattered on the floor. Worst of all was the furniture. The pillows had been torn apart. The cotton and kapok stuffing strewn, the frames of the sofas and chairs cut and gutted. I'd seen places tossed a couple of times before, but I'd never known this kind of systematic destruction. As I stood there looking around, I didn't know quite what to feel—disgust, or maybe awe at the cold fury that must have gone into all this. Then I became aware of sounds behind me, a kind of hiccup followed by a groan.

I knew the room they had come from. I walked over to the door I had crashed through the afternoon before and pushed it open. Eduardo sat there on a folding chair in the middle of the room, surrounded by his broken easel and three or four ripped canvases. One of them I recognized as the nearly abstract desert scene that had hung in the living room. Tubes of paint had been emptied and smeared on the walls, brushes broken and tossed down on the floor.

He looked up at me, and I saw that he was crying. The

94

hiccup was a sob. The groan was a groan. "You see?" he managed to get out. "You see what the police do?"

"Digame qué pasó," I said to him. Tell me what happened.

He responded to the invitation and spoke in Spanish, telling me that he had come back this morning to pick up a few more things, moving out more or less by stages. He had found the police seal on the front door and gone around to the back, just as I had. He had found the seal on the back door broken and the door standing wide open.

"Then I came inside," he said, "and found this earthquake destruction! No, worse than an earthquake. An earthquake does not destroy art like this"—he waved a hand at the broken canvases on the floor—"or break brushes and waste paint. This is a devil who did this—a devil!"

I listened, nodding sympathetically, then shaking my head in dismay where it seemed appropriate. But I couldn't help noting that he was not nearly as broken up about Worley's death. He took that too matter-of-factly. Well, that was his problem, not mine, not now.

"Eduardo," I said, "let me tell you something. The police did not do this."

He looked at me doubtfully. "No?"

"No." Warnecky was obviously pretty pissed off when he guessed rightly that I'd been there before him. But he wasn't pissed enough to do this. I didn't think he had enough energy for this kind of sustained assault. "The police here are not always good, but they do not do such things." I hoped this was true. "Besides, the band across the back door was broken. They would not leave it so."

"Then who?" he said, *"who?"*

"Somebody who was looking for something. You've been here over an hour. You've been through the house. Is there anything missing?"

He looked at me a little strangely then, as though there was something he was trying to understand—but couldn't. "Sí," he said, "tapes."

"Really?" I turned this over in my mind. "What kind?"

"Every kind. Jimmy had many tapes he worked with, the

big thick kind for the cinema. I looked in his workroom. They are all gone. The videotapes also are missing, even the little cassettes we play on the stereo—you know, Michael Jackson, Janet Jackson, Streisand, all disappeared."

I had to think about this. It wasn't exactly what I expected. To tell you the truth, I'm not sure what I expected. But I turned my attention to Eduardo. "Look," I said to him, "whoever did this thing may come back looking for you. If he did not find what he searches for among the tapes, then he may come for you, believing you know. Do you know?"

He looked shocked, frightened. "No!" I believed him.

"So you must now gather together all that belongs to you." I gestured to the floor. "All that remains. We will pack it in the car, and you must not return here. It could be dangerous for you. Understand?"

He listened closely and nodded. "I understand," he said.

So he set to work filling boxes, talking to himself as he did. Or was he praying?

And what was I doing? I was thinking.

As he came out of the bedroom with an armful of clothes, I turned to him, sort of confronted him, and asked, "Do you know anybody named Alex Wakefield?"

He stood a moment, pouched his lips, and shook his head. "No," he said, "but Jimmy did. I heard him talking about him that night."

"What night?"

"That night when Clay was here. Yes, I decided that was his name—Clay."

Ten

When at last I rolled up to the studio gate, it was well into the lunch hour. Alta Jean waved me down from the guard post and moved her ample body through the doors of the booth and over to my car. She leaned down to talk. She wasn't smiling.

"I understand you're responsible for this," she said, then swung her hip around and pointed down at a holstered Smith and Wesson .38 Police Special just like mine.

"Well, not really," I said.

"That's what I heard. And I just want you to know I don't like it. I ain't ever shot one of these things, and I don't ever want to."

"Uh . . . I don't like them either, Alta Jean."

"Okay. Just so you know." She still wasn't smiling. "Wiggins wants to see you."

She slapped the window frame, nodded me through, then turned away. I hung on there a moment, looking after her as she pushed back inside the booth. Feeling guilty, I pulled away and drove to the parking space with my name on it.

I guess she was right. In a way, I was responsible—but not a hundred percent. Honest, Alta Jean. I just gave some dumb off-the-cuff response to some dumb question from a reporter—and look what happened. Somebody else made the decision. Probably Wiggins.

As I climbed the stairs to his office, I decided that whatever he had to say to me, I had to talk to him about this business of the sidearms. Maybe some other things, too.

Wiggins's secretary waved me right through. He was on the phone. Sitting down in the chair he pointed to, I leaned back and listened in on his conversation. It seemed he was talking to one of the cops, probably Warnecky or Pell, very reassuringly. He was telling them that, no, there was absolutely nothing to worry about. Because of the precautions they'd taken, nobody was going to get hurt. It was all just for show. He listened, nodded, made some more convincing noises, then ended by saying, "I'll tell him, sure. You bet I'll tell him." Then he hung up.

"That was the cops," he said. I didn't register any real surprise at that. "They seem to think you've got the address book that belonged to that guy who got killed."

"Worley," I put in, "James Worley."

"Yeah. Worley." He looked at me and waited. "Well, do you?"

This was getting to be a problem. "I might," I said. "I'll have to look around."

He gave me a kind of baffled frown. "They said if they don't get it, they can get a search warrant in five minutes and pull your license in ten." Then he added, "They also said the only reason they put up with your shit so far is they checked up on you, and you were a pretty good cop."

"Who was this? Warnecky?"

"No. The other guy."

"Pell?"

"Yeah."

They could have the address book. It wasn't much help anyway. The problem was just getting it to them without directly incriminating myself. Right now it was at home, tucked beneath a drawer in my desk.

"Tomorrow morning by ten o'clock," Wiggins said.

"That's the deadline?"

He nodded. "You know, Cervantes, I'm really grateful to you for saving my neck at that press conference yesterday, but

I can't have you impeding a police investigation. It makes the studio look bad."

"Okay," I said. "Don't worry about it. But listen, what's this about the studio guards going around armed? If that was Pell you were talking to just now, he didn't seem to think it was a good idea. Neither do I."

"Well, you suggested it."

"No, I didn't. I said it was an option. Your decision."

Wiggins smiled at that. "Well, actually, it wasn't." He laughed, just a sort of chuckle. "You know, I really gotta hand it to those Germans. That young Mr. Geisel, he's a pretty smart fella. He's not exactly your biggest fan, Cervantes, but when he saw you on TV and heard what you said about arming the guards, he thought that was a pretty good idea.

"I *didn't* say that. The reporter asked if—"

"Okay, okay. Anyway, he called up and asked me how much that would cost. I gave him some kind of rough estimate and he said, oh, that's too much. But I said it would also take a while because we'd have to train a lot of the guards, you know, at the shooting range. Then he said, that's no good because what they're really after is publicity. You know, show the TV and the newspaper people right away we were taking this seriously—armed response and so on. Then he got this idea that I thought was just absolutely brilliant."

"Don't tell me," I said. I had an idea what was coming. "Or maybe you'd better."

"He said, since this is just for show, we'll rent them from a prop house! Is that smart or not? A lot cheaper than buying them."

"They're not real guns?"

"Oh, they're real, but they just fire blanks. They've been fixed for the movies."

"Do the guards know what they've got?" Alta Jean sure didn't.

"Well, they ought to. A blank charge doesn't look like a bullet. You know that. We figured we wouldn't say anything so word wouldn't get out."

I sighed, wondering who was more dangerous, Hans-Dieter

Geisel or this guy. Probably Hans-Dieter, because he was the boss. "You know, Wiggins, you can kill somebody with a blank charge."

He shrugged, dismissing it. "Oh," he said, "you hear about it. But it's very rare."

I got up slowly and pointed at him, making a pistol of my thumb and forefinger just for emphasis. "Wiggins, I've got two things to say to that. One—you better tell those guards what they're carrying around in their holsters. Two—you better get a prop man, or whoever it is takes care of that stuff, to give them lessons on handling blank-firing weapons."

"Hey," he said, "what is that? A threat or something?"

"No threat. Just a strong recommendation." I turned around and started out of there.

But Wiggins called me back so loudly and insistently that I was forced to blow a good exit, turning around halfway across the outer office and backtracking to his door. "Yeah?"

"We never got around to what I was supposed to tell you," he said.

"And what was that?"

"I was supposed to tell you you've got a date to drop by and see Heinrich Toller this afternoon around four o'clock. You know where to go? Up Benedict Canyon?"

I nodded. "I know where."

He shook his head then, like he really couldn't believe it. "You must really be in tight with the old man," he said.

"Why?"

"Well, because you're working here, drawing dough. The rest of them—the daughter and that Geisel fella—they really seem to hate your guts."

Not, perhaps, a nice note on which to leave, but that's the one I left on.

With a shrug and a devil-may-care wave to that poor, chairborne timeserver, our hero departs, making his way hastily down the stairs, out into the brilliant daylight, and on to his personalized parking space (which may not be personalized for long).

As I unlocked the Alfa and was folding myself into the entry

100

position, I suddenly realized what I didn't like about this deal at Majestic: it was guys like Norbert Wiggins wondering how I got it.

"Cervantes! Hey, Cervantes!"

At the sound of the voice, I looked around and saw Tom Beatty quite close by. I thought at first that he was returning from lunch, but then it occurred to me that he was headed in the wrong direction, and I noticed the box of personal effects in his arms. What's more, Beatty noticed me noticing. He looked angry.

"That's right," he called over to me from the side of the studio street. "You're drawing a fair conclusion. I'm off the picture, as of this moment. If you want to hear any more about it, you'll have to call my lawyer."

"Your lawyer?" I heaved myself out from under the steering wheel and went over to talk.

Beatty stopped and heaved the box up on his hip. "And furthermore," he said. "I'm filing a suit for wrongful dismissal. Now, don't try to talk me out of it."

"Why should I want to do that?"

"Well, you work for the studio, don't you?"

"Not the way you mean. I'm a consultant, whatever that means."

"Oh, well, okay." He looked me up and down, then kicked at the pavement in frustration. "I guess I'm just looking for a fight. It's this AIDS hysteria that's got everyone freaking out. Emmett and all of them. Or just general homophobia, I don't know. It's all so awful, Jimmy dying, murdered, and now this."

He fell silent, as though for the moment he had run out of complaints. Then, without quite looking my way, he said, "I shouldn't take it out on you, though, Cervantes. You were the only person who treated me decently yesterday."

"Well . . . I . . . ." There wasn't really much to say to that.

"No, it's true. And as I said last night, I should have taken your advice and kept my theory to myself." He shrugged. "Well, anyway."

"Look," I said, "why don't you let me drive you to your car? You've got that box."

"It's not heavy," he said, "just big enough to be awkward. Pictures, a notebook, odds and ends, a couple of books. I'll manage." He slung the box around and shuffled his feet, getting ready to go.

By this time I had my wallet out and had pulled a business card from it. "Take this," I said. "If you think of something that might help, something about Worley, just give me a call. Okay?" I tucked the card into his shirt pocket.

"You're really concerned about trying to find out who killed Jimmy, aren't you? Not just in hushing it up?"

"Yeah, I really am."

He shook his head and gave me a crooked smile. "Amazing," he said, "just amazing."

I stood there for a moment and watched him go. I was glad I'd given him the card. Angry as he was, something might come of it. In his own way, Tom Beatty was a pretty tough little guy, hundred-dollar haircut and all.

I jumped into the Alfa and got out of there in a hurry. On my way through the gate, I got a stony look from Alta Jean but managed to return it with a smile.

There was plenty of time to kill before reporting to old man Toller, and so I stopped at a bookstore on Sunset and browsed until I found that biography Alex Wakefield had mentioned—*Rock Avatar: The Life and Turbulent Times of Tommy Osborne*. It looked promising. What I had in hand was the paperback edition of a book that had appeared a couple of years ago. Looking it over, I seemed to remember ads, maybe even a review or two. But it certainly never made the bestseller list: people who buy records, even CDs, don't necessarily buy books. They go to movies, though. That was the bet there at Majestic, and it was a good one.

I walked down to the corner, took a table at one of those places on the Strip that insists on presenting itself as a sidewalk cafe. Settling down in the shade, I ordered a sandwich and opened the book to the back to see if I could find Clay in the index. No index. So I started reading. This one plunged right into the action in the first chapter, the way these pop biographies do, dramatically describing the events leading up to that wild night ride that led to Osborne's death. The author—what was this guy's name? Kelly Klinger—really seemed to have the inside dope. He let you know the layout of that hideaway in the Cascades, the view from the deck as the sun set behind Mount Shasta, the angry words that passed between Osborne and his girlfriend, even the thoughts that ran through his head as he roared out into the night in his month-old Corvette.

There was more, of course—the fiery plunge down the mountainside witnessed only by a single driver far up the road; the next day, the precarious climb down the face of the mountain by the Siskiyou County sheriff's deputy and the Klamath Indian guide. All described graphically, just like this guy Klinger had been present at the scene, details right down to the state of the body, burned beyond recognition, when it was recovered from the wreckage. It was enough to take away your appetite for ham and cheese on rye.

But at the same time, this stuff fascinated me, and I wasn't quite sure why. Sure, it was ancient history—it had all happened twenty years before—but I hoped to find some answers among the facts of Osborne's life. Maybe I had concentrated too much on this guy Clay who had been with Worley just before Worley was killed. Maybe it was just because he was the missing piece that I had focused so much attention on him. Maybe I should just read the book through and see what might turn up.

But later, I looked at my watch and decided it was time to head up the road to Toller's place. It wouldn't do to keep the old guy waiting.

I liked him. I really did, even though I was fairly certain that made me a member of a tiny minority. Heinrich Toller had a reputation in the movie business as a pirate, and it was probably well deserved. But luckily for me, I never had to deal with him on that level. I wasn't his friend; I don't believe he had any

103

real friends. But I believed he trusted me, and it wouldn't be long until I proved that trust misplaced.

When I turned in to the driveway of the Toller estate, the gate opened up, and the guard waved me through. He knew the car, and he knew my face. I had become a regular visitor.

Parking off to the side of the house in front of the Mercedes limo, I went to the door and rapped loudly with the hand-shaped knocker. A moment or two later, the door swung open and revealed the ample form of Ilse, the maid. She smiled broadly. I was one of her favorites, probably because she was under the mistaken impression that I spoke German fairly fluently. I remembered a little from my tour of duty with the MPs in Frankfurt twenty years before, and I worked that little for all I could with Ilse.

I gave her a *"Grüss' Gott,* Fräulein Ilse" (since I knew she was from Bavaria), and that was really all it took.

She flung the door wide and answered me with a flood of German, a lot of it in Bavarian dialect which I had no hope of understanding. I got the drift: the *Willkommen,* the inquiry after my health that I answered politely, and the invitation to wait in the library. What I didn't quite get was where Herr Toller was and how long he would be. It had something to do with *"die Dame"*—the Dutch woman with the world-class laugh—and her shopping trip to Beverly Hills. Presumably she was modeling her purchases for him.

In the library, alone, I browsed, as I always did there. I had met Heinrich Toller there for the first time months ago with an edition of De Quincey in my hand, open to "Murder Considered as One of the Fine Arts." That impressed him, or amused him at least, because from that day on he nearly always addressed me as De Quincey. Remembering that, I was a little uneasy when I realized I had just pulled down a copy of *The Tragical History of the Life and Death of Doctor Faustus.* After all, I didn't want him to start calling me Marlowe.

Little chance of that. When Toller came through the double-door, he fairly swept into the room, moving about as swiftly as his game right knee would allow. He came directly to me, pumped my hand strongly, and gave no notice at all to

104

the book I had open. "De Quincey," he said, "how very good it is to see you." He gestured to a chair on the other side of the big desk. "Please," he said, "please sit down."

That's what I did, putting the book aside, folding my hands, waiting.

"So," he said, "things go well? The checks arrive on time?"

I said they did and added that they were honored at the bank, too. "It's a very nice arrangement."

Toller chuckled. "Not like at first, huh? You were afraid our checks would bounce!"

"No, well, I . . ."

"You and everybody else!" He laughed hard at that, so hard, in fact, that he was forced to pull the powder blue silk handkerchief from the breast pocket of his dark blue suit and wipe the tears from his eyes. When he had recovered, he replaced the handkerchief and shook his finger at me in a kind of professorial way. "But you—you took a chance, and you got us out of trouble." He shrugged. "Well, you helped, anyway. *I* got us out of trouble."

"No question," I said. "It was you."

A smile spread on his face. It was a joke between us. "But you certainly helped. So what happens then? I reward you, right?"

"Right. A check—good check. I liked all the zeros on that check. Very artistic."

"Not only that very generous contribution to your welfare, and your lady friend's, and now the baby's, too—not only that, but a job at the studio, the best kind of job ever."

I frowned. This I didn't quite follow. "How is security consultant for Majestic Pictures 'the best kind of job ever'?"

Enough of this kidding around. *Bang!* He brought his fist down on the desk. "It's the best because you don't have to work at it," he growled. "We don't even *want* you to work at it. Just accept your checks as they are mailed to you, why don't you? Stay at home, or the office, or wherever it is you go when you're not bothering people at the studio!" He was fairly shouting there at the end.

"This is crazy," I said. "Who's been after you to get me to back off?"

"Nobody."

"Bullshit."

He looked at me furiously. He wasn't used to being answered back, except perhaps by his daughter, and he could handle her. But he calmed himself in a moment and even managed a phony smile. Again he poked his finger in my direction. "I know you, De Quincey. You think it is dishonest to take our money and do nothing. That is, in a way, admirable. But keep in mind, this is not *our* money. It belongs to the parent organization. If it did not go to you, it would go into the pocket of that war criminal who sits at the top of it. Think about that. Better you than he, uh?" He pulled back then, let me think it over.

After all, why not? I had a little money in the bank for the first time in years. Maybe I could satisfy him and my conscience both.

"Seriously," I said to him, "is it Ursula who wants me to stay away?"

He laughed at that. "Nooo. She wants you out of there and off the payroll."

"Then it's got to be one of two people. Or Wiggins—it could be Wiggins."

"Who is this Wiggins?"

"It couldn't be Wiggins, I guess." I sighed. "Okay, look. I'll try it your way. Maybe I can build up my business instead of just waiting around the office for the phone to ring."

"Maybe later on you come, uh? On special occasions."

"Like that, huh?"

"Like that. The checks still come every month, just like before."

I nodded, but even as I did, I was thinking that at this point I could probably work the case better from the outside anyway. What was it Alex Wakefield said?

So I lied.

106

Eleven

Since Detective Pell's deadline was ten A.M., I got there by
9:30. Pulling up at a meter just down from the Hollywood
station, I sat there behind the wheel for a little while trying to
decide just what I could say to him when he asked me why I
had kept Worley's address book. I knew why I had taken it.
I wanted a look inside. I wanted to see if I could find some
trace in it of the mysterious Clay. But I hadn't. Then why
hadn't I turned it over to the cops right away? Because it
contained names of certain public figures and notes on their
sexual preferences, information that would be, to say the least,
embarrassing to them. I was afraid that somebody at Hollywood Division might get hold of the book and put the squeeze
on certain public figures—that guy on the Dodgers in particular. But I couldn't tell Detective Pell that, could I?

Why should I care? I was pretty sure I had my man Clay,
anyway. I had found him the night before, reading through
Rock Avatar. He had been there all the time, just waiting for
me to do my homework.

Alicia was annoyed with me, sulking because I wouldn't
read through her lines with her the way I'd done before.

"But you jus' sit with a book," she had said, pushing out her
lower lip in a stage pout. "How can you be a detective like
that?"

"I'm being a detective inside my head," I told her.

107

"Ah, el profesor detective, uh?"

"Something like that."

She stared at me suspiciously for a long moment. "You know what I think, Chico?" Then she waited.

So I had to ask: "Okay. What do you think?"

"I think maybe you don' wan' me to get this part. You wan' me to stay jus' how I am."

Okay. Looking back now on that whole episode, I have to admit that there was something—not much, but something—to what she said. I mean, I wanted her to succeed. I really did. But I thought she was kidding herself if she thought she could just walk in and then walk right out again with the lead in a TV series—even with Ursula Toller behind her. This was her fantasy and not real life. How could I tell her that? I was afraid she'd get hurt, if not by this guy Gresham, then by circumstances.

And I'll admit it, beneath it all was the fear that if fantasy won out over reality, then I might lose her.

But I denied what she'd said, of course: "Eres loca."

"Speak English, please."

"All right, you're crazy. I want only the best for you."

"If is true, tha's nice." She spoke very seriously. "But I tell you one thing. I got a career, or I gonna have one. And nobody gonna stop me, Chico, not you or nobody."

And then Alicia punished me by doing her lines over and over again as I tried to read. She tried different readings—monotone, with feeling, and then full voice. She had me, and she knew it. I couldn't go into the bedroom. The light might wake the baby. It had happened before. I wasn't going to be chased into the bathroom to do my reading. I had to stay right where I was in order to prove a point. It would have been easier, better, smarter to let her have her way, to sit down and just go through the twenty-odd pages of the script with her and then return to the book. But we draw lines and take positions, and we seldom do what's best in such situations. And afterwards we may wonder why we acted the way we did.

I gritted my teeth and read on, repeating sentences, paragraphs, whole pages in silent, self-righteous rage. And eventu-

108

ally I outlasted her. The baby began to cry for her ten o'clock feeding. We looked up. Our eyes met. Alicia slammed down her copy of the script on the sofa, jumped up, and headed into the bedroom to feed the kid. That was how it was.

Somehow, with all this, in spite of it, I managed to locate Clay Weston. He made his appearance toward the end of the book's third chapter. Or I think it was then. It's possible he was mentioned earlier, and in the state I was in I failed to notice. Anyway, there he was at Cass Tech in Detroit—with Tommy Osborne in 1963, both of them seniors, cutting classes to jam in Clay's garage, or maybe just hanging out at his place after school listening to his prize collection of blues and rhythm-and-blues records. Even in high school, Clay Weston was a good guitar player. He conducted Osborne's musical education, taught the nerdy, abnormally quiet kid how to turn his poems into songs.

They stuck together after high school and formed a band. The first time around they called themselves the Tunebusters. Clay Weston was featured on Fender guitar—he was the leader then—and Osborne on rhythm guitar and vocals. The bass and drums came and went, came and went, changing about as often as they changed the name of the band. As they gigged around Detroit—then Windsor, Ann Arbor, and Toledo—they were known at different times as the Fairlanes, the Freaky-Deakies, and finally, from 1967 on, as the DMZ. Brilliant! The DeMilitarized Zone—the name suggested the violence of war and gave a nod at peace all in three letters. And it was as the DMZ that they made it to Los Angeles on a record contract, caused a riot on Sunset when they played the Whisky a Go Go the first time, and began the national tours that made them infamous. There was big bucks in infamy back then, just as there is today. And it wasn't long before the DMZ was one of the top groups in the country, rocking up there right alongside Big Brother and the Holding Company and the Jefferson Airplane.

That was about as far as I got that night. I'd outlasted Alicia. After the ten o'clock feeding she'd announced that she was tired and was going to bed. If that was an invitation, it

109

lacked a certain warmth, and so I gave her a kiss and sent her on her way. That only seemed to annoy her more, but after what I'd endured from her, I didn't much care. So I stayed up reading for a while, even reread some of what I'd gone through earlier while she was proving to me that her career was just as important as mine.

I went nearly halfway through *Rock Avatar* before I got tired of all the gushing over Tommy Osborne. When the guy who wrote the book—this Kelly Klinger—when he wasn't gushing, he was psychologizing, explaining Osborne's traumatic childhood, going back to it over and over again to account for erratic behavior and irrational episodes. My man Clay hardly counted in it at all after his first few appearances. And I noticed, too, that in a book heavy with quotations from anyone who had known Osborne even casually, there were none from Clay Weston. I looked in the front of the book at the long list of people Klinger had talked to and saw that that particular name was missing. Was I disappointed? You bet I was. I'd hoped I might be able to contact Weston through Klinger.

After marking my place, I tossed the book aside, promising myself I'd get back to it the next day. Then I turned off the lights and went quietly into the bedroom, where I undressed and climbed into bed beside Alicia. She was breathing lightly, and I suspected she was awake. But she didn't say a word and neither did I.

I went into Hollywood Division and asked for Detective Pell. The desk sergeant was just phoning to see if he was upstairs when Pell burst through the door. He almost ran into me, but then he pulled back, recognized me, and said, "Come on." Just like that.

There was no arguing with the guy, no telling him I had places to go and people to see, so I just followed him on out to his car, an unmarked GM something. And then he said, "Get in."

I got in.

We were off and running before I had the door shut tight.

He zoomed out into traffic, took a hard left that set us in a direction away from the studio. "Where are we headed?" I asked.

He didn't answer.

About a block later I sort of cleared my throat and said, "Look, if this is about that address book, I can explain about that." I didn't know how, but I'd think of something.

Again he didn't answer. He just gave me an annoyed glance, and kept right on driving.

All right, I thought, be like that. If you don't want to hear my excuses, then you won't.

He took Fountain and headed west, taking the kind of chances in traffic that only a cop will. I held on and watched the blocks spin by. When I realized we were in West Hollywood, I wondered if we were on the way to Worley's place. Maybe they'd gone back and seen the condition of the place. Maybe they were blaming me for that. But I didn't ask. Finally we turned left on Havenhurst, and he slowed down. Ahead of us I could see a black and white double-parked and sensed immediately that it was bad news.

Pell pulled to a halt behind the black and white, killed the motor, and spoke up at last. "Cervantes," he said, "I took you along to show you something. Not because I think you have any particular right to, but because this way, it's going to get you out of our hair at last. Do I make myself clear?"

No, but he had my attention anyway.

There was a little crowd outside the building, a kind of garden-apartment setup that was the most common in this section of West Hollywood. Pell grabbed on to the sleeve of my jacket and pulled me through it before I had a chance to take it all in. The sheriff's cop at the door waved us through when Pell flashed his shield, and we headed down a short hallway.

Warnecky was there. He was standing just this side of an open door talking to a woman in her fifties. Behind her, sort of peeking out, was a little dog on a leash. He seemed more than a little intimidated by what was going on. Maybe it was Warnecky and his cigar; he intimidated me.

111

There was some noise out on the street behind us, and the cop at the door called out, "The coroner's wagon's here."

"Good," Pell answered and then to me: "Come on in here. I want you to see him before they cut him down."

I winced at that but followed him around Warnecky, the woman, and her dog. Warnecky gave me a dirty look. She looked at me as I passed, sizing me up. She was a tough old broad, almost enjoying the attention she was getting. The dog—what they call a schnauzer, I guess—shrunk further back, almost wrapping the leash around the woman's ankles. She jerked hard at it. "For Christ's sake, Oscar, don't be so damned scared. Nobody's going to hurt you."

I was with Oscar. I was scared. Or I guess *apprehensive* is a better word. I hung back at the door. Detective Pell looked back at me, annoyed, and gave a swift short movement with his hand, the one that says, Let's go.

I followed him in. There was another detective in there, one I hadn't seen before. Pell walked up to him and shook his hand. "Charlie, I really want to thank you," he said. "I don't know how you guessed this had to do with this shit at the movie studio, but you were right on the money."

"It was easy," the detective said. "It was right on the screen. I remembered the name." He nodded toward another door that stood open. "He's right in there. Go on in."

We walked through the room, a modest living room with only the usual comforts—except for a huge electronic setup against one wall. It seemed to contain every device for musical reproduction known to man, with speakers scattered around that seemed to focus right into the center.

I must have stopped to take that in, or maybe I was just hanging back again, but the next thing I knew, Pell was standing at the other door, rasping a nasty, "Cervantes, will you come on in here?" He waited for me. "That guy, Charlie, he's a sheriff's cop. We owe him. He saved us at least a day."

I didn't quite understand why that would be so, but I followed him into the room. It was a workroom that looked a lot like the one in Worley's little bungalow before it was torn apart. There were stacks of printouts, a few books, a video

112

monitor, and a computer. A chair lay on the floor. In the middle of it all, his feet not far from the overturned chair, Tom Beatty hung from a rope attached at the upper end to a light fixture.

The body was completely still, turned so that the face was more or less in my direction. They talk about faces turning black from strangulation. Well, that's not really the way it is. It's more like purple. Everything above the rope was swollen and livid like one huge bruise. The mouth was open in an ugly grin; and the tongue stuck out, extended beyond the point you would think possible. And yes, the tongue was black. The amazing thing was that, distorted and discolored as his face was, you could still tell that it belonged to Tom Beatty. It was Beatty, all right, hundred-dollar haircut and all.

"The lady with the dog came out of the rear entrance to the building," said Pell. "She was out, you know, taking her morning constitutional or something. She just looked in, and there he was."

He pointed to the window. The drapes were parted. You could look right out at the next building about twelve feet away, or of course someone passing by could look right in.

"How long has he been up there?"

Pell shrugged. "Your guess is as good as mine." He took a step forward and gave a tap to an arm. The body swayed slightly on the rope, but the arm stayed rigid. "We got rigor mortis here, so it's been awhile. I guess you'd have to ask the medical examiner that one." He turned and stared at me for a moment, then he added, "But don't do it."

"Don't do what?"

"Don't ask the medical examiner. Don't ask anybody anything. As of right now, as far as we're concerned, the case is closed."

I was confused. "Wait a minute," I said. "Which case are you talking about?"

"The one at the studio. That guy, James Worley."

"I still don't understand. You mean this—"

He interrupted me: "I mean this guy killed Worley and then killed himself."

"How do you figure that? I mean, it's possible, but isn't that pretty neat? A little *too* neat?"

There was noise out in the hall, then in the next room. The meat crew from the morgue had arrived.

"Just take a look at the computer," Pell said to me.

I had to walk around Beatty to get there. I gave him a wide berth, and just as I got to it, the sheriff's cop came to the door and asked us to clear out. "The forensic team has to get in here before the guys from the coroner cut him down and take him away," he said.

So there was just enough time to take a look at the screen before Pell dragged me out. There, in green letters on a smoky black background, was this message:

I KILLED JAMES WORLEY.

The letters shimmered slightly, but they didn't change.

"Okay, Cervantes," said Pell. "You heard the man."

I started to turn away, and then I looked back. I was right. Something was missing—tapes—floppy disks, and the audio-tapes and videotapes these guys work with. The shelf above the computer had been cleaned out.

I turned back to Pell. "Hey, listen! You know what—"

"Come on. Out!"

Reluctantly I followed. There was quite a crowd in the living room. Charlie, the county detective, pushed past me and led three plainclothesmen into the room. The two guys from the morgue stood around looking at each other. One of them tossed the black body bag down on the sofa and lighted a cigarette. Pell stood by the door. He was ready to leave.

But I wanted to check something first. I went to that impressive audio system and found beside it what should have been a four-tier rack of cassettes. It was empty, too.

I beckoned Pell over. I wanted him to see this. But he just stood there at the door, shaking his head. "Let's get out of here," he said. "Now." He stepped out into the hall.

What could I do? I followed him, of course. He was halfway

down the hall before I caught up with him. Warnecky was gone and so was the woman with the dog.

"Hey, look, Pell, come on back there." I was almost pleading with the guy. "There's something I want to show you."

He wasn't buying any. He just kept walking.

"Something's been stolen out of that apartment."

That stopped him. He looked at me. "How do you know? Have you ever been inside there before?"

"No, of course not."

"Then how do you know something's missing?"

A reasonable question. Could I tell him that I had been into Worley's place a second time and seen that it had been ransacked for tapes? And that's how I happened to notice Beatty's tapes were missing, too? No, I couldn't exactly tell Detective Pell that, could I?

"Cut the shit, Cervantes," he said. "What's this all about?"

"The tapes are missing."

"What?"

I tried logic. "Listen, when I looked at the computer, like you told me to, I noticed there weren't any disks around—no audiotapes, either. He's got a video monitor in there, too. It's what he worked with—but no videotapes."

"So?"

"Then in the living room, by that monster audio setup, there was a big rack for cassettes. They'd been cleaned out, too."

"Wait a minute. Are you trying to tell me Beatty was murdered, made to look like a suicide, just so someone could walk away with his tape collection?"

"Maybe they were looking for one tape in particular and just took them all to be on the safe side."

He looked at me like I was a little bit crazy. Maybe I was.

"Then why bother to take the computer disks?" Pell wanted to know.

He had me there. "I don't know. But you'd better tell those guys in there to print out what's on that remaining disc, the one that's in the computer now."

Pell shook his head. He seemed almost angry. "I'm not

going to tell them to do anything. It's their show." He stared at me, lips pressed together, as if he was afraid what might come out if he relaxed them. But gradually they did relax. He sighed in exasperation and tried to look sympathetic. "You know what's wrong with you, Cervantes?" he asked—then went right ahead and told me: "You're trying to make a big mystery out of something that's really pretty simple."

Well, there was no use trying to convince him, not there and then. So I just shrugged. He took that to mean he'd convinced me. He turned then and led the way outside and on to his car. I followed him without a word.

And that was how it was all the way back to Hollywood Division. Total silence. Not a word from either one of us during that drive down Fountain.

But I still had something to say. So when he pulled up in front of the station house, I turned to him and said, "Look, do you think it's completely reasonable that a guy would write a suicide note—a confession, for God's sake!—on a *computer?*"

He rolled his eyes like this was the last straw or something. Then he came on like he was talking to a slow learner: "I think it's unusual, yes, but it's possible, more than possible. Some of these guys, they get so attached to those things they can't write any other way."

It was my turn to sigh. "Well, I hope they dust the keys for prints," I said. Opening the door, I started to climb out of the car. Then I remembered why I'd come in the first place. "There was something I had that you wanted," I said.

I dug into my jacket pocket and tossed Worley's address book on the seat between us.

Pell looked at it a moment and then pushed it in my direction a few inches. "Keep it," he said. "I told you, as far as we're concerned, the case is closed. That's what Warnecky and I are going to tell the lieutenant. That's what the lieutenant's going to tell the captain, and that's what we're all going to tell those idiots at the studio. Closed. Over. Finito. Keep it."

I grabbed it off the seat, slammed the car door, and just managed to jump clear as Pell gunned down on the accelerator and roared out of there.

116

Twelve

Okay, I'm back at the studio gate. Alta Jean waves me down again, pushes out of the booth, and heads over to my car. I notice that she's still wearing that .38 on her ample hip, and I wonder if Norbert Wiggins has gotten around to telling her that it only shoots blanks. I'm about to ask about that when she stops me cold.

"Got bad news for you, Chico. You barred from the lot."

At first I thought she was putting me on. But that solemn, no-nonsense expression on her face remained unchanged. "What?" I said. "What is this? Since when?"

"Word came down this morning when I started my shift. They real serious about it. Took away your park space and everything."

"Whose authorization?"

"The top—the very top."

So Heinrich Toller didn't trust me after all. That hurt—although it shouldn't have. He had just proven himself a better judge of character than I had even known.

"Well, look, Alta Jean, I just have to dash in and get something from Casimir—you know, Casimir Urbanski? in Development?"

"I know. The answer is no, Chico."

"I'll park on the street. Just let me walk through. You can look the other way."

"No."

I realized then for the first time that this was her job—keeping out people who didn't belong—and she was good at it. There was no arguing with her. I sighed. "Okay."

She nodded, satisfied. "Now," she said, "if you will just proceed ten yards beyond the gate, you will find there is plenty of room to make a turnaround. If you go beyond that point, I will be forced to shoot you with the blanks in my pistol."

Well, at least she'd gotten the news about that. "Okay, Alta Jean."

"Sorry, Chico."

I believed she was, but that didn't change things at all. I pulled ahead, as she had directed, and made the turnaround in a single sweep, something no Mercedes sedan could accomplish. I was just heading toward the street on the other side when I happened to look over at the line of cars that had formed while I had my talk with Alta Jean, and I noticed a familiar old Ford—and at the wheel, a familiar driver.

"Pilar!" I called across to her. "What are you doing here?"

She saw me and waved excitedly. "Oh, Mr. Cervantes, is the big day!"

Then Alicia appeared, her face thrust next to Pilar's. "I got the call! I got my reading, Chico! Wish me buena suerte!"

"Sure, of course," I said without much enthusiasm. "Good luck."

Then, with another wave, Pilar bumped forward to the guard booth. I looked back as Alta Jean listened to them a moment, checked her list, then waved them through. I just sat there in the Alfa, half turned around, watching them go. Then somebody behind me gave me the horn, I gave him the finger, and I drove on out of there.

But not very far. There was a bar down the block and across the street where Casimir and I had eaten a couple of times. I hung a *U*-turn and pulled up in front of the place. There was still parking there, it was still too early for lunch. But not too early to give Casimir a call.

I yelled down to the bartender for a cup of coffee, then went

118

straight to the telephone. Dialing Casimir, I got his secretary, of course.

"Lorraine, this is Chico. Let me talk to him if he's in, okay?"

"He's with somebody now. Could you call back?"

"How long will it be? I mean, sure, I can call back, but could I talk to him just for a minute? It's important."

"Hold on."

There was a pause, and then Casimir came on the line, sounding maybe just a little abrupt. "Yeah, Chico."

"Did you get that report from the medical examiner's office?"

"Yeah, I got a copy. You can pick it up by Lorraine any time."

"That's just it, Casimir. I can't. They won't let me through the gate."

Again, a pause, as he tried to figure that one out. "What did you do?" he asked at last.

"Nothing!" No, I had to level with him: "Well, maybe something. I'll tell you about it later. But look, could you bring it over to me? I'm just across the street at the Backlot—you know, we ate here before."

"Yeah, okay. It's almost lunch. I'll see you then."

He hung up before I could thank him.

The place was almost empty when I came in, but in the short space of that phone call six or eight people had walked in. So I grabbed my coffee off the bar and headed for a booth near the door. The waitress saw what I was up to and nodded her okay, and I settled in.

Think about it, I told myself. Just sit here. Try to block out everything else. Drink your coffee, and keep an open mind.

The first thing that came to me was the last thing I'd tossed at Pell. Nobody, but nobody would ever write his last words down on a computer screen. That would be too impersonal, too mechanical. It just didn't make sense in human terms.

Then I thought back to the last time I had seen Tom Beatty alive. It had been right there across the street in the studio parking lot the day before. He was indignant, angry, talking about suing Emmett and the studio. You'd never expect a guy in that state to commit suicide a few hours later.

But just say, for argument's sake, that he decided to commit suicide. Would he choose to hang himself? Not a chance. He'd overdose on Seconal, or whatever it is they take. He would know that death by strangulation was painful, and Tom Beatty struck me as the kind of guy who would do all he could to avoid pain. Unless . . . it brought him sexual pleasure. Hadn't I read once about guys who got their kicks by hanging themselves—a little bit? Maybe I was being naive. Maybe Beatty was one of those. But my single experience with the pain of strangulation made me wonder how there was any kind of pleasure, even perverse pleasure, to be gotten from it.

Okay. What about motive? The guy who wept over the death of his friend, Worley, couldn't have killed him. He couldn't have killed himself in regret for something he hadn't done in the first place. No, it didn't make sense, none of it did.

Any way you looked at it, even if you kept an open mind and tried to see it Pell's way, it seemed a lot more likely that Beatty had been murdered and the murder made to look like suicide. All of a sudden, I knew I wanted to see the medical examiner's report on Beatty, too.

Then it occurred to me that maybe it was dumb to try to change Pell's mind on Beatty—Warnecky I considered beyond communication—because it was really to my advantage if the case was closed. I could work on it then without the cops or the studio coming down on me. I could make kind of a hobby out of it, if I wanted to, just keep nibbling around it at the edges until I came up with something.

It was obvious that what was on some tapes was the key to all this. That was why someone had wrecked Worley's house looking for them and killed Tom Beatty to get them. Someone was looking for them and what was on them. Wherever Clay Weston was, I bet he knew what it was. I was still chewing on that when Casimir walked in.

And not a moment too soon. The waitress had been around a couple of times to fill up my coffee cup, looking at me kind of dubiously, and the place had filled up fast so that about the

120

only empty spot in it was the one across from me in that booth. I felt relieved when he filled it.

He tossed the medical examiner's report down on the table—thick, three or four pages, folded twice. "This is it," he said. "You can have it. Just don't tell you got it by me. Anybody." He seemed uneasy, like he wanted to get up and leave.

"Have a beer," I said. "I'll have one, too. And let's eat something."

He was looking around the place, not like he was trying to flag the waitress down, but like he was really uncomfortable. Was it me? I picked up the medical examiner's report and tucked it away inside my jacket. I was eager to read it, but this didn't seem to be the time.

"This time it's definitely on me," I said. "I owe you."

He nodded and seemed about to say something when the waitress appeared, order pad out and pencil poised. I ordered a bowl of chili and a Dos Equis. Casimir called for a cup of coffee and a cheeseburger.

"Only one?" I asked. I'd seen him eat three at a sitting.

"Yeah, I'm not doing zero exercise at all no more. So I gotta watch what I eat. I never had to before. It's hard."

It probably was. Casimir Urbanski had changed his life in more ways than he could have imagined when he left the LAPD to become a movie mogul. The strain was beginning to show. He was comfortable being a cop. He had all the moves down. He was good at it. But now they were asking him to become someone he never was, someone he'd never even imagined. Yeah, it must really have been hard.

"You probably want to know why I asked for this," I said, patting my jacket where I'd tucked away the report.

"Yeah, well . . ."

"Maybe I'd better tell you the whole story." And that's what I did, leaving nothing important out, but sparing him some colorful but unimportant details.

He listened, nodding, taking it all in. About halfway through my recitation our food arrived. He picked up the ketchup bottle, hinged up the lid of the cheeseburger, and nearly drowned the yellow-covered patty in red, then dumped about half the bottle on the french fries. I broke off and stared. He looked up and said, kind of sheepishly, "It makes it more to eat this way. But it's still, you know, just one cheeseburger."

I nodded and kept on talking. I'd gotten to the part about Tom Beatty. After telling him about the condition of the body, the missing tapes, and all, I laid down all the reasons that Beatty couldn't have committed suicide, and I sounded pretty convincing, if I do say so myself.

I sat back and waited for him to say something. He just kept eating. Finally I shrugged and said, "Well, what do you think?"

He shrugged back at me and said, "What do I think? I think the cops want to close it."

"Well . . . obviously. That's what I'm saying. But it—"

"And you know why?"

"Okay, why?"

"Then I'm telling you why. Since this one happened by the studio, they got maybe six or seven homicides more to work on, only they can't, because this one is big because it happened on TV. Right?"

More or less. "Yeah, I suppose so."

"Okay. They close this one they work on the other ones. Right?"

"Right."

"Who can say the other ones aren't more important? Maybe some old babe got raped and murdered. You got no sympathy on her? You think your guy—okay, your two guys—are more important than her?"

"Well, I . . ."

"Sure you do. You know why?"

I sighed. "Tell me."

"Because they're yours. Because these are your stiffs you got a vestige interest on them. Am I right? Think about it."

I didn't need to think about it. Sure, he was right in what he'd just said, but wrong, dead wrong, in what he seemed to be suggesting. I tossed back a big gulp of Dos Equis and gave him a long look, trying to figure him out. He didn't seem to be on my side anymore.

"The cops want to close this up because they got not enough time," he continued. "You, you want to keep it open because you got too much." Then he added, by way of clarification: "Time. You said so yourself."

"Well, you're right about one thing and wrong about another," I said.

"How's that?"

"You're right I want to work on it because I've had a lot of time on my hands. I admit it. But I'm not so sure I want it kept open. See, I'm not supposed to work on active police cases."

"I know that, too. So?"

"So I can keep working on it, and nobody's going to pull my PI license."

"Yeah, but nobody wants you to, right? That's why they won't let you inside."

"You've been on the phone," I said, "haven't you?"

"Okay, sure. I called Uschi."

"And she told you her father said I should drop it."

"Right. And he was the one shut the gate on you so you would." Then, after the kind of brief pause actors call a "beat": "Drop it."

"You're really in the organization now, aren't you?" That didn't sound right, even to me. "Okay, look, forget I said that." But he didn't look like he would. His lips were thin, pursed, like he might bite down on them and draw blood. "I know you're working for them, Casimir," I said. "I know what you're doing now is a big strain. It's tough. You don't know your way. And I promise I won't put the squeeze on you again if you'll do just one more thing for me."

"Yeah?" He looked skeptical, almost hostile. "What's that?"

"I'd like you to go back to that same guy who gave you the medical examiner's report on Worley and get the one on Beatty."

He looked pained, really uncomfortable. He pushed his empty plate off to one side. He'd finished minutes before, so

123

this was a gesture, one I couldn't quite read. He looked like he was about to make a speech, but all he said was, "Chico, I found a script."

That confused me. "I don't quite get what you mean," I said at last.

"The deal with Uschi," he explained, "she said I should go into development and start reading scripts so I could get ideas from them, you know? That when I found one, I could produce it. It's a cop one, this one. That's what they expect from me is cop ones. But it's pretty good, you know? That's what I was doing when you called, I was talking to the guy who wrote it. I mean, he was never a cop, but he did research, so it's not, like, total bullshit, you know?"

"I understand," I said. I did, too.

"Where I came from—Hamtramck, Detroit, you know—I never thought I could ever do something like this. I would never have the chance. Now I got the chance, I don't want to fuck it up. Right? You see what I mean?"

"Yeah, I see."

"I hope so," he said, "because it's because of you I got this chance, and I really want you to understand. I don't forget what you did for me, hooking me up with Uschi, but I gotta play it their way. I'm sorry, Chico. I really am, but I can't get involved in it any way. Not no more."

Through all of it I was doing the nodding this time. I even managed to put a smile on my face, just to let him know that, yes, it really was okay.

He slid out from the booth seat and stood up. If he was getting fat, I couldn't see it. I had to look at all this from his side, and when I did that, I really did understand. "It's okay, Casimir." That was all I could say.

He tossed a twenty down on the table. I picked it up and handed it back to him. "I said this one's on me. Remember?"

He nodded and accepted it. "Sure, Chico. I forgot." Then he gave me a look of sadness and a little envy that said he knew that things were very different between us now. Then he turned and walked quickly out the door.

I watched him go and waited, thinking how much I liked the

124

guy and how little I envied him. I took another swig from the Dos Equis bottle and then pulled the bowl of chili over and dipped my spoon into it at last. It was cold. I pushed it aside. Who wants to eat cold chili, anyway?

I drove around aimlessly for a while, thinking that the smart thing to do would be to go up to the office and wait for the phone to ring. But I didn't do that.

Eventually my driving, if not my mind, took some direction. I headed up Cahuenga, where it runs parallel to the Hollywood Freeway, and took the turnoff where Mulholland Drive begins. Accelerating up the grade, I was soon up in the Hollywood Hills, riding the ridge, driving those twisting curves, shifting down and up automatically as I took a kind of pure pleasure in the road. Release—this was what I needed. I used to come up here in the old Toyota and drive too fast, pushing it around the bends and switchbacks, driving out my frustrations with the business, with my wife, with whatever it was that had me feeling sorry for myself at the moment. That's not how it was today. No, it wasn't desperation that drove me, but just the desire to be free for a while, to put it all behind me, or maybe just to let things cook for a while at the back of my brain.

So I drove—past Coldwater Canyon, along the stretch where the movie stars' houses are shelved into the hillside, precariously supported on stilts; past Laurel Canyon, where the sweeping curves rise and fall with the terrain; and finally, just a bit past Benedict Canyon, near the firehouse, where I knew I would stop.

This used to be the place where I did my thinking. It was here I decided to leave the LAPD and try it on my own. It was also here, one night all alone, that I said good-bye to my wife, decided that yes, she was right, it wasn't working and maybe we should just be friends. I remember that night very well. I was smoking more then, and I must have gone through nearly half a pack as I sat in the car at that pull-off. I stared down at the lights of the Valley, quite a sight blinking below me, reviewing the last five years, the good and bad, and decided finally that it was okay, okay for both of us. After the divorce, she went back to Seattle. Now she's my friend in Seattle. I get letters from her once in a while, and a couple of times she's called.

But again, this time it was different. It was midafternoon. The Valley is a lot prettier at night than it is in the daytime. The smog hangs over it like a fuzzy brown blanket. The air is murky. As I looked across that expanse, about the size of the city of Denver, I could barely make out the mountains that formed the north wall. But that was okay. I didn't come up here to admire the scenery. I came up here to think.

What came into my mind immediately was what I'd been keeping out ever since I left the bar across from the studio. Just this: that most of what Casimir had said to me made perfect sense—not only from his point of view, but from mine, too. If I went ahead with the case, I'd get no encouragement from anybody. I stood a good chance of ruining my relationship with Heinrich Toller and losing a lot of money in the bargain. Everybody said drop it, so why not drop it?

What was I, one of these TV private eyes who's going to solve the case whether he's got a client or not? I remember watching those shows one night with Dee Dee Lazarus and positively hooting when the guy got fired by his client and made this speech about how he was going to get to the bottom of this, no matter what. I told her that was bullshit, nobody works without getting paid. It's not professional.

And I always prided myself on being professional. So what was I doing, sitting up here in my car on Mulholland Drive, even considering pushing ahead with this on my own? Was it some personal regard for Worley and Beatty? Of course not. I never even knew Worley, and Beatty was just a guy, a gay guy at that. Not exactly my cup of tea. Casimir was right: they were only special because they were *my* stiffs, and right now I had time and energy to burn, a great unfocused need to keep busy.

Thinking about Casimir, I at last remembered the medical examiner's report I had in my jacket pocket. I pulled it out and began browsing through it, just looking to see if something would turn up. Something did. At the bottom of the second page, the ME concluded that the initial knife thrust was delivered from behind, over the victim's shoulder, and with considerable force to the center of the chest, piercing the sternum, and—

Piercing the sternum? It would take a hell of a blow to do that, and a hell of a sharp knife. I couldn't drive a knife through the bone that holds the rib cage together. Not many men could. As far as I could tell, there was only one man I'd seen in the past few days who was likely to have that kind of strength—the kind it would also take to lift an unconscious man up and wrap a noose around his neck. That was Alex Wakefield's driver. And I didn't even know his name. I wondered how I could find out.

I hadn't been doing so well with names lately. There was no Clay Weston listed in either of Los Angeles's two area codes, and my one and only contact at the Department of Motor Vehicles wasn't due back from vacation until day after tomorrow. Maybe I'd lose interest by that time. Somehow I hoped that I would.

I started the Alfa, drove the half block to Beverly Glen, took a left there, and headed for home.

By the time six o'clock rolled around and Alicia hadn't shown up, I was kind of worried. Pilar, after all, was not the slickest driver I knew. She was one of those women who kept to the right lane on the freeway, no matter what, and played kamikaze with every car entering the race from the surface streets below. But there was no freeway driving necessary from Majestic Studios. All she had to do was head west on Santa Monica, and she'd have Alicia and the baby home in a matter of minutes. So, yes, I was worried. Too many minutes had gone by. I went to the telephone, checked in the book, and dialed Pilar's number in Silverlake. She answered on the second ring.

"Oh, yes, Meester Cervantes," she explained, "I lef' her and the baby there. That Meester Gresham said it was okay. He drive them home. Is nothing to worry about, I'm sure."

"Why are you so sure?" I asked her. Sitcom producers could have auto accidents, too, couldn't they?

"Because he's, how my kids say, a nerd, not muy macho, like you."

"That wasn't what I meant."

"Oh. What was it you meant?"

"Never mind."

I said good-bye and hung up, leaving Pilar free to wonder why I'd bothered to call her at all. I wondered that myself. I picked up *Rock Avatar* from the telephone table and settled back into the chair where I'd started reading an hour or two before.

I was getting toward the end of the book, past the point where Clay Weston seemed to figure in the story anymore. The writer, this guy Kelly Klinger, was pretty vague about Weston's final break with Tommy Osborne. Which seemed pretty peculiar, considering the two of them had been together since high school. He just quoted Alex Wakefield to the effect that Clay Weston had made "unreasonable demands" on Osborne. (You could sure tell where Klinger got most of his information.) Anyway, he placed their falling-out, or whatever it was, up in Osborne's place in northern California. And it was about a year before Osborne's death.

I kept on reading in hopes that Weston might pop up again, but, no, it was just stuff about the making of that last album, the one released simply as *Tommy Osborne,* with no mention of the DMZ. And then there was some stuff about the girl-friend, Rachel Klein, leading up to a rerun of the death scene in the first chapter.

By the time I finished, it was about eight-thirty, and still no Alicia. She had the baby and had gone through one feeding already. I was about ready to start calling all the Greshams on the west side, when I heard a key in the door. Alicia signaled quiet. The baby was asleep. She tiptoed with her into the bedroom, and I waited. Alicia came out after a minute or two with a smile on her face from here to there.

Closing the door quietly after her, she came running up to me and gave me a hug and a kiss and another hug, while all the time she was talking, saying, "Chico, Chico, Chico! Ay, qué suerte! Is the bes', the mos' bee-you-ti-fool."

"What is it?" I said. "What?"

"I got the part!" Then she added, "Almos'."

Then, well, I didn't exactly push her away, but I stepped back and studied her for a moment. "What does that mean? You got the part, almost?"

The way she looked, she wasn't sure whether to give me an exasperated look or a pout, so she split the difference and gave me an exasperated pout. She pulled herself erect, put her hands on her hips, and said, "It mean' that *Arnie* like' me jus' fine. Only I got to go back an' read for another guy."

"Who?"

"I don' know, some guy. Is head of TV at the studio."

She wasn't kidding, was she? Even if Gresham had an okay on the pilot script, casting couldn't be his call alone, not for the lead. I still had the feeling that this was totally unreal, that she, or I, or maybe both of us, were just being strung along.

"Only one thing," she said. "I gotta work on my blocking. Was okay when I read for Arnie at the office, but at his house I got all mix' up when he had me walk on it."

"Walk through it," I corrected automatically.

"Sí. Walk true it."

"You went to his *house?*"

"Sí. Por qué no?"

"Without Pilar."

"Sure, withou' Pilar." Then her eyes widened in something like shock. "Chico, you're jealous, huh? Celoso!"

"No, I'm not."

"Then why you ac' like this? You think I do something with him to get the part? Well, I tell you one thing. I don' have to do that stuff. I'm an ac'ress. I make it on my own."

Was I really hearing this? How could I explain to her that in this business it was easy to get hurt by a guy like Gresham? How could I explain that, when chances were pretty good that she was right—I *was* jealous? "Now you're going to tell me all about his big house, I suppose."

"Not so big."

"And his big car."

"Little. Very little. Pequeño. But faster than yours!" She was taunting me now.

"He whipped up a little supper? An omelet? Candlelight?"

"No. He sen' out for Chinese."

I threw up my hands, turned, and started to walk away. But she grabbed me by the arm, held me, made me face her.

"You think I do this thing? Es verdad?" She looked at me like she couldn't believe it. "Is not *profesional.*" She said it like the Spanish word, meaning the same. "If I do this, Ursula, she wouldn' like it."

Maybe. But then again, it seemed to me that Ursula Toller would be pleased at anything that would separate us. But I looked at Alicia, and I had to admit that she probably thought what she said was true. And really, I had to admit that I believed her. Of course I believed her. She was right. I was jealous. "Okay," I said at least. "I'm sorry."

"You un'erstan'. Good. Chico, I need your help."

"Sure. Okay."

"This blocking. This—qué quiere decir—hit the mark? You help me, huh?"

I sighed. "We'll see. Maybe tomorrow."

Then she threw her hands up and stamped her foot in anger. "Oh, tomorrow? Mañana, mañana, mañana, siempre así. I thought you American, but you *really* Mexican, huh? I'm gonna tell you something." She stood, shaking her finger at me—and then she stopped. "No. I tell you nothing. I go to bed now."

With that, she turned and headed straight for the bedroom. A moment later she disappeared inside. So it was another one of those nights, was it? I could live with it—with a little help from my friend José Cuervo.

I marched into the kitchen, broke out a few cubes from the freezer, and filled a glass from that gold bottle I took from the cupboard shelf. I took a big, long gulp of it and stood waiting, as if I expected it to cool me out immediately. It didn't. So I took another gulp and opened up the bottle and filled it up again.

Then, as I stood looking at the glass in my hand, what she had said suddenly struck me: "It's not *profesional*." No, it was what she hadn't said. Not, "Oh, no. I love you too much to do such a thing, Chico." And then I realized there hadn't been much talk of love between us for quite a while. How did I get into this crazy, nowhere situation, anyway?

All of a sudden I felt the need to talk to someone, anyone, about practically anything. It wasn't late. I looked at my watch and saw that it wasn't even nine o'clock yet. But there was no one I could call, and certainly no one I could talk to about this. It was grin-and-bear-it time.

Then I remembered I hadn't talked to my answering service for a day or two. Is not *profesional*. So I walked to the telephone—a little unsteadily, I admit, for the Cuervo Gold had hit me and my empty stomach harder than I'd realized. I dialed the number and got the night operator on the line.

"Anything for me, Darlene?"

"Oh, hi, Chico. Long time no talkee. How you doin', honey?"

"Don't ask."

"Like that, huh?"

"Like that."

"Well, yeah, I got a couple of things here for you. Lady named Dee Dee—have I got that right?—she called this afternoon and said you two should get together because she's got some stuff to tell you about a certain party. You'll know who. You know who?"

"I know. It's okay."

"She said call her back. You've got the number. Okay?"

"Okay."

"And then there's this one from yesterday evening about seven-thirty. You know, you really ought to call in more often."

"I know."

"It's from—hold it a minute. I have to take a call." And she went off the line. It couldn't be much fun doing what Darlene did. I got the feeling she wanted to talk to me as much as I wanted to talk to her.

It was almost exactly a minute, or maybe ten seconds more, and she was back: "Where was I? Oh, yeah, well, this fella called—I took it myself. He was all worked up, wanted your home phone number and all. I told him we didn't give out that information."

I'd gone unlisted when I opened up the office on Hollywood Boulevard. So far I liked it that way.

"Who was he? What was his name?"

"Wait a minute. I've got the slip right here. A Tom Beatty. You know somebody by that name?"

My mouth went dry. I set the glass down next to the cradle of the telephone. "I used to," I said. "What's the message?"

"Well," said Darlene, "it's really not much at all. Just a name and a phone number. I tried to get him to give me more, but he said this was what you wanted."

"What *is* it, Darlene,? For God's sake, *please.*"

"Oh, now, don't you start in, Chico. Here it is. 'Clay Weston. Area code 805, 637–7749.' "

Thirteen

I lined up early at the box office and got one of the few remaining tickets to the show. It's not that Maya Kester was such a hot act, but she had gotten a lot of press. And while she couldn't fill the Universal Amphitheatre, and maybe never would, her record company must have figured she was too big for anything but the Roxy. It's the little club on the strip where the class acts all play. Club Lingerie, the Whisky—well, they're okay, but the groups that play there are looking for attention from critics, record companies, managers, and so on; they're looking to get discovered. By the time they hit the Roxy they're beyond that. Maya Kester was after attention, too, and with her second album just going into release, DBR, her label, was going to make sure she got it with a big block of tickets to the press, the deejays, and all the movers and shakers of the music industry. It was all but a private party. The few tickets that were left went on sale before the show, and that's why I lined up early to get one.

Was I a big Maya Kester fan? No. You might say I was vaguely aware of her as a name but had no idea what she sounded like. The big attraction was Clay Weston.

After I got the number from Darlene the night before, I'd thanked her politely and then hung up. Then I actually started to shake. Maybe it was the Cuervo Gold, but I don't think so. I sat down in the chair beside the phone and felt a kind of

133

electricity in my hand. I held it up and saw that there was a steady little tremor there. There was this ugly image I had of Tom Beatty at the end of the rope, a mental picture that I had pretty successfully kept out of my head until that moment. But there he was, and he was talking to me through Darlene, telling me what I wanted to know.

I took another drink of the tequila. Just a sip, I thought, to steady me. But I wasn't high. My pulse was racing. I sat there, trying to calm down before I took the next step.

What was it going to be? Sure, of course, I would call the number that Beatty had left for me. The 805 area code said that it was probably someplace in Ventura County. But for whatever reason, I wanted to know where. I dialed 805 information and asked the operator the location of the 637 exchange. She told me that would be in the Ojai area.

Well, okay. I knew approximately where: Ojai—tucked high up in the Ventura Mountains, a community of artists and people who pretended they were. There were some ranches up there, but most of it was laid out along dusty streets that surrounded a center that was about equal parts country town and boutiqueland. You didn't have to be rich to live in Ojai, but it helped.

I sat there a moment staring at the telephone, then with a sigh, almost as if it were something I dreaded, I dialed the number.

A woman picked up, and I asked for Clay Weston.

"He's not here," she said.

"Well, when will he be in?" I asked. "It's pretty important."

"It always is, isn't it?" She laughed at that. I'd noticed she was slurring her words. She sounded drunk. Maybe they'd just had a fight, too.

"When can I call back?"

"Not tonight. He's in L.A. tonight. He said he'd be back tomorrow night late, but don't count on it."

"Well, look," I said, "I'm calling from Los Angeles. Is there a number here where I could reach him?"

"If there is, I don't know it. He's probably with one of his girlfriends. Leaves me with the kids, no way to reach him,

134

nothin'. I mean, what if something happened, if there was a fire or somethin'? What would I do, up here all alone? What would I do?"

She really wanted to know. What could I tell her? "Uh, call the fire department?"

"That's what he says. Just call nine one one, he says."

"There's no way I can reach him, huh?"

"Who are you? What's this about?"

"I'm an old friend of his from Detroit," I said. "I knew him in high school."

"Yeah?" She sounded skeptical. "What high school was that?"

I was afraid she'd ask. What was it the book said? I reached out—and suddenly there it was: "Cass Tech."

"Hey-y-y! That's right! I guess maybe you do know him then. So . . . listen, he's at the Roxy tomorrow night."

"He's playing there."

"Yeah, right." As if to say, who in his right mind would go there for any other reason? "There's this chick, I forget her name—he did backup on her album. Now they want the same licks in the same places. Same old bullshit, you know?"

I didn't know, exactly, but I said, "Sure. Anyway, I'll try him there."

"Yeah. Do that. It's been nice talking to you . . . uh, what did you say your name was?"

"Marlowe," I said, "Phil Marlowe." That just popped out. I wished it hadn't.

"Okay, Phil. Just see he goes home tomorrow night, okay?"

"Right, and thanks."

So that was why I was at the Roxy. I waited around out in front of the place for a few minutes, more than a few, trying to get some sense of the people who were moving through the entrance in a steady stream. A girl stood there with a guest list, checking them off, one by one. The movers and shakers were present in full regalia, their dates adorned for the occasion in net, sequins, and gold lame. Mixed in among them was another group, unisex, definitely scruffier, that seemed to favor jeans, T-shirts, and unwashed hair; these, I was pretty sure, were the journalists. The others? Well, they must have been the deejays; mostly, they looked the way I did—jacket, slacks, no tie, and an indifferent expression.

I looked at my watch and decided I ought to go inside. There was plenty of time left before the show, but if I had any hope of getting up close to the stage, I couldn't wait too long. So I headed through the entrance with my ticket and tried to push it at the girl with the guest list. She shook her head and pointed over to a guy on the right and he let me through.

I did manage to get pretty close to the stage—over on the left side. All I could do was hope I could attract Weston's attention from there. I ordered a beer and waited.

It occurred to me that I'd been doing a lot of waiting that day. First of all, I waited for Alicia to get up. She never did, not while I was around, anyway. The baby woke up for a feeding sometime in the early morning, probably around five. I was vaguely aware of that, and sort of semiconscious, too, when Alicia climbed over me and went back to bed. But a couple of hours later when I got up, she was sleeping soundly, and I didn't wake her. I fixed breakfast for myself and let Pilar in when she showed up. Still not a sound from the bedroom.

I made a phone call and got a name and a number. I called the number, talked to the name, and made an appointment for later in the day. Then I wrote it all down on a piece of paper and handed the paper over to Pilar.

"What is this, senor?"

"It's something . . . well, it's for Alicia."

"You have a fight with her?"

"Maybe you could call it that."

"It happens. My husband and I, when he was alive, all the time."

I shrugged and then gave a little tap to the paper in her hand. "Tell her this person can give her what she wants."

"And what is that?" She was as nosy as my mother used to be. Are all women like that? Or just all women of a certain age?

"Tell her this person will show her how to hit the mark. Got that?"

136

"Hit the mark," she repeated.

"Right. You can drive her over at one o'clock, can't you?"

"Sure. Is no problem."

"This person is an acting coach. Not exactly a teacher. She helps with specific problems. Maybe Alicia should see her a few times."

"I tell her that, too."

"Yeah." I didn't see any point in hanging around any longer, so I headed for the door.

"Senor Cervantes?" I turned and found Pilar staring at me very seriously. "These things work out," she said. "You will see."

I nodded and walked out the door.

There wasn't much for me to do that day, or anything at all, really, so I headed over to the office, opened the place up, and sat around for a while. Oh, I tried to read *Don Quixote* but found that I couldn't keep my mind on the page. So I just leaned forward on the desk and stared out the window, south across Hollywood, acres and acres of urban sprawl as far as you could see, about as dismal a view as you would find anywhere this side of Mexico City. I was thinking about Alicia and me, about Clay Weston, about a lot of things. None of it led anyplace, of course. I came to no conclusions, reached no decisions, just provided time and space to allow some unconnected notions to circulate through my brain. I sat there a long time like that, as if I were waiting for something.

The telephone rang. I grabbed it, thinking it might be Alicia. But no. It was Dee Dee Lazarus.

"How come you didn't call, Chico? I got all this good information for you, and you didn't call."

Yeah, why hadn't I? Partly, of course, it was the shock of getting that message from Tom Beatty. A message from the dead. That shocked me, even scared me a little. But by the time I heard that Dee Dee was trying to reach me, I was beginning to feel guilty about my suspicions. Maybe I thought I could just drop the whole thing. But with Dee Dee, there was no chance of that. "Well," I said at last, "I've been pretty busy on this case."

"The one that involves Arnie Gresham?" I had sort of led her to believe that, hadn't I?

"Well . . ."

"It's not *really* a divorce case, is it Chico?"

"Uh . . ."

"How about that lunch? Remember? You promised."

I hadn't, really. But just try telling Dee Dee that. Besides, what else did I have to do the rest of the day, except stare out the window? "Okay," I said, "sure. How about Butterfield's at one o'clock?"

"Butterfield's! I haven't been there for ages! Not since that time you—well, we won't go into that."

It was agreed then. We would meet. I spent the rest of the morning looking forward to it and dreading it, trying to get my story straight, wondering if I could get away with telling her nothing at all. Not likely, not with Dee Dee.

As it turned out, there was some need to worry. It started out an easy occasion, but getting started took a while. I arrived a few minutes early, took a table, and waited with a beer.

Butterfield's is the kind of place—you have to know it's there. Strictly speaking, I guess, it's on Sunset. But you go in the back way, leave your car, climb some steps, and find yourself in a garden. Nice. Women like it. The sun beats down. If it gets a little too warm, each table is equipped with a parasol. There's a fish pond with a few gold carp, and an energetic crew of waiters and waitresses who want you to know their first names and are ready to tell you all about the day's specials.

I like it, too. It's a nice place to wait. I waited. With Dee Dee you always do. Conversation flowed around me—movie stuff, mostly. But it's not one of those places where you recognize faces. Just people in the industry.

I made a concession and drank my beer from a glass. It is, after all, a pretty classy place. As I waited for Dee Dee, I tried to remember the last time I was here with her, maybe a year ago, maybe not quite that long. But I couldn't remember what I'd done or said that was so awful that she didn't want to talk about it on the telephone. It also occurred to me that even

138

though my place was only a couple of blocks away, I'd never brought Alicia here. I wondered why.

By the time Dee Dee made her appearance, it was pretty close to one-thirty, and I was on my second beer. She bustled over to the table, showering a lot of unfocused energy in every direction. I got up, put out my hand to greet her, but she threw her arms around me and gave me a kiss, right on the mouth.

"There!" she said. "We've got that out of the way."

Well, there was a lot of how-have-you-been, what-have-you-been-up-to talk that took us right up to the food. Most of the time, what Dee Dee wants to talk about is Dee Dee, and that was just the way it went there in the beginning. In fact, she seemed to be avoiding any mention of Arnie Gresham. I heard more about the cancellation of her cop show. Then she told me about what she had "in development." That's right—Rossi—a drug series. Only he'd disappointed her by refusing to talk about active cases and not saying much about the ones they'd closed. Anyway, they'd had a couple of "meetings," and she'd taken a lot of notes. Now she was trying to find the right writer for the pilot—meaning, I guess, one who would do it on spec.

"And then, of course," she said, pausing over her seafood salad to raise her wineglass, "there's always *our* series, the one about you."

"Well, let's talk about that later."

I must have sounded kind of touchy, because the next thing she said was, "You're always putting me off on that. That's how it was the last time we were here. That's right—here at Butterfield's. I mean, I just asked you for a few details about something you were working on, and you got angry. You said—and I quote—'My life is not a TV show, Dee Dee.' Like a TV show was about the lowest thing there was. Honestly, Chico!" She made some effort at looking hurt, then she suddenly turned sly. "Do you still feel that way?"

"Well, I don't know. I—"

"Because I'm beginning to wonder about your sudden interest in this guy, Arnie Gresham," she continued. "I know you're working over at Majestic now. I saw you on the news—

quite a performance, I must say. And I just got to wondering about that. Gresham has this development deal at Majestic Television, and it occurred to me—well, I could be way off base on this, but it did occur to me that maybe he's developing a show with you—kind of a 'Barney Miller' sort of private-eye show. Is your life a *sitcom,* Chico?"

That hurt. And the reason it hurt was that the way I felt now, my life *was* kind of a sitcom. These scenes with Alicia might be funny to everybody but me. And I'd managed to shoot myself in the foot so often on this Worley thing that it was a wonder that I could walk at all. Barney Miller? More like Maxwell Smart.

So maybe it took me a little longer to answer than it should have. And maybe I didn't sound completely convincing when I said, "No, it's nothing like that, Dee Dee. Honestly."

She took a sip of wine and looked at me coolly. "I know you asked me all that stuff about, was he married, was he a womanizer, and so forth. But then it occurred to me maybe that was just to throw me off. Maybe what you really wanted to know was, Can I trust this guy? What kind of a business rep has he got? Now, Chico, if you're doing business with this guy, I have only one piece of advice for you." She paused then and leaned forward and rasped out in a stage whisper. *"Get an agent!"*

She seemed to have convinced herself that this was what was going on. And as far as she was concerned, it was just the latest betrayal. First the cancellation, then Rossi, and now me.

"Look," I said to her, "I've never even met the man."

"Oh? Who're you dealing with then?"

"I'm not dealing with *anybody,"* I said. "That just isn't happening."

"Chico," she said with a sigh, "I thought we had a special understanding on this. How much are they offering you?"

This was crazy. She wasn't listening to me at all. "Dee, Dee, I'm trying to—"

"Whatever it is, *get it in writing!* It doesn't have to be one of those big studio contracts with a lot of boilerplate. Just a simple letter of agreement between you and Gresham—or

140

whoever it is you're dealing with. You could probably write it up yourself—or maybe one of your lawyer buddies."

This time I didn't try to say anything. I just sat back and looked at her. Amazing. The way she saw it, she was giving me good advice. I had to give her credit for that. This was altruism, Hollywood-style. The fact that it had no relationship to any sort of reality didn't change that. She looked so damned earnest, staring across the table at me, that I felt a kind of sudden wave of affection for her—friendship, whatever, call it what you want to.

So maybe it was that. Or maybe it was because I didn't want her to number me among her betrayers. Or maybe it was just because I felt like I had to tell somebody. Anyway, I told *her.* What I did, I gave her an edited version of this situation with Alicia and Arnie Gresham. The way I presented it, Alicia had been an actress in Mexico with some experience—though not as much as she'd let on to him. She was talented, all right, but she lacked some of the basics. Anyway, Gresham was acting like she was just what he was looking for—but it was just happening too fast. I didn't want her to get hurt. Yeah, sure, I told Dee Dee that, but she saw right through it.

"You're afraid of losing her, aren't you, Chico?" Women have this sixth sense about stuff like that.

"Yeah," I said. "I guess I am."

"And that's why you wanted to know if he was married and all that."

"Yeah. Pitiful, huh?"

"It sounds like you're really in love with the lady." She put her hand over mine.

"Well, we haven't talked about that much lately."

"Maybe you should."

"Maybe. It's not so easy sometimes."

Dee Dee nodded. She understood. Then she suddenly brightened and gave me a rough pat on the hand. "I've got good news for you," she said. "The word is, Arnie Gresham is gay."

*   *   *

That gave me a lot to think about. Only I'm afraid not much of it was very rational. You remember those old movie serials? No, maybe you don't. I was just a kid, very young, when they were still showing them on Saturday afternoons downtown. Anyway, each week they'd end with the hero in some horrible predicament, and you had to come back the next Saturday to find out how he got out of it. The one I remember, the one that used to give me nightmares as a kid, was when the hero— maybe it was Flash Gordon, maybe Jungle Jim—got locked in some room, and suddenly the room started closing in on him. The ceiling came down, the floor came up, and on either side the walls began moving in. It was obvious he was going to be crushed, squashed, turned into one great big spot of Jell-O. How did he get out of it? It's funny, but I don't remember. All I remember is that room closing in on him very slowly, and that feeling that there was nothing anyone could do to stop it.

What's this got to do with Arnie Gresham? Well, these questions started coming without me really thinking them— and they all had to do with Gresham being gay. Did he know Worley? Did he know Beatty? Or worse, was he a friend of Alex Wakefield's? How did he fit in?

Well, of course he didn't fit in. I was trying to turn this whole experience into some sort of gay conspiracy aimed at me, closing in on me from every side, the way it was in that old Saturday afternoon serial. That was kind of paranoid, wasn't it? Yes, and maybe more than kind of. There's a lot of that latent paranoia circulating through Los Angeles these days. At best, with so many out of the closet and filled with gay pride, it more or less isolates them from the straight majority. At worst, with the threat of AIDS, it makes lepers of them and makes—what was the word Beatty used?—homophobes of the rest of us.

I remember I was still chewing that over while I was waiting for the show to start that night at the Roxy. The place had filled up fast. I was lucky to get a chair at a ringside table. With no apologies, I crowded in with a threesome from DBR Records. They never missed a beat in their rapid-fire conversation and managed to ignore me completely all the time we sat

142

together. Which was all right with me, because I really didn't have much to say to them, anyway. They were talking promo and publicity, saturation and focus. I wasn't sure whether they were trying to impress each other or somebody at the next table.

But they shut up fast when the lights went down and somebody from DBR—I guess he was the boss—came out and introduced "a vibrant new star who . . ." Well, you can imagine how the rest of it went.

Then the music.

There was this little girl with pink hair who was dressed in, well, sort of a black-lace jumpsuit, and she stormed up and down the stage, mike in hand, like she was really angry. And all the while, the band is going crazy behind her. This is no intro. It's the real thing—sixty-four bars of solid fury—and finally she takes a big leap and lands right in the middle of the stage and starts shouting into the microphone. She was so full of rage I couldn't understand a word she said. But it was very impressive noise. You remember Brenda Lee? Probably not. But everybody remembers Janis Joplin; even kids born the year she died know her from the golden-oldie stations. Well, Maya Kester sounded a little like both of them, only she was singing a full octave lower. We're talking about a five-foot female baritone, who's holding absolutely nothing back—a big voice, miked at state-of-the-art that's coming on so loud I halfway expected to see the walls start quivering.

And, oh, yeah, the band. There were really four of them, but amplified, they sounded like a whole army in hot pursuit. Bass, drums, a keyboard man with a complete electronic workshop at his disposal, and there he was on guitar, my man, Clay Weston.

He was just about as Eduardo had described him—a throwback to the sixties, with long, dark hair in a ponytail, a Vandyke, a western shirt, faded jeans, and a bent hand. It was his left, the one that moved up and down the neck of the guitar, finding the chords, as the pick in his right hand blurred through the strings. He'd given up his Fender guitar for a Les Paul Gibson, and what he played on it was different, too. My

143

memory of the DMZ told me that musically they were like a lot of other bands from the late sixties, a little more rhythm-and-bluesy than most; it was Tommy Osborne who made them different from the rest. Back then, Weston supplied a lot of clash and grind, raw sound that was just right behind Osborne's shouted threats. But now it was different—a lot different. The keyboard man provided a kind of basic floor on the synthesizer, while Weston moved in and out, down and around it, counterpointing with the little girl in the black jumpsuit about half the time, and driving hard behind her when she needed it. It was quite a performance, but I don't think anybody but the musicians up on the stage realized what Weston was up to. And what he was up to was pretty close to jazz.

They romped through a whole string of numbers, most of them up-tempo and hell-for-leather like the first—but no carbon copies. She did a blues and a couple of ballads, too, mixed in with the rest, and on one of these Weston came up front and did some cute stuff, trading off with her. That was when I got a good look at that left hand of his. It was a wonder he could do anything with it at all. The fingers were gnarled, two joints permanently swollen, and I actually saw him cross his index finger over his middle finger to hit one position. But he played. And there was good rapport between him and the girl. I got the sense he'd taught her a few things.

The basic idea was to present the new album in live performance. They got through that without a hitch. But the audience kept them up there for two or three more—from the first album, I guess. Then at last, bowing, showering sweat down on the tables front and center, Maya Kester left the stage. The members of the band unhooked from their amps, squirmed out from behind their equipment, and began shuffling off the stage.

I stood up. The way it looked to me, Weston would pass about four feet away from me. Applause had died down. I called to him, *"Clay Weston!"* He looked over at me and gave me a little wave and a tentative smile. I beckoned him over. He frowned and came a couple of steps closer. "I want to talk to you about Jimmy Worley." I said it as quietly as I could and still be heard.

He stepped back and looked at me. He was sizing me up. There was something in his eyes—not exactly distrust, or even suspicion, but caution. He leaned down and gave one short nod of his head. "Over at the Rainbow," he said, then he turned and walked off.

I knew where he meant. It was the bar next door. He would talk to me, anyway. Whether he would tell me what I wanted to know was something else again. But I was satisfied. I turned and started out. Some of the crowd stayed on to finish their drinks. Some of those leaving stood and talked, shook hands at the tables, and stood and talked some more.

I squeezed around them and past them and had just about reached the rear of the place when I looked down on a group of four at a table and straight into the face of Alex Wakefield.

Our eyes met. He smiled his dazzling smile. But he didn't say anything, and neither did I.

Fourteen

Upset? Sure I was upset. I sat at the bar in the Rainbow keeping my eyes on the door, waiting for Clay Weston. Music—Motown stuff from the sixties—hummed out loudly from speakers in the bar and the big room beyond. So I waited and watched as the kids came in ones and twos and fours and headed for the big room or the party room upstairs. But more clearly than them I saw the face of Alex Wakefield in my mind's eye and that smile he had flashed at me. It was a smile that said, I know all about you—I know everything, and I'm three steps ahead of you. It was what you'd call a supercilious smile.

Of course he had seen me talking to Weston. From his rear-table vantage point, he could hardly have missed it when I called out and got Weston's attention. Just seeing us there in the same room would have made him suspicious. But of what? He knew me, and he almost certainly knew Weston, but did he know the connection through Worley and Beatty? But wouldn't he guess? And what was Alex Wakefield doing at the Roxy, anyway? Had somebody tipped him off I was there? And at that point I began wondering just how much thinking I was doing and how much of this was pure paranoia. Because, after all, a showcase performance like this one was just the sort of function he'd be invited to and would attend. He was in the business, after all—very big in the business. It just hadn't occurred to me that he would be there, too.

I took a pull at my beer and noticed I was sweating. The barmaid, a blondie in jean shorts, came over and asked how I was doing on that beer. I told her I was doing just fine and watched her walk away.

That was all it took. I'd looked away from the door maybe ten seconds, and suddenly Clay Weston was there right in front of me when I looked back.

"Who are you?" he demanded.

"My name is Antonio Cervantes. I'm a private investigator." We had to talk pretty loud to be heard over the music. I didn't like that.

"Let me see your ID"

I pulled out my wallet and showed it to him.

He handed it back, not impressed but at least satisfied that I was who I said I was. "Who're you working for?" he wanted to know.

"Majestic Pictures," I said. It wasn't really a lie. "Worley was—"

"I know," he cut me off. "I know all about it." He took a step back, sizing me up again. "Why did you want to talk to me?"

"Because of Worley," I said, "and Tom Beatty. Eduardo said you talked to Worley a couple of nights before he got killed, and Beatty gave me your number in Ojai just before he . . ."

"Yeah, I heard about that. Suicide. It was bullshit."

"I agree."

He gave me that searching look again. "Who's Eduardo?"

"Little guy. Mexican. Lived with Worley."

He nodded. "Oh, yeah. The artist. But that still doesn't tell me why you want to talk to me."

I looked him straight in the eye. "Because I think you know why Worley was killed and who it was arranged Beatty's suicide."

At that, he seemed to have come to some sort of decision. But he looked around, annoyed, or at least disapproving. "We

147

can't talk here," he said. "Too noisy." Then he half turned and beckoned me to come along. "Come on. I know where we can go."

He led the way out of the Rainbow Bar and Grill, turned left, and headed down the alley that the place shared with the Roxy. "We'll take my car," he said. "That's better than trying to meet somplace."

I thought so, too, but my motive was simpler. I just wanted to get the hell away from the Roxy—and Alex Wakefield—in a hurry.

It was a short drive to the Mondrian Hotel, just down Sunset a few blocks, about as short as the elevator ride up to the terrace lounge. He hadn't said much on the way over, but he remarked as he pulled up to the entrance, "I've already checked out of here, but it's okay." Then he unbuckled and hauled out his guitar case. He told the parking attendant not to bury the car too deep. Not likely. The "car" was a beat-up Jeep at least a decade old. The kid would probably hide it out on the side street.

The lounge was quiet, all right. There was a piano over in one corner, tinkling jazz in imitation of Bill Evans. We sat at the bar, well removed from three solitary drinkers at the far end but within sight of a wide view of the west side spread out in lights all across the LA Basin. I'd never been here before. It was okay.

Weston took a gulp of his ginger ale, then turned to me and said, "How do I know which side you're on?"

I thought about that. "I don't know," I said honestly. "What can I say to convince you?"

"Well, you can start by telling me everything you know."

I did that, and it took a while, even keeping it down to the facts and the specific conclusions I'd drawn from them. I left my speculations out of it.

He listened soberly, nodding from time to time, not saying a word, just sipping from his drink. The only real response I got from him was at the end, when I told him that about the message that Tom Beatty had left with my answering service—just Weston's name and phone number.

"So that's how you found me, huh? It's unlisted. But you got the number and called it, and she told you where I was."

"Well, it wasn't as simple as that."

"No?"

"No. I said I knew you in high school. I conned her, I guess."

"It ain't that hard to do, not when she's drinking." He sighed. "I don't know. I kept Rachel out of this, didn't tell her a thing, didn't want to scare her. Just asked her not to talk to anybody, and I wouldn't tell her where I was staying. But I guess she gets lonesome up there."

Rachel? That rang a bell. "Wait a minute," I said. "Wasn't she . . ."

"Yeah, that's right. Tommy's old girlfriend, sort of. We're both survivors of the same war. They put it out she was with him right up until he died. They had this big fight and all. Well, that was all bullshit, too. She was long gone by then, turned up pregnant, and Tommy kicked her out. We found each other a year later, her blasted out of her gourd on any kinda drug she could find, and trying to take care of the kid, Tommy's kid. We've been together ever since, just holdin' on. I got her off everything but liquor. I got a little problem with that myself." He raised the glass of ginger ale, like he was toasting sobriety. "Anyway, she pretty much only drinks when I'm away—and I guess that's to punish me for leavin'. But leavin's how I make my livin'."

"What happened to the kid?" I asked.

"Tommy Junior? Yeah, she named him after his father. I don't know. He's down in Mexico someplace last I heard—and that was a couple of years ago. He's just like his old man, though—might even be dead, for all I know." But then he brightened a bit and said, "We got two of our own, though. They're turning out pretty good, considering the parents they got."

He smiled at that and then grew thoughtful again. He put his left hand up on the bar and held it there for me to see. It

149

was the first real look at it that I had had since I'd gotten that look at it up on the stage. He had a way of keeping it out of sight—behind him or shoved down in his jacket pocket. When he drove, I noticed he kept his palm up with his thumb hooked in the steering wheel. But now it was there, palm down, flat on the bar for my inspection. If you looked at it, you'd say he had a crippled hand. The middle knuckles on two fingers were about twice the size they should have been, and the index finger was bent in at a slight angle. But how could you call that fret hand of his crippled when he'd played the way he had that night?

"Want to know how I got that?" he asked.

"If you want to tell me, I do."

"That was the night," he said with a kind of bitter smile. "The night of the 'Big Fight.' " In quotation marks. "It was up north at Tommy's place in the mountains. I was up there, and so was Rachel and Alex and Ferdy."

"Who was he?"

"Oh, you've met Ferdy. You've seen his work. Ferdinand Petko."

"The big guy? Wakefield's driver?"

"When he's around, yes. And Tommy was there, too, of course. I flew all the way up there to have it out with them."

"What was this about?" I asked. The way he was staring off into space, I could tell it was all real to him at that moment; it was happening all over again. I needed details.

He looked at me and nodded. "Well, it was about the DMZ. It was always a partnership, Tommy and me. The others in the band sort of came and went. But ever since Detroit in high school it was him and me. We wrote the songs. We fronted the band. It was just us two together, but we never had anything on paper, never needed to.

"But then Tommy signed with Alex Wakefield—not the band, not the two of us. Wakefield just wanted Tommy, and he got him. From that moment on, he was trying to drive a wedge between us. The whole thing came to a head with that last album we did together. To this day, I don't know how he pulled it off, but Alex got it released more or less under

150

Tommy's name. Not 'the DMZ,' the way it always was before, but 'Tommy Osborne and the DMZ,' That's what I went up there about."

Petko—Ferdy—met the plane in Redding. Weston hadn't expected that and should have been suspicious, but the big guy had been driving the band's equipment van for over a year, and he was trusted—up to a point. So Weston went along for the ride—and a long one it was, up into the mountains, well off the highway, miles from any town.

"But I remember," he said, "we'd been driving on this old ridge road, and it was after sundown but not quite dark, and there were these lights high up there above the trees. Ferdy points and says, 'That's it,' and he takes a left, and then we were really driving on some kinda rough road, up and up, but all the time there were those lights there, and that's where we were headed."

As Weston had anticipated, Alex Wakefield was there. The only one he hadn't expected to see was Rachel. She'd been hanging around the band for a while—more than a groupie but not what you'd call "Tommy's girl." Tommy didn't have one—he had thousands.

After some drinking, a little eating, and continual sparring, Weston got down to cases with Wakefield. He wanted to know what this shit, "Tommy Osborne and the DMZ," was all about.

"It means," Alex had said, "that Tommy is now number one, and my job is looking out for number one."

Weston looked to Osborne then. It was up to him at that point to confirm or deny what Wakefield had just said. But he was out of it completely. "He hadn't said a word, hardly even knew I was there," said Weston then, and he demonstrated by putting on a stone face with vacant eyes. "I don't know whether it was downers or maybe he was off on LSD someplace. He was into that then, everybody was. Anyway, he wasn't around when I needed him. Rachel seemed to know what was going on, though—at least that's what she said afterward."

Wakefield said Weston could stay on "more or less as an

151

employee" if he wanted to, and if he didn't, well, that was the end of it.

"But then," Weston continued, "I started in on him. I guess I came on pretty strong. I told him that even if it wasn't down on paper, Tommy and I had a contract. There were lots of people who would testify to that, and I'd take him to court if I had to.

"He said, 'A verbal contract isn't worth the paper it's printed on.'"

"Old joke," I said. "Popularly credited to Sam Goldwyn."

Weston slapped the bar with his bad hand. "That's it!" he said. "He was joking with me. He was so sure of himself he wasn't even taking me seriously. That drove me crazy! So I went after him. I jumped him, got him down, hit him in the face a couple of times, banged his head on the floor, and then all of a sudden I feel myself lifted up and off him. It's Ferdy. He's got my arms pinned to my sides, and my feet are off the floor. You know how big he is."

"Yeah." I nodded. "I know."

"Anyway, Alex gets up, and he's dabbing away at his lip, which is bleeding, with a handkerchief. The way he looked at me then, I've never seen anybody look. If he'd killed me, I wouldn't've been surprised. But he said in this shaky voice, 'Let me tell you about contracts. They are based on the idea that both parties will deliver as promised. If Tommy lost his voice in some accident, then there would be no more contract. And if you . . .' And then he told Ferdy to put me down on the floor, flat. And Ferdy stretched me out. I started fighting and trying to get away, but it didn't do any good. Ferdy put my left hand out, and Alex stomped down on the fingers real hard with the heel of his boot two or three times. I don't know, maybe more. Rachel started screaming then. But Tommy never came out of it.

"Alex yelled at me, 'The contract is void!' And then he said to Ferdy, 'Get him out of here.' Ferdy just picked me up, hauled me to the door and pushed me out. I banged on the door with my good hand for a while, but then I understood I

152

was on my own. No ride to the airport. No coat. A broken hand. It was survival time.

"What can I say? I survived. It was October and, God, it gets cold at night up in those mountains that time of year. But I didn't have any choice, I staggered down that old dirt road to the county road, and I started hiking back the way we came. The shock gradually wore off, and that's when the pain started. They say you can't remember pain, but, man, I remember that! I might not've made it at all, but this old trucker came along with a load of logs and dropped me off in Mount Shasta City, the nearest town.

"That whole year, that was pretty bad. The doctors said, sure, they could operate, but they'd have to break my fingers again, and they couldn't guarantee the results anyway. So I said, 'No, thanks.' "

He seemed to have come to a stopping point, so I asked him, "Did you sue? bring charges? anything?"

He sighed. "No, I'll be honest with you. I'd had the fight scared out of me, I guess. Or maybe that wasn't it. Maybe I just started drinking and couldn't get it together enough to do anything more than feel sorry for myself. Money wasn't a problem. BMI and the label kept paying me royalties. So I just stayed drunk for a year."

"But you came back," I put in. "What happened?"

"Django Reinhardt happened."

"What do you mean?"

"Well, back before the war, there was this French Gypsy guitar player who—"

"I know who he was," I interrupted. "I know about him."

"Well, I didn't," said Weston. "And this one morning I woke up all hung over and hating myself—but sober—and this guy I know showed up at my door. Well, I'd only just met him once or twice before, but I got to know him pretty good eventually. He was a guitar teacher, and when I first hit L.A., I had the idea I'd take lessons. Like everybody in rock back then, I was self-taught, and I thought it'd be neat if I really learned how to play. But I let it go after a couple of times with him.

"Anyway, this same guy showed up at my door, and he had a pile of records under his arm. He didn't wait to be asked. He just walked right in. He'd heard about my situation, but he didn't try to give me a pep talk or anything. He just walked over to my phonograph and put one of those records on. 'Sit down and listen to this,' he said. Well, it was jazz, sort of, but all strings, and this solo guitar was like nothin' I ever heard before. Real fast, but with rolls and runs, the kind of jazz you might expect a gypsy to play. It just sort of stunned me.

"I listened and listened, and when that side was over, the guitar teacher said, 'You've just listened to one of the greatest guitarists of all time. It's a miracle that Django Reinhardt and Andrés Segovia were playing in the same century, like having two Paganinis.' And then he whipped out this picture of Django from one of the albums, and he put it in front of me, and he said, 'Now, take a look at his fret hand.' And there it was, all scarred up, and you could see Django's got one finger, the middle one, crossed over the other to make a position, looked like G-natural. I began to get the message. Then this fella, his name's Carl, and he's pretty old now, he told me how Django got his hand burned in a fire and pretty much lost the use of two fingers when he was about twenty. So he said to me then, 'Now, you can either sit here and drink yourself to death, or you can take charge of your life and do what Django did. Either way. It's up to you.' He left the records and told me to bring them back to him in a week and let him know what I'd decided.

"Didn't take a week. I got a rubber ball and started working with that, like the doctor told me to in the first place, and then I began working with Carl."

The place had become pretty quiet. The piano player had stopped a while ago, I guess, and I hadn't even noticed. All but one of the other drinkers had left. The bartender stood polishing glasses at the other end of the bar.

"That's quite a story," I said at last. Understatement of the year.

He nodded soberly. "I may not be Django, because I ain't

154

a genius the way he was, but I am the best damned studio guitarist in L.A., and I don't care who knows it."

He said it like he meant it. He also said it like that was his last word. We weren't through talking, though—and he knew it. Just to underline it, though, I ordered another round—beer for me, ginger ale for my friend.

"Okay, what do you want to know?" he asked, then he answered his own question: "You want to know about the tape, right?"

"Yeah, I guess I do."

"All right, yes, there is a tape, and where I've got it hid, nobody's going to find it."

"Next question—what's on it?"

"Yeah, that's the big one, isn't it?"

The bartender trudged over and put our drinks before us. He looked at me kind of questioningly, and I shook my head. He shrugged and walked off to polish more glasses.

"What's on it?" Weston echoed my question. "Enough to blow friend Alex right out of the water. Look, I knew Jimmy Worley—not well, just casually—for about twenty years. He was a recording engineer, then he produced a little, and finally he got into the movie business as a music editor. He was real good at it, I understand. Anyway, a little over a week ago, he got hold of me on the phone, and he asked me to come down and listen to a tape. Well, that didn't interest me much, but then he told me it was some of the stuff for this movie they're making on Tommy. That interested me a whole lot.

"So I drive down from Ojai, and he played it for me, said he'd smuggled it out from the studio. The way he put it, he said, 'Tell me what's wrong with this.' And after I heard it, I didn't hardly know where to begin. See, it was supposed to be one of these famous *Garage Tapes* Alex had been putting out, one with new material from our earlier sessions. Or not even that, really. Studio time was nothin' to us then. We'd just go in and fool around for weeks and weeks at a time. The record company didn't care just as long as the album went gold. So in the beginning this was all this stuff we didn't use, jamming other people's tunes, trying out new things that never made it

155

onto an album. I was on all of the early *Garage Tapes.* Sure, I signed a release. I needed the money then.

"But then they came out with stuff that sure wasn't the DMZ. I thought it was kind of funny, but after all, Tommy cut an album without the group. He must have fooled around for about a year on that one. The thing was, nobody but Tommy was identified on the album—no recording information, when, where, nothin'. But people bought it. The critics never questioned it.

"That was a while ago. But now Alex comes up with this new material for the movie. Worley's supposed to use two pieces of it for a couple of montage sequences, he tells me. Anyway, I listen to it, and the first thing I notice is the synthesizer on it. Now, we never used a keyboard in the group. It was just me on lead guitar, Tommy on rhythm, bass, and drums. But there was a synthesizer on that album he cut without us, so that's cool. *Except!* Except you listen to this one on Worley's tape, and you can tell it's a Yamaha DX-7. It's a digital synthesizer, and it's got a different tone—sharper, more of an edge, but the most important thing is it's polyphonic—you can play chords on it. And the DX-7 didn't come in until the early eighties.

"Okay. Then I noticed the drums—very tricky—the guy's playing patterns against himself. Impossible. Two drummers? Not likely. No, you listen and you can tell it's a drum machine in there with the drummer. But they didn't start using drum machines until—what?—the late seventies or so. See? None of it works out."

If I could see through this, then Clay Weston certainly could. What did he think this proved? "Look," I said, "we're talking about multitrack recording, aren't we? I mean, they could have lifted the vocal track from someplace else, any place, and just had the instrumental stuff recorded last month or something."

"Sure," he said, "sure, and maybe that's just what they did. Maybe they had it recorded someplace nobody would ever know, like Japan or Korea or someplace. Only I know Tommy, and I know how he works, and he's gotta work

156

against the band. He can use earphones, but all the time he's pulling his phrasing from what's going on behind him. And there's a couple of times, well, more than a couple, when he picks up the rhythm pattern this drum machine is laying down. No, the instrumental track had to be recorded first.

"But Worley hadn't noticed any of this. To tell you the truth, he isn't that much of a musician—or wasn't. Sound repro is what he knew about. And that's what had him going. When Alex delivered the tape to him, he told him it was badly recorded. He knew Worley's background in recording, and he told him to bring up the quality of Tommy's voice, get it to sound 'right.' What he meant was, get it to sound like Tommy Osborne."

I thought I was following all this—but he left me here. "You mean they're trying to pass somebody else off as Osborne?"

"No, no, no. It's Tommy, all right, but his voice has *changed!* The upper register isn't there. He's gone deeper and kind of gravelly. Worley was supposed to feed in all this treble to get him to sound the way he used to. Look, it happens. You get older. Your pipes get rusty. You don't sound the same. Right away I thought back to that last batch of *Garage Tapes,* and I wondered if maybe there was some of that on it, too. I've checked the album out since, and it's true. You listen, and you can hear his voice going."

"Look," I said, "you tell me. You spell it out for me. What does all this prove?"

"It proves Tommy Osborne's still alive."

This complicated my life considerably. Clay Weston had convinced me, but the idea of going to someone else, to the cops, and trying to prove this theory to them just because a drum machine had been used, or a certain synthesizer, or because Osborne's voice didn't sound quite the same—well, chances of making that work seemed pretty remote. But on the other hand, two men had died, hadn't they? Alex Wakefield seemed to take this theory pretty seriously.

"Okay, say you're right. Say they're recording Osborne today. But where? They couldn't take him down here to do it. Not anyplace. He'd be recognized, or his voice, or—"

He cut me off. "Up there," he said. "They gotta have a little studio up there in the mountains. Alex owns it now. He knew enough to run a mixing board—the basics. He did a little of that in England before he came over. He didn't know shit about music, though. That's how what's on the tape got past him."

He took a deep gulp of ginger ale and went on: "I'm afraid friend Worley had a little blackmail in mind," he said. "I believe he wanted to leave something for his young friend, the artist. I guess you must have heard Jimmy had AIDS?"

"Yeah," I said, "but what about Tom Beatty?"

"I don't know," he admitted, "unless he was in on it, too. I never knew him, but he gave you my number, and he must have gotten it from Worley and have known something about it."

"But you say you've got the tape?"

"Well, what I've got is a copy. Worley made one for me. When I told him all this stuff about the synthesizer and the drum machine, he just about flipped. But I let on I was a lot less sure about it than I was. Told him I had to check it out with some people. He bought that and made me a copy. Maybe Alex and Ferdy found the original—and then again, maybe they didn't. Like I said, they'll never find mine, where I got it hid. I ain't tellin' you or anybody else where that is."

"And what're you going to do with it? Blackmail?"

"Not me. I don't want Alex's money. I just want to destroy him."

Lots of luck, I thought. "Tell me something. You think Wakefield has put you together with Worley? If Worley put the squeeze on him, the way you think he did, you think he mentioned you?"

"I don't think so. No."

"Well, I hate to tell you, but he was there tonight."

"So?" He shrugged. "That's not unusual for a show like this one."

"Yeah, but he saw us talking, probably saw me call you over on the stage."

"I still don't get the connection."

"Yeah, well, he probably does. That's what I'm getting at. He knows I'm interested in the case. I've even talked to him briefly about it a couple of times."

"So he puts you together with that, and you together with me. Is that it?"

"Yeah, more or less."

He sat there thinking that over. "Well," he said at last, "I won't pretend I like hearing that. But the way I see it, Alex and I been in this town for twenty years or so. Well, the last five I been up in Ojai, but I work here all the time. We keep our distance. As long as he doesn't know I've got a copy of that tape, everything's cool."

"You really think that?"

"I have to. I got a date with a drunken woman I gotta keep."

"Let her wait. Stay here tonight."

"No, I already checked out."

He pushed away from the bar. I tossed twenty down as he clambered off the stool.

"Just one more thing," I said. "I'd like to hear that tape."

Clay Weston sighed. "Well, why not? Come on up tomorrow. Not too early, though. I want to get some sleep. I'll play it for you, show you how it checks out exactly how I said." He grabbed a bar napkin and drew a map: "Off one-oh-one at Carpinteria, then up Casitas Pass Road," and so on, then he handed it over.

He grabbed up his guitar case. "Come on," he said, "I'll drive you back to your car."

Fifteen

I was on the road for Ojai by ten o'clock the next morning. The way I figured it, that would put me at Weston's a little after eleven, just about the time he would want to see me.

I liked the guy. You couldn't call him a survivor of the sixties, not Clay Weston. He had more than survived. He had prevailed. Here was a guy who had overcome failure, and a drinking problem, and toughest of all, success, to become what he was—a decent human being, a guy who took pride in what he was and what he did, who took care of his family. My father would have called him muy hombre. So what if Weston wanted revenge? That also fit my father's conception of manhood. And deep down, it fit mine, too.

When he had dropped me off on the side street where I'd left my car a few hours before, Weston offered me his hand. "We in this together?" he had asked.

I took it and gave it the old high wigwag shake from the sixties. There was strength in that right hand of his, and without testing it, I knew that the other hand, the crippled one, was even stronger. "Together," I said, then climbed out of the Jeep. "But do me a favor, okay?"

"What's that?"

"Cuidase." Take care of yourself.

He winked and gave me a thumbs-up to let me know he'd

understood. Then he threw the Jeep in gear and roared off down the dark street.

The drive I had ahead of me was mostly pretty boring. It only got really interesting toward the end. A straight shot up 101 would take me beyond Ventura and just over the Santa Barbara County line. That's the fast way. You could meander along the ocean on the Pacific Coast Highway for most of that distance if you had the time and the taste for it, but that morning I had neither. This was business.

Still, even 101, with its miles of suburban roadside clutter, had its rewards. They came a little later on, just after I'd left the city limits and emerged into open country. There they were, those soft California hills, burnt yellow in the bright sun, some of them dotted with a few scrub trees—but with them or without, they looked like woolen yellow blankets, one after another, in low peaks and long wrinkles jumbled on an unmade bed.

I never thought too much about Los Angeles. It was home, where I'd grown up, where I'd lived and worked all my life except for that stretch in the army. I don't think I'd ever really thought seriously about living anywhere else. Why was it then that whenever I got out of the city, just far enough to see these hills, I got such a rush of pleasure?

Although the hills went on for miles, they were gradually replaced by more mountainous terrain, and it had its own sort of threatening beauty. The road climbed high, then dropped swiftly, heading north and west in a sweeping loop. And before I knew it I was in the flats, heading into Camarillo with Oxnard and Ventura ahead. There wasn't much to look at along here, and that gave me time to think.

Clay Weston had convinced me last night. I was a believer. There was no arging with him on that technical stuff, and he did know Osborne's style and mannerisms. So, sure, I accepted his conclusion: Tommy Osborne was alive. What did that mean? Well, it meant, for one thing, that somebody was dead in his place. They found a body in that Corvette of his nineteen years ago, or however long ago it was, burned beyond recognition. If it wasn't Osborne, it had to be some-one. They couldn't fake that.

That was reason enough for Alex Wakefield to keep it all a big secret. But I had it in mind that a live Tommy Osborne wasn't worth nearly as much to him as a dead one. He'd said as much himself, hadn't he? If Osborne were to be produced, in whatever shape, there would be a lot of explaining to do and maybe a new ending for the movie to be shot—at the very least. As for why Worley and Beatty had been killed, maybe it wasn't enough that they knew—but they got in the way. I bought Weston's blackmail theory, too. But Wakefield sure wanted that tape back, didn't he? What did he expect to do with it—fix it? I'd have to ask Clay Weston about that.

Things got interesting again just out of Ventura. I passed the first turnoff to Ojai, just as I'd been told to do, aiming at the one down the line right around Carpinteria. Between the two lay the best twenty miles of highway to be found south of Big Sur. The Pacific Coast Highway had joined 101 back in Oxnard someplace, and 101 had taken the place of PCH next to the ocean. But it wasn't just the ocean and that long stretch of beach off to the left—you could get that hundreds of places along the coast highway. No, it was the line of cliffs that mountained up on your right as far as you could see that made the view, well, sort of startling.

The road was wide and fast, an open invitation to open up the Alfa and blow out the accumulated carbon. I accepted. The car surged forward as I cut into the far left lane, leaving behind a line of assorted overpowered American and under-powered Japanese cars. The gulls swept down from the cliffs. The morning sun sparkled on the water. God's in his heaven, all's right with the world.

At the end of that line of cliffs, with Santa Barbara in sight, the highway narrowed down to two lanes, and just ahead lay Casitas Pass Road. I turned off there, headed east, and began heading up in a twisting two-lane road. Weston had been very specific. I had the map he had drawn on the cocktail napkin flattened out on the seat beside me. His point was that since he lived just off this road a few miles west of Ojai proper, I might as well stay on 101 and enjoy the view. It was just as fast and twice as scenic. It would give me an idea of why he had chosen to live up here, so far away from work.

I'd been up this way a couple of times before, but that was years ago, so I was almost surprised when I found water on my left, then on my right, as I drove through the rough, rocky hills. Then I remembered: this was so-called Lake Casitas. There was a dam up there just to the north in the Santa Barbara Mountains, and the man-made lake behind extended far down here into little fingers and inlets covering all the low separations and little valleys between the hills. It was all kind of picturesque, I guess, but somehow you got the feeling that it didn't belong.

Because I had gotten off onto Casitas Pass Road from 101 all alone and hadn't encountered many other cars along the way in either direction, I had the mistaken notion that there wasn't much traffic up there with me. I found out differently when I swung around a bend and was suddenly forced to jam on the brakes to keep from crawling up a Buick's trunk. He was just the last in a long line of cars.

We crept. I counted eight up ahead, but then there was another curve, so there was no telling where the line ended, or why it was there. Time wasn't a factor, but I felt rattled by the sudden halt, uneasy at what might lie ahead.

You could call it a premonition, I guess, but it was certainly late in coming. When at last I lugged around that curve in first, I saw some yards ahead of me just what it was all about. There were a couple of California Highway Patrol cars parked indifferently on the narrow shoulder and half on the road, a county ambulance, and up ahead of them all, half-hidden by the ambulance, a wrecker with a car. One of the CHP cops was directing traffic, keeping two lanes moving through one.

So we crept some more. But by the time I had pulled up beside the ambulance, my worst fears were realized. The car at the end of the tow truck's long cable was a ten-year-old black Jeep. Clay Weston's. The mud on the tires and the drying wet grunge all over it said that it had been in the water.

163

When I came up to the cop who was directing traffic, I yelled at him, "Hey! What about the driver?"

But he wasn't listening. He just shook his head, and waved me through. Okay. I accelerated around the tow truck, swerved over to the shoulder some distance ahead of it, and parked.

I jumped out of the car and ran back toward the CHP cruisers. On the way, I saw what I dreaded seeing. Between the ambulance and the steep bank leading down to the lake was a black body bag. It was full.

I didn't stop. There was no one to talk to but the cop nearby who was filling out a form on a clipboard.

"Hey, excuse me, officer."

He looked up, ready to be annoyed. "Yeah? What is it? We're pretty busy here right now."

"I know that, but, look, I know that car," jerking a thumb back toward the Jeep, "and I know the driver. Is he . . ."

"What's his name?"

"Clay Weston."

"That's him, all right," he said, shaking his head in a stolid show of sympathy. He pointed with his ballpoint pen. "He's in the bag over there."

"How did it happen? When? He knows the road. He lives up here."

He hesitated, looking me over. "What's your relationship to the deceased?"

"Friend," I said, "back in Los Angeles. I was driving up to see him."

"Well, okay, *friend,* he got pushed off the road and down into the drink by a big pickup. It all happened late last night. About one a.m. We wouldn't know that, except somebody coming down the other way got a glimpse of it. The guy saw there was nothing he could do to help your buddy, but he phoned it in right away and left a flare to mark the place. We had to get a diver down there this morning to attach the cable and pull out the body. Diver said he was still strapped in. Must have gone unconscious at impact. He drowned."

He stopped then and waited, watching me.

"Jesus," was all I could manage. I must have looked shocked. I was.

"You got any idea who could have done this? We're putting it down as highway homicide."

"No," I said, lying through my teeth.

"Any enemies?"

"None that I know of."

"Could have been a crazy, of course. God knows we get a lot of them. Maybe your friend Weston cut him off, or the pickup driver just wanted to have some fun." He grimaced, wrinkling his nose. "Jesus," he said, "people today."

I knew what he meant. We worked different sides of the street, but we both had a sense of the violence out there. It was like a disease, an epidemic. "There's a lot of that going around," I said.

"You said it. Look, let me have your name and address. Your phone number, too. There'll be an investigation on this. Somebody may want to talk to you."

"Sure." I pulled out my wallet and reached for one of my cards—then thought better of it. No need to let him know I was a PI. I handed him my driver's license instead.

He copied down the address, and I gave him my phone number.

As he handed it back, he said, "You said you were driving up to see this guy, Weston. Any special reason?"

"No. Just a visit."

"He knew you were coming?"

"Yes."

"Well, okay. Look, I guess you know his wife. She's over there across the road. Maybe you could calm her down."

He pointed. I looked. There, beyond the tow truck, just past the cop who was directing traffic, in front of a Cherokee, stood a little group gathered around a woman whose head was bowed and covered by her hands. Her shoulders jerked at irregular intervals. She was sobbing. There was a girl almost as tall as she was, and a boy who was about four inches shorter and a couple of years younger. Away from them there was

165

another CHP cop; even at this distance he looked helpless and embarrassed.

"Okay," I said to my cop. "I'll see what I can do."

I started over to the other side, signaling to the cop in the road that I wanted to get over to that bunch at the Cherokee. He nodded and held traffic so I could get across. I wasn't looking forward to this, but I had a message to deliver.

I went to the cop first. I explained to him that I was a friend of "the deceased," and that I'd like to talk to the widow. He assumed I meant privately—I did—and he stepped away, with a nod, more than happy to let me have a try at a situation he couldn't handle. "She's in no condition to drive" was all he said.

I had to deal with the kids first. The boy, who was about ten, just looked at me blankly; he seemed stunned. The girl was suspicious, almost hostile. She was her father's daughter in more than looks. She reminded me of Weston when we were shouting at each other over the music at the Rainbow the night before. No bullshit. Put up or shut up. "I have to talk to your mother," I said to her.

She frowned at me. I half expected her to ask to see my ID. But she decided in my favor. "Mama," she said, "this man wants to talk."

Rachel Weston pulled down her hands just far enough to take a look. She couldn't have seen me very clearly. Tears had swollen her eyelids. Her eyes were bleary with them. Then she nodded.

"Look," I said, "Mrs. Weston, Rachel, I knew your husband. I was with him last night."

She pulled her hands from her face. Her cheeks were tear-stained. Snot dripped from her nose. She didn't care. "It wasn't an accident," she moaned.

"I know that. The police know that, too."

She didn't say anything, just waited for me to say what I had to say.

"Whoever did this to Clay wants something he's got," I said. "A tape. I don't want it. If you know where it is, then give it to the police for safekeeping. It's evidence." I glanced at the

166

girl. This was partly for her benefit, too. What would she be? About twelve? But she was listening, and she knew what I was saying.

"Now, do you have friends you could stay with?"

Rachel looked at me for a long moment, concentrating, as though she was translating what I had said from a foreign language into her own.

"Anyone?" I asked. "For a while?"

At last she nodded.

"Good," I said, and I gave a strong look at her daughter. Listen to this, kid. "Because you should know that whoever killed your husband may come looking for this tape. If you're around, they'll threaten you, and they'll threaten your children. You'll have to get out of your house for a little while."

"Who's that?" the girl asked. "Who's coming?" I could tell she had murder on her mind.

"Don't worry about that now," I said to her. "Just stay out of the house for a while. And I'll tell the cops about it. They'll keep an eye on things."

The girl nodded, satisfied.

I turned to her mother then. "Is that all right with you, Rachel?"

She said nothing, just stared at me through those swollen eyes. I turned around and started over to the cop. I was going to explain the situation to him, some of it anyway, and ask him to drive them home. But an awful croaking yell sounded out from behind me. It was Rachel Weston. *"Tommy did it!"*

She meant Tommy Osborne and, in a way, she was right.

By the time I got back to West Hollywood, it was midafternoon. The apartment was empty. I had no idea where Alicia and Pilar and the kid were, and to tell the truth, I didn't think much about it either. I had other things on my mind.

The more I told the CHP and the Ojai cops, the more they wanted to know. How did I know the house would be burglarized or maybe even raided? I didn't know. I only suspected it. What were they after? A tape. What was on the tape? I didn't know. (Another lie, compounding the rest I told.) Why hadn't I told the first cop about this?

On and on it went. If I thought that I could get protection for the Westons without risking my own neck, then I'd forgotten how cops operate. But at last, telling as little as I could to make it sound convincing, I managed to talk my way out of Ojai, satisfied that Rachel and the kids would be safe at a friend's house in Santa Paula. And, yes, the Ojai police agreed grudgingly to keep an eye on the Westons' place.

That left me free to do what I'd decided to do about the time I crossed Casitas Pass Road and headed for that little group of mourners next to the Cherokee. I meant to get out of town in one hell of a hurry.

Packing wouldn't take me long. Nothing fancy, just jeans, some heavy shirts, a sweater, and biggest and bulkiest of all a fleece-lined, rawhide short coat I'd hardly worn at all. It was going to be hard to close the suitcase over it, but where I was going, I'd need it. I was headed north.

But I wasn't through yet. I went into the top drawer of the dresser and dug out my Smith and Wesson .38 Police Special, checked it to make sure it was empty, then took out the full box of loads. Would I need more? I hoped not.

While I was rummaging around the bottom drawers looking for the lead cloth to wrap the bundle in, I heard the door open in the front room. The women were back.

Alicia came bustling into the bedroom, stowed little Marilyn in her bed, then looked across at me curiously. The suitcase laid open between us. I stood there with the .38 in one hand and the lead cloth in the other.

"You make a trip?" she asked. She didn't seem to like the idea much at all.

"Yeah," I said, "a trip."

"Where you goin'?"

The baby let out a couple of cranky little exclamations. Maybe she could sense the tension that was suddenly there between us. Or maybe she was only hungry.

"Just away. On a case." I decided to tell her as little as possible. The less she knew, the better.

168

She nodded, her lips pouched judiciously. "On a case," she repeated. "So. You make beeg business, uh?"

"Alicia, it's what I do. You know that."

"Oh, I know, I know. But maybe you forget I got work, too."

"What do you mean?"

"Chico, I need your help."

I didn't understand. "How can I help you? I don't know anything about acting. That's what Mrs. Lubovitch is for. You went yesterday. You said she was good, she helped a lot. Now all of a sudden she's not helping you?"

Alicia came over close and looked me in the eye. "She helps," she said. "I was there now. She show me movement. Alexander Technique. Is very good."

"So what do you need me for?"

"I need your support. Ursula, she say, you don' give me support. I think maybe she's right."

Ursula again! How was it that the production head of a major motion picture studio always managed to find time in her busy schedule to stick her nose in our business? I was annoyed. I must have looked it. But all I said was, "What does she mean by that?"

"*Support!*" she exploded. "Don' you know support? You got to be *there* for me. If you're not there for me, is bad for my career. If you don' give me support, is bad for our relationship."

Oh, Jesus, spare me. I'd been around actresses enough to have heard that before. Egomaniacs, all of them. Where was that simple little puta I knew and loved down in Culiacán? Probably never existed—or was there only in my imagination. No, Alicia had been up-front about it from the start. She let me know that she was a woman with a mission—stardom or bust! It's just that I hadn't taken her seriously—and I had reckoned without the intercession of Ursula Toller.

I didn't say anything for a while. I was thinking about it. And as I did, I went about the business of wrapping the .38 in the lead cloth, tucking in the box of cartridges, and placing the package in the suitcase, there in the folds of the coat.

169

When I looked up again at Alicia, I could tell that all that deliberate care had irritated her. She had expected, probably even hoped, that I would explode right back at her. Not Chico, not Mr. Control.

"Cariña," I said at last, and I spoke to her in Spanish, "listen to me. When I met you, when I fell in love with you— oh, yes, believe it!—I said to myself, 'Here is a woman who can look after herself. She is strong. She can take what life has to offer. She knows what matters!' Now you come to me, and you say that was not you down in Mexico. 'Chico,' you say, 'I am weak. I need your help. I no longer respect what *you* do. What *I* do is more important.' That is what you say. You use different words, words you have heard from someone else. But that is what you say to me."

I waited, looking for some response from her. Nothing. She stood, staring me down, her face quite expressionless.

So I pushed on: "You tell me. Do I listen to that woman I fell in love with, or do I listen to this woman who tells me what others say?"

I waited again, carefully folding my arms as a sign that I was prepared to stand there a long, long time. But, as it turned out, there was no need for that.

She said coldly, "I don' un'erstan' you. You're speaking a foreign language."

That's when I might have exploded—except that just then the telephone rang. I looked from the door to her and back to the door again. I might have run to pick it up, but I heard Pilar answer, and a moment later she called for me: "Senor Cervantes. Is for you. I take the number or you talk?"

I turned away from Alicia and walked out of the room.

Pilar held the telephone out to me. She looked at me a little too searchingly. I supposed she had been listening to us there in the bedroom, as she usually did. Well, all right. I'd gotten used to that. I didn't even mind.

I took the receiver and turned away from her. "Yes? This is Cervantes."

A kind of downhome voice came over the wire—country-with-smarts. "Yeah, hi, Cervantes. This here's Jimmy Al-

170

bright. I'm an investigator with the Ventura County Sheriff's Office, and I'd like to talk to you."

"That may be kind of difficult," I said.

"Oh? How come?"

"I'm leaving town," I said.

"Don't know as I like hearing that," said Albright. "Cops in Ojai told me you had a lot to say about this Weston business, and probably knew more than you were tellin'."

"Yeah, well . . ."

"This has all of a sudden got lots more interesting, see," he continued. "Because once they got that fella Weston's body in the morgue and undressed him, they found he had a bullet wound in his side. Small caliber, and no exit wound, so I guess that's how they missed it at the scene. Anyway, that just about washes it as a hit-and-run accident. Looks like it was intentional—very intentional." He waited.

"Yeah," I said. "I guess it does."

"Since you seem to know more about this than anybody else, I'd like to talk to you."

"Well, like I say, I'm going out of town. Probably not for long."

"We could come and get you, Cervantes. Hold you as a material witness."

"I won't be here." I sighed. "Look, I'm not trying to impede you. Honest. I'll stay in contact. Maybe we can have a long talk on the phone tomorrow."

For a moment he didn't say anything. Then: "It says here you're a PI. Your trip related to this matter?"

"Yes. Okay, look, who you should talk to is Detective Pell of Homicide in the Hollywood Division LAPD. Get him to tell you about a couple of homicides—James Worley and Thomas Beatty. He'll tell you they're closed cases—but they're related to the one you're handling, believe me. You'll get some background there, and then we'll talk tomorrow."

"I suppose it wouldn't do any good to ask you where you're headed."

"No, it wouldn't."

"Well, if that's the best we can do." No threats. No bluster-

171

ing. I liked his style. He gave me his telephone number at the Ventura County Sheriff's Office, and that was that.

The rest was up to me. And the rest was up there around Mount Shasta someplace.

Sixteen

It was long after dark by the time I arrived in Mount Shasta City. Clay Weston had said that was the town nearest Osborne's mountain hideaway, so it seemed like that was the best place to set up base camp. After a long layover in San Jose, I had caught an American Eagle flight north to Redding. The prop-driven Fairchild Metro III we flew up in is one of those small, pencil-shaped jobs that you see taxiing around the big Boeings at the major airports. You look at them, and you say, "Hey, it might be fun to ride in one of those. I'll have to try it sometime." And it is fun, in a way, but it's a lot different from going anyplace in a DC-9 or a 737. You're one of eighteen or twenty airborne pilgrims who have joined together to participate in the miracle of flight. You see a lot more of the country, even at night, because you're flying closer to it. You feel the air around you as a presence, buffeting you a bit, resisting progress.

Redding lies at the very top of the Sacramento Valley. Beyond it are mountains, the big ones that make those around the Los Angeles Basin seem like so many hills. By the light of a nearly full moon I could see them in the distance as the Fairchild settled down for a landing. There they were. That's where I was headed.

Once on the road I began to feel like I was doing something for a change. I had wheels under me, four-wheel-drive wheels.

173

I'd had to fight the girl at the Hertz booth to get that Ford Bronco, but it was mine for as long as I needed it.

There wasn't anything wrong with the road I was on: Interstate 5 runs from the bottom of California right up to the top and beyond, a solid, four-lane double ribbon of concrete. Mount Shasta City was about an hour out of Redding in the next county north. The drive gave me a chance to do a little reasoning. I'd spent most of the time since I left Los Angeles telling myself what an idiot I was, taking off like this on the half-chance I might be able to find Ferdy and bring him back—or better yet, find Tommy Osborne and prove he was alive, just as Clay Weston had said he was. I was making this trip for Weston, and for his wife and kids. When I saw that body bag and then got a look at Rachel's face, destroyed by grief, I knew I had to do something. And all I could think of doing was going up and proving Weston was right. But not knowing the territory, chances were pretty slim I'd find anything or anyone. I knew that. I'd been telling myself that for hours now. So there on Interstate 5 I made a bargain: I'd take just three days, starting tomorrow. If I hadn't accomplished anything in that time, I'd turn around and go back home. I made a promise to myself.

Then, as if solemnizing it, a vision appeared in the windshield before me. I was just rounding a curve when this . . . vast something suddenly came into sight. It was white and fairly shone in the bright moonlight—a double-peaked mountain, snow-covered, alone. The thing must have been miles and miles away, but it filled a full foot or more of the windshield just above the steering wheel. I'd never seen anything like it. I had this impulse, I almost blessed myself, like it was God up there on that mountain looking down at me. And God was saying to me, Okay, Chico, give it three days, but also give it the best you've got.

As I walked down the hall, unbuttoning the fleece-lined coat I'd crammed into the suitcase, I heard the familiar squawk of a police radio. I knew this was the right place.

I stopped at the service window and looked over the room

174

inside. It was medium-sized and had a couple of offices at the back. There were a few desks and chairs there—old gray-steel office furniture. At one of them sat the night-duty man, and off in one corner an old-timer, seventy if he was a day, was hunched over a two-way radio. Both of them had turned and were looking at me. The night-duty man got up and walked over to the window. He was tall and lean in his khakis. His brows were flexed in a frown, but the corners of his mouth were turned up in a polite smile.

"Yes sir. What can I do for you, sir?"

I pulled a card out from my wallet, the one that said I was security consultant for Majestic Pictures, and put it on the board between us. "I'm up looking for a guy who's supposed to live here in the area," I said.

"Oh? Who's that?"

"Ferdinand Petko."

His face suddenly relaxed into a grin. "Oh, Lord," he said, "what kind of trouble's Ferdy got himself into now?"

"No trouble. It's his boss, Alex Wakefield. Man was in an auto accident, a bad one, and he's in a coma at Cedars-Sinai." It's those details that make a story convincing.

"And they sent you up to bring him back?" He sounded a bit skeptical.

"Not just that. Wakefield's producing a picture at the studio—the one about Tommy Osborne?"

The night-duty man nodded. He'd heard something about it.

"Well, it seems that Wakefield had a tape with material that was supposed to go on the soundtrack. It's essential. Now nobody can locate it. They figure Petko might know where it is since he'd been driving his boss around until yesterday."

"But a security consultant?" He was puzzled. "What's that mean?"

"It means I used to be a private detective, and I'm supposed to be good at finding people. This is my first stop."

He nodded then, satisfied at last, then turned back to the radioman who was taking all this in from the corner. "Louie,"

175

said the night-duty man, "you know where Ferdy lives? I sure don't."

"I don't know," said the radioman, "supposed to be some big place out in the county somewhere. Heard tell of it. Don't know where it is, though."

"This Alex Wakefield," said the night-duty man. "He English or something?"

"That's him."

"Yeah, I've seen Ferdy driving him around town in some sort of fancy four-wheel-drive setup. Guess it was English, too." He turned back to the radioman. He owns that place, doesn't he, Louie?"

"That's what I hear. Used to belong to that rock-and-roll guy got killed when he drove off White Ridge Road. That was about five years before you come out here, Frank." That last to the night-duty man.

"But you don't know where it is?" I asked.

"Sure don't," said the dispatcher. "But I know—" The radio squawked again, and a message came in from a patrol car, probably the only one out that night. "Just a minute," said the radioman. "Gotta handle this."

And as he did, the night-duty man made an attempt at small talk. "You with the movie studio, huh?"

"That's right."

"What's that like? See all the movie stars?"

"See them. That's all."

"Clint Eastwood. Ever seen him?"

"Once or twice, I guess."

"Is he as big as he looks? Everybody says those fellas are lots shorter than you'd think, seein' them up there on the screen."

"Not him. He's big."

"I thought so." He nodded wisely. "Yeah, that's just what I thought."

The radioman signed off, got up from his chair, and ambled over. "I was just gonna say that I don't know where Ferdy lives, but I know where he drinks."

A lead? Well, maybe the hope of one. "Where's that?" I asked, just showing professional interest.

"The Wild Goose in Modoc."

"Is that far from here?"

"Naw." The dispatcher wrinkled his nose in disdain. "A few miles back down the road is all. If you drove up from Redding, you passed right by it."

I seemed to recall an exit off the interstate. "Okay," I said. "How do I find it once I get there?"

The two men looked at each other and chuckled. "You can't miss it once you get there," the dispatcher said. "Ain't much more than one street in that town—Modoc Avenue— and the Wild Goose is right there on it. It used to be the big town, and we was the small one. Now it's the other way around." The two stood, looking at me, nodding and grinning, as though pleased at the justice of that.

They were right, though. There really wasn't much to the town of Modoc. I took the exit, swung left then right, and found myself on the main street. There were a couple of residential blocks, a filling station closed for the night, but ahead I saw a few lights on—and one of them announced the Wild Goose Tavern. The message wasn't lost on me: here I was on a wild goose chase.

But maybe not. I parked three or four cars down from the bar, leaned over and got the .38 out of the glove compartment. Then I sat there, trying to think through what might lie ahead. What if Ferdy was inside? Not likely. For all I knew, he was still back in L.A. I'd decided the best-case scenario would put Ferdy out of the picture and give me a clear shot at getting inside that place, wherever it was, and finding out if Osborne really was still alive. But Ferdy was my only link. I had to find someone who knew that place out in the county and was willing to tell me where it was located.

But then, though I hadn't thought it through, there had to be a worst-case scenario, too. That was why I jammed the .38 in the deep pocket of my coat before I climbed out of the Bronco and headed for the entrance to the bar. I hesitated

177

there for a few seconds, then opened the door and stepped inside.

The place was dimly lit and murky with tobacco smoke. A few heads turned in my direction. I didn't wait to give them a look back but walked straight to the oval bar and climbed up on an empty stool. I figured if Ferdy was there, I might as well look at him from across the bar as let him see me in the doorway. I hadn't spotted him yet.

The bartender, a big, heavyset guy, came over while I was busy checking out his clientele. It was a sorry-looking bunch. Still, no Ferdy. He asked what I'd have, and I told him a beer. The bar was pretty crowded for this time on a weekday night, about half full or better. I went from face to face, making a complete circuit, and found four of them staring back at me, two of them women, but no Ferdy—definitely no Ferdinand Petko present. I let out a sigh and unbuttoned my coat. My right hand released the butt of the .38 and found its way up to the bar.

The bartender came back and put a bottle of Coors in front of me. He asked me if I wanted a glass. I shook my head no and waited. I realized I was waiting—but for what?

You go into places like the Wild Goose, and you get a sense of what those saloons in the old West must have been. There wasn't any big mirror or a picture of a painted lady on the wall. No, it looked about the same inside as any bar in the dingier parts of Los Angeles, or San Pedro, or Torrance. But there was something there in the atmosphere, something brought in with them by the people at the bar. A few of them were talking in low tones but seemed always aware of others— looking over their shoulders at them, glancing across the way. One guy down at the other end raised his voice and slapped the bar to make a point. Eyes turned to him. He looked around, taking this in, and continued in a quieter tone. I realized that they seemed to be waiting, too—but for what? Something to happen. Violence, I supposed. There seemed to be more than a potential for it there—more like an expectation.

I picked up the bottle of Coors with my left hand and took a swig. My right hand went back down into my pocket and

178

grasped the butt of the pistol lightly. The bartender was talking to a woman at the bar, one of the two who watched me so intently when I came in. She climbed off her bar stool then and disappeared into the darker recesses of the place. There was a dim orange light on back there, probably marking the location of the toilets, and in a corner, an object lit in red and yellow, unmistakably a jukebox. She went to the jukebox and dropped in some coins, then without pausing to choose, punched in her selections. She was a regular. She knew the board by heart.

To the accompaniment of Tammy Wynette's "Stand by Your Man," she walked back to the bar, worked her way around it, and headed straight for me. She was dressed in tight slacks and a bulky sweater. Blond, round-faced, and about thirty-five. She had average good looks and an average good figure, but I suspected that around here that put her way ahead of the pack.

"Hi," she said. "You're new in town, ain'tcha?"

"I guess so," I said as I swung around on my stool. I wasn't so much interested in giving her the full benefit of my radiant smile as I was in keeping her away from my right pocket. "My first time in here, anyway." Then I added, because I knew it was expected of me, "Want to sit down? I'll buy you a drink."

"Why not?" She clambered up on the bar stool to my right and gave me a kind of sly look. "Where you from?"

"Sacramento," I said. It's a town I know a little about from visits to my sister. The next thing she would want to know was what I was doing here. My mind raced as I tried to come up with something. But she surprised me."

"I thought it'd be someplace south," she said. "We ain't got too many of your kind up here."

"Yeah? What kind is that?"

"You Latin lovers. That's what they say about you guys. You know that, don'tcha?"

She was hustling me. I knew that. But what was the hustle? Were there hookers in a little town like this? I was pretty sure the bartender had sent her over. Why?

He appeared. If she ordered a bottle of champagne, then everything would be clear. Again she surprised me, asking for a B & B, a drink that had long been out of style. Maybe they didn't know that up here. The funny thing was that while the bartender was listening to her, his eyes were on me. I capped the bottle of beer in front of me with the palm of my hand and gave a slight shake of my head. But that wasn't it. He kept right on looking—until he broke away suddenly and headed off to get her drink.

"What's your name?" she asked me.

"Tony," I said. "Call me Tony."

"Well, okay, Tony. I'm Diane." Then it came: "Whatta you do down there in Sacramento?"

"Work for the state, like everybody does." I was ready for her by this time. I simply described my sister's job, as well as I knew it, as an assessor in the Department of Motor Vehicles. I went on about it long enough to bore her and make it seem convincing. Her drink appeared in the middle of my recitation. The bartender hung around long enough to get some idea of what I was talking about, then turned around and headed for the other end of the bar. I guess he got bored, too.

Finally she cut me off: "Sure sounds like an important job." She raised her glass. "Well, here's to the old DMV."

I raised my bottle, and we drank to it. She tossed hers down in one big gulp.

"Hey, Tony, wanna dance?" The jukebox had gone through Tammy and George Jones and was now giving forth with Patsy Cline—"I Fall to Pieces." Nice stuff, as good as country music gets.

"No, I'm not much good at that."

"Slow dancin'? Anybody can do that. Come one, Tony, we can snuggle!" And with that, she aimed a playful punch at me—directly at the right pocket of my coat. I saw it coming and twisted and took it in my belly.

"Hey," I said, forcing a laugh, "you're pretty tough, huh?"

"Tough as I need to be." That came out suddenly and from some other place. It was as if she was saying, Let's drop the bullshit. But she didn't say that. Instead, she smiled sweetly and said, "One thing I don't understand, Tony."

"What's that?"

180

"What's that big important job of yours got to do with you bein' here in Modoc?"

"Not much," I said, "I'm on vacation."

"Vacation? Here? There's nothin' here but fishing, honey, and that's out of season."

"Well, yeah, okay. I'm headed up to Portland, but I stopped off because I heard that a guy I knew in the army was living in this area. Don't know exactly where, though."

"Who's that?" She looked skeptical and sounded dubious.

"His name is Ferdinand Petko. Big guy. We used to call him Ferdy. You know him?"

A strange sort of expression had crept over her face, like I'd said something funny. "Sure do," she said.

"You know him pretty well? You know where he lives?"

"Oh, I know him real well—so good that I know old Ferdy was in the marines and not the army. No doubt about that. Anybody talks to Ferdy ten minutes know that about him."

Before I could think how to respond to her—why hadn't I stuck to the story I gave to the Mount Shasta cops?—I felt a strong hand tight on my arm, squeezing right through the sleeve of that heavy coat. It was the bartender. He was giving me one of those flat, hard Lee Van Cleef looks, right out of a western movie.

"Listen," he said, "maybe you think we're so dumb up here we can't spot a cop when we see one. Well, I got news for you. Unless you got a warrant or a badge or something else you want to show us to make it official, you take yourself and that piece you got in your pocket and get the goddamn hell outta here. And if you got the idea you're gonna pull that piece out instead of some paper, there's about three or four guys at this bar carrying just as good as you and maybe better. Now, git!"

With that, the hand on my arm released me with a shove that sent me sprawling off the bar stool. I looked around. Diane had her back to me. The bartender was setting her up with another drink, but he had his eyes on me. So did everybody else in the house—smirks, smiles, grins. I guess I was what they'd been waiting for. The night's entertainment. Having no other choice, and without a look back, I got.

181

Back in my motel room, I stood for a minute or two in front of the mirror, trying to decide if they really could tell that the .38 was there in the pocket just looking at it. There was a slight bulge, sure, but that could be gloves—or just anything. Maybe it was me—the way I appeared, the way I was dressed. Well, I could change that—and maybe I'd have to.

Seventeen

That big—oh, enormously big—double-peaked mountain was still up there. If it seemed vast when I first viewed it thirty-five or forty miles away, then from a distance of ten miles or so it was an inescapable presence, dominating the townscape, blotting out everything else. You had to turn your back on it and face a ridge of mountains off to the west in order to avoid seeing it.

Mount Shasta, of course. There was some literature about it left out for visitors in the motel room. The usual stuff, I guess—volcanic in origin, thought last to have erupted in the seventeenth century, fourteen-thousand-odd feet high, the lesser of the two peaks known as Shastina (a bit cutesy for something so grand). But at the end of the brochure there was a kind of pitch to the New Age people about the mystery of the place, lessons to be learned there by those who had visited Sedona, Arizona, or other spots sacred to the UFO crowd.

All of which put me in mind of my promise to stay there just three days but give it my best shot. Last night I was definitely not at my best. But how much of that was really my fault? Sure, maybe I should have given them the same story I gave the cops—but why didn't I? Because I wanted to come in low-key, and not the man from the movie studio. I hadn't wanted to attract attention, but I had attracted a lot. Again, why? I could only judge that they had been visited by cops

183

before; they knew just how far they could go and went a little farther. Chances are, I thought, they're dealing more than wine, spirits, and beer there in the Wild Goose. And maybe Ferdy, with his frequent trips back and forth from Los Angeles, played an important part in the operation.

This was what was running through my head during my second cup of coffee at a bakery-and-breakfast shop just off the main street of Mount Shasta City. It seemed to be frequented by hippies left over from the early seventies. They had sought higher ground and found it here, away from Vietnam and Watergate and all the thrills and chills of that desperate time we all remember but try to forget. Well, they had chosen pretty well. They, and their undisciplined kids, seemed to fit right in. Anyway, the banana bread they baked here was good, and once in a while I liked my coffee with cinnamon in it, too.

I hung around a little longer than I needed to, studying the crowd, wondering if any of them knew how to get to that place out in the county that Ferdinand Petko called home, but afraid, after last night, to go around asking. At last I finished off my cup of coffee, pulled on my coat, and started for the exit. But I stopped on the way out and took a look at a big bulletin board right by the door. It was filled with notices, a lot of them out of date—for a film series at the community college in Weed that had ended last month, for vans and jeeps and pickup trucks that were offered for sale, for guru lectures and courses in deep massage. About what you'd expect. But one item on the board took my eye. It was a picture of a girl around fifteen or sixteen, one of those high school yearbook pictures. She was sort of pretty the way most girls that age are, but with a forced smile that could only be called sullen. And above the photo a lettered caption: HAVE YOU SEEN ME? Below, typed in with a few strikeovers, was her name, Karen Valesko and a physical description. At the bottom was a note: LAST HEARD FROM IN MOUNT SHASTA CITY, AUGUST 21ST. IF YOU HAVE SEEN HER, OR KNOW SOMEBODY WHO HAS, PLEASE CALL COLLECT, and then a number with the 415 area code.

Jesus, I hated seeing an item like that and thinking of all the pain behind it. Karen Valesko was just another runaway—or

184

maybe not quite that, since she'd been in touch with home. There may have been an argument with her parents. Or maybe she'd just put an extra pair of jeans and a blouse in her backpack one day, gone to the highway, and stuck out her thumb to see where it would lead her. Well, it didn't look like it had led her anywhere she wanted to go. There were hundreds, maybe thousands of girls like her in Los Angeles. Once in a while I got a call to find one of them. I never turned them down.

I walked to the car with some semblance of a plan in mind. In spite of last night's bad beginning, I'd already taken a couple of constructive steps. The first thing I'd done that morning was to call my sister at the DMV in Sacramento and give her Ferdinand Petko's name and his approximate age—in the unlikely event there were two by that name in the state—to see if she could come up with an address for him. If he was using his own address up here, then it would probably only be a rural route number, but that might be all I'd need. It would help, anyway. She hates doing stuff like that for me; she never lets me down, though.

Then I called Jimmy Albright of the Ventura County Sheriff's Office, just as I'd said I would. He told me what he'd heard from Detective Pell, which wasn't much, and what he thought of it. I told him how Worley's and Beatty's deaths fit in with Clay Weston's. After that, I told him I was up here looking for Ferdinand Petko—not strictly true, but not stretching things too far—and what had gone down at the Wild Goose the night before. If the worst happened, I wanted to leave some record of where I'd been and who I'd talked to. Just as I would have told him, he told me to be careful. And that was all we had to say to each other.

I'd gotten hold of a map of the county in the motel office, one of those that show the recreation areas and camping sites and so on. But it also showed named and numbered routes and little squiggles and lines that were . . . what? streams? creeks? trails? Most of them didn't seem to lead anywhere. Looking at the map, I saw that there was a little town named Everett between Mount Shasta City and Modoc, off the interstate and a little to the east. If Weston had been taken to Mount Shasta because it was the nearest town all those years ago, and Ferdy hung out in Modoc all the time these days, then it might be that the place I was looking for was somewhere in the vicinity of Everett. I decided to go there and take a look around, anyway.

A bell over the door jingled as I walked in, just as they used to do in shops and walk-in offices back in the old days. A lot of Everett was like the old days.

"Good day to you, sir. How can I help you?"

That sounded pretty old-fashioned, too. The man behind the desk didn't bother to get up, but the smile he wore seemed genuine, and he pointed to a chair opposite like he'd really be pleased if I sat down in it.

I did, and at the same time tossed down one of the Majestic Pictures cards on his desk. He picked it up and looked it over. "Mmm," he said, "that's one of the big Hollywood studios, isn't it?" He gave me a wink then, like we were both in on the joke. "All right, Mr. Cervantes, my name's Jack Tonelli, but I guess you know that from the sign outside. I repeat, how can I help you?"

"I'm looking for a guy," I said, a great big guy, hard to miss, named Ferdinand Petko. People call him Ferdy."

Tonelli thought a moment and shook his head. "Well," he said, "I'm afraid I've missed him."

"What I'd really like to know is where he lives."

"In my business, real estate, I get to know where most people live around here, always on the lookout for sellers."

"Yeah," I said, "that's why I stopped by."

"But Petko . . . no, that's a new one on me."

He wasn't lying. You could tell. I sat there frowning.

"You might try across the street at the general store," he said. "Old Frank's been here so long he knows just about everybody."

"I already did," I said. "From my description he said he thought he might have seen him around town a couple of times, but that's all."

186

"Hmm," he mused. "Well, of course there's one place would probably give you what you're looking for. Might take some digging, though."

"I know," I said, "the county recorder of deeds."

"That's right. Up in Yreka. Got every active deed in the county registered and filed right there. Might take a day or two because the files are organized by area and not alphabetical, but you'd find Grace Pickthorn in that office real helpful. She might even be able to suggest some kind of shortcut."

"I guess that's what I'd better do," I agreed. "I've been putting it off, thinking I might get a lucky break or something."

"Sometimes you have to do things the hard way."

"Don't I know that!" I sighed and got up from the chair, getting ready to go.

"Why not let me sell you a house while you're here?" He sat there, grinning at me. "Lot of folks come up here from L.A. and are just amazed at the prices."

"Yeah, what is it about this town? The houses seem well-built and in good shape, but they're mostly all alike. Only about two kinds around here, it seems."

"Three, actually. Plus some new ones that don't conform to pattern. Everett's an old company town. Founded by the Everett Lumber Company, used to be owned lock, stock, and barrel by it."

"Even the stores?"

"Oh, especially the stores. My dad used to tell how the company police would put up roadblocks on payday nights just to keep people from leaving Everett to spend their money."

"I've heard about places like that," I said. Then I thought a moment about what he'd said. "You said your dad told you that. Did he used to work here?"

"You bet he did. I grew up here, but I found it, well, kind of restrictive, so I left just as soon as I could and wound up working for the state in Redding. That wasn't much fun, so when the company pulled out and everything went up for sale,

I came back and set up in real estate." He hesitated, then added, "Done pretty well, too."

"Glad to hear it," I said, and I was. I liked the guy. But my attention had been taken by a map of the immediate area that was hanging on a side wall. "Something I was curious about." I walked over to the map and traced a few of those squiggles I'd seen on the county map. Here, however, they seemed to connect. There seemed to be a whole network of them there. "What're these? No names, no numbers. Are they roads or what?"

"Sure they are, or they used to be. They're the old logging roads. They cut those trees down, they had to haul them out. Some of them are still in pretty fair condition, some of them are just about impassable. None of them are paved, of course."

"How about up around here?" I pointed to White Ridge Road. The cop in Mount Shasta City had identified that as the place Tommy Osborne was supposed to have driven to his death. A few of the old logging roads fed into it from the north. I wondered about them. "Did they work this area, too? It says Shasta-Trinity National Forest."

"Yeah, they went in there, too. There were some restrictions, but they cut and replanted all around there in that one tract where you see the roads and trails marked."

"Would there be any houses up there? Any private homes?"

"Well, not in the park itself," he said, "but there could be a few just off White Ridge, I suppose. I'm not too familiar with the area, frankly. Just about everything I've handled has been here in town—this side of the interstate, generally.

I took one last look at the map and turned back to him with a nod. "Well, thanks," I said. "I was just curious."

"Sure you were." With that, he gave me another wink.

When I got back to the motel, there was a message to call my sister in Sacramento. I dialed her at the office and got right through to her.

"I hope you're not going to make a habit of this, Chico." We always have to go through this.

188

"No, Lulu, this is important. He's one of the bad guys, for sure." Her name is Luisa-Esmerelda. I gave her the name Lulu when I was two.

"Sometimes I wonder about you and this business you're in. I liked it better when you were with the police." Always the big sister.

"He probably killed three guys—three that I know about."

"How do you get mixed up with people like this?"

"It's a dirty, rotten job, I admit, but—"

"I know, I know. Somebody's got to do it."

"He also deals drugs. Probably." That would do it. If there's anything that makes my sister Lulu crazy, it's drugs. All you have to do is say "heroin," "cocaine," or "crack," and you get this tirade from her. I wasn't ready to listen to that, so I added, "Come on. Time's important. I have to catch this guy."

"Well, you're at the wrong end of the state to do it," she said.

"What do you mean?"

"You were right, there's only one Ferdinand Petko registered as a driver in the state of California, but he's in Los Angeles.

"No, he isn't. He's up here—or he's supposed to be most of the time."

"Chico, all I can tell you is what it says on his driver's license." And she told me. It was an address on Hollywood Boulevard, west of the zoo. I knew the area, of course. It was all condos and garden apartments. He probably did keep a place there. "That's his legal residence," she said. It was also a good cover for wherever it was he holed up here in Siskiyou County.

I sighed, admitting to myself I'd gone up another blind alley. "Okay, Lulu," I said weakly, "thanks."

There was silence for a moment at the other end of the line. Then: "Not good, huh?"

"You did your best. I appreciate it."

"I hope you catch the guy, Chico."

"I do, too, big sister. Say one for me."

189

We said our good-byes then and hung up. I sat there a moment on the bed with my hand resting on the telephone receiver, trying to remember the name of that woman Tonelli had mentioned in the county deeds office, wondering if I should call her before heading up there. Then I glanced at my reflection in the mirror on the opposite wall and decided that whether I called her or not, I'd better get dressed up for the occasion. I was going to need all the help I could get, and I'd be more likely to get it if I wore a shirt and tie and jacket and pants to match. The only thing was, I had been so sure I was going to come in here like a commando that I'd left all that stuff behind. Well, I'd been thinking about changing my appearance some way or other. This was my chance to do it.

A new me? Well, maybe not quite that, but I certainly looked different in a cheap tweed jacket, suntans, blue button-down shirt and an acrylic paisley tie. I'd even stopped in at a barbershop and had my hair trimmed for the occasion. About the time I stood looking myself over in the barber's full-length mirror, I wondered if I wasn't doing all this to delay my arrival up there at the county seat. It was all Majestic's money anyway—my time and Majestic's money.

I slipped on my sunglasses, and the transformation was complete. Chico, I told myself, you look like executive material. Out on the street, I even bounced along with a spring in my step that wasn't there before. Who was I trying to fool? Myself, maybe.

When I got back to the car, I tossed in the bundle that held the clothes I'd worn into the clothing shop, and I took one last look around. And in that look, my eyes took in something I hadn't really noticed before.

It was a music shop. I mulled that over for a moment, then slammed the car door and started across the street. At least I was dressed for the role I wanted to play.

Inside, there were a couple of kids going through the record bins, and the guy behind the counter—about thirty, lean and hungry-looking—was talking eagerly to a good-looking blonde who seemed pretty interested in him, too. I started to remove my sunglasses, then thought better of it and left them on. I waited.

At last he pulled himself away from the blonde and stepped over toward me. "Was there something special?" he asked.

"Yeah, I guess there is," I said. "My name's Cervantes, Tony Cervantes, with Starlight Management—down in Los Angeles?"

"Hey! I'm from L.A., too! Jack Josephson's the name. I've had this shop here two years now."

"Great, Jack, then what I'm going to ask won't seem so weird to you."

"What's that?" I had him interested. For the first time he turned his back on the blonde and leaned over the counter in my direction.

"Well, here's the situation. We just signed this group, the Mucous Membranes—I saw the expression on his face. "Yeah, crazy name, right? Anyway, they've got this recording contract, but you know how it is, bunch of street kids from Echo Park, they aren't ready. My thought was, we get them out of that environment to someplace where they can work on their material without the usual, uh, distractions?" I made an invisible syringe out of my thumb and first two fingers, then squeezed down the thumb against them. "You copying?"

"Oh, absolutely. Totally."

I noticed the blond girl had edged a step or two closer. Let her listen.

"Anyway," I continued, "this place, Mount Shasta, seems ideal. I've been through here a couple of times, and I thought it would be. Only one problem. And that's maybe where you could help me."

"Yeah? How's that?"

"We want to put them someplace where they can record. You know. They jam around, and 'Hey! That sounds pretty good. How did we do that?' See, they can play it back, hear what they did, maybe work up some new material that way. You copy?"

"Right. Sure. And I think I've got just the answer to your problem."

"Oh, yeah?" I said. "You do?"

"Absolutely. I've got the greatest little twelve-track setup you ever saw in my basement."

This wasn't the kind of help I was looking for. "Well, uh, that sounds great," I said, "but we want to expose those kids to a completely professional setup," I said. "Is there a twenty-four-track facility in the area?" I saw his face set a little. I didn't want to lose him, so I added, "Look, you can run the board for us. You've handled twenty-four-track, haven't you?"

"Oh, sure. Back in Los Angeles."

"I thought so. We can make it worth your while. Don't worry about that."

"Uh-huh." He seemed to be weighing things, making a decision. He turned to the blonde, who was now just behind him, taking it all in. "Laurie," he said to her, "you could fill in for me behind the counter here, couldn't you?"

"Oh, sure, Jack. Like I did last time you went to L.A."

"Right," he said. Then to me: "Okay, there is just one twenty-four-track setup around here. It's private, kind of a weird situation, in somebody's house, so they may not let you use it, no matter how much you offer. The fact is, they're pretty weird."

"Oh? How do you mean?"

"Well, the way I found out about it, this big guy came in one day a few months ago, and he wanted to know if I knew anything about twenty-four-track. And then, you know, I told him I worked with it back in L.A. Then he wanted to know, could I fix a twenty-four-track board. Well, that depended on the problem, and the way he described it to me, it sounded like a basic wiring problem that screwed up its mixing capability, which I thought I might be able to handle. So the end of the day, I closed down the shop, and he's ready to take me there, only it turns out he wants me to wear a blindfold."

"A *blindfold!*" I yelped. Shock, surprise, indignation—I can really turn it on when I want to.

"Yeah, that was my reaction, too. I said to the guy, 'Hey, no way. I'll follow you in my van,' you know? So that's what

192

we did." He came to a full stop then, like that was the end of the story.

"And?"

"I fixed it."

"Well . . . great," I said, "but what was so secret about the place they didn't want you to know where it was?"

"You got me. I mean, it was just this big old redwood place. I didn't see much of it, just the studio. There wasn't much to that." He frowned a moment. "How big is that group you wanted to put in there?"

"Uh, four. There's four of them."

"Well, you might just fit them in there. But *just*. You know what I mean?"

"Small?"

"Small."

The blonde punched him lightly on the arm. "Tell him about that weird guy you saw," she said. "You know, the one you said really looked gross."

He nodded emphatically. "Oh, yeah. The guy I followed in there left me alone for a while. I guess he got bored watching me work. Anyway, while I'm alone in there, this other guy came to the doorway, and he just stood and stared at me. He didn't say anything. Just stared."

"What did he look like?"

"Yeah, well, that—that was the weird part. He was huge. I mean fat, real fat, and his hair was down into his eyes. He was real dirty, and he had snot running down his nose, you know? Anyway, he was only there a minute or two, and then the other guy came, the one who wanted to blindfold me, and he hustled him out of there. I definitely got the idea I'd seen something I wasn't supposed to, like he was the castle monster or something."

"Were there other people there?" I asked.

"Yeah," he said, "at least one that I could hear. I didn't see anybody else, though." He looked at me then kind of dubiously, like he was starting to wonder what this was all about. I didn't want to lose him. I couldn't afford to. Then he said,

"I think your chances of getting in there and renting their setup are about zero, you know?"

I nodded, like I was thinking it over. "You're probably right. But my boss told me to try for twenty-four-track, so I have to at least make the effort," I said. "That twelve-track setup you've got will probably do just fine. And however it turns out, you run the board. That's a commitment. Thousand a day sound right?"

His face relaxed. "Sounds great." He was hungry.

"But like I say, Jack, I've got to make the effort, so maybe you could take me up there and maybe point the place out to me."

His lips pursed, and he glanced back at the blonde. "Laurie," he said to her, "why don't you go over and ask those kids what they want?"

She made a face at that but left us without a word.

He leaned close then and whispered, "I'd rather not take you out there, see? I've seen the guy, the big guy, around town a couple of times since then, and the way he looks at me, he's kind of threatening, you know? His name's Ferdy, and he's got a reputation as kind of a heavy dude. Into stuff, you know? Anyway, when you talk to him, don't let him know I told you any of this. There's other places you could've found out. Just leave me out of it, okay?"

"Well . . . okay, but how am I going to find my way up there?"

He thought about that a moment. "I could draw you a map," he said.

That was when I made another mistake. Armed with the map Jack Josephson had drawn for me and the instructions he had given me, I decided to go right out there and locate the place while it was still daylight. Not a bad idea. If I'd left it at that, things might have worked out better later on.

By the time I got going, it was early afternoon. I'd left the .38 hidden in the motel room and wanted it with me—just in case. I dug it out from the dust and fuzz balls beneath the bed, well protected in its lead-cloth wrapper, checked it over, and

194

tucked it away. As an afterthought, I took six loose rounds from the box of fifty I had with me and dropped them into the pocket of the new tweed jacket. I'd decided to go up there dressed as I was.

Then I stood there for a moment, looking at the telephone, wondering if I shouldn't make a call or two—but to who? and to what purpose? One last look around, and I left.

According to the map, I was headed for White Ridge Road, west of Shasta City. Somehow that failed to surprise me. From the time the cop had mentioned it as the site of Osborne's supposedly fatal accident, it had seemed likely that his hideaway might be somewhere nearby. Nearby, but again according to the map, the location, which Josephson had marked with a big *X,* was off on one of those logging roads only vaguely marked on the county map.

As I headed out from town beyond Interstate 5, the road began to rise, snaking up and up in long, looping switchback curves that kept me busy at the steering wheel—so busy that I almost missed the turnoff to White Ridge Road. In fact, I did miss it, saw it flash by, and had to stop and reverse to pick it up. At that point I looked back the way I'd come and saw it really wasn't so far. The town was nestled down below beyond the interstate. I glanced down at the odometer and saw that it registered just over four miles—4.2, to be exact. I made a mental note of that and accelerated off down White Ridge Road.

True to its name, it followed the ridge line, curving here and there as it followed the contours of the mountain topography but not rising or falling much along the way. If the loggers had been here, they had left plenty. Pine covered the mountains ahead, but you could see stands off to the left where full trees had been cut and young trees were planted to be harvested in—what? twenty or thirty years, maybe.

Josephson said the correct turnoff from White Ridge Road was about ten or eleven miles down the line, the last left before the Shasta Trinity Forest, which, according to the map, cut across a big portion of the western part of the county. If I came to the sign marking the entrance to the national park, then I'd know I'd gone too far.

As I drove along, I noticed how steeply the ridge dropped off to my right. For one stretch of well over a mile I seemed to be driving along on the edge of a cliff without much in the way of a shoulder to hold me on the road. At last I came to a spot wide enough to pull over. I came to a halt there and got out of the car. Walking to the edge in short, careful steps, I looked down and saw a sharp fall below of a good five hundred feet—or maybe more. I'm not good at judging vertical distances. But then, who is? It was enough, anyway, to make me feel a little dizzy, just looking down. I turned away and took a giant step back from the edge. It was probably along here somewhere that Osborne's Corvette went over the side, I told myself. It must have taken days to get down there and recover the body. Whose body—and why?

As I climbed back into the Ford, I happened to look back to the east and caught sight of Mount Shasta. It seemed to loom just as large from that distance as it had from the town below. Was that some trick of perspective, or was it the way that it seemed to address me personally? I couldn't see the top of it because it was covered by a cloud. Was it my imagination, or was there more snow up there than I had seen on it before? Maybe it was then that I noticed a slight chill in the air. I stood there with the car door open, staring across at the lonely old mountain and suddenly got the feeling that I could do just about anything. Or, no, it wasn't that, exactly. It was more like, no matter what, things were going to turn out all right. Anyway, it was a surge of self-confidence, and I don't get those very often. I blame what followed on that.

Back on the road, even the Bronco seemed to move along with a greater sense of purpose, like it had caught my mood and was ready to respond. The two of us zoomed on together until suddenly I caught sight of a green sign just ahead announcing the Shasta Trinity National Forest. I hit the brakes and stopped just beyond it. So, okay, I'd overshot the logging road on the map. I checked the odometer again and noted the figure, then wrestled with the steering wheel and managed to get turned around in that narrow space. Then I headed back carefully the way I had come, looking for the turnoff that I'd missed.

It was there, all right, but no wonder I had driven past it. Somebody—Ferdy, I supposed—had gone to a lot of trouble to camouflage the entrance to the road, laying brush and branches from the surrounding pines across it, making it look like there was no road there at all—just a trail or a mountain track. But when I got out and cleared the way, I saw that it was wide enough and led up to where I wanted to go. Not paved, of course, but dirt, with an old overlay of gravel ground into it, like a private driveway. It was clear that was how it was being used.

I proceeded carefully in first gear, studying the high ground on my left. According to the map beside me on the seat, the place was about a quarter mile up this road and not easy to see among the trees.

But there it was. The sun glinted on the windows. There was no missing it, even though its redwood exterior blended perfectly with the surrounding pines. I pulled up opposite the place and sat gazing up at it. Even this close, with only a forty-yard drive separating me from it, the place was half-obscured. They had sure gone to a lot of trouble to make it invisible. You'd never find it by accident.

There was a Jeep parked off to one side. Yet the house—two stories, with a raised deck running the width of it—seemed deserted. Of course it couldn't be, not if I was right about who and what was inside, and not if I hadn't wasted my time coming up here. But something told me that Ferdy, at least, wasn't around, and that this might be a good time to take a closer look.

Well, there's confidence and overconfidence, courage and bravado. In other words, every upside has its downside, every positive its negative. And when I marched up that hill to that big, imposing redwood structure, I must have known deep down that I was doing something foolish. Call it acting on a negative impulse.

The first bullet hit a tree about eight feet to my right. The

197

thud of it and the crack of the rifle were just about simultaneous.

I decided that was a warning shot and stayed on my feet. "Hey," I yelled, "I just want to talk!"

There was no response, so I took a couple of tentative steps forward.

The second bullet hit just a yard in front of me. If the driveway had been paved, even blacktopped, it would probably have ricocheted right up into my abdomen. As it was, it sent a sharp spray of dirt and gravel up as high as my crotch.

That was enough for me. I took a running dive for cover at the side of the road. I kept rolling until I was down beneath a low-boughed spruce with ground brush in front of me. Still, I had a pretty good view of the house, and I could see the rifle barrel sticking out just inches from an upstairs window right above the front door.

Then, just to let me know he knew right where I was, the shooter put one through the tree branches just above my head and another into the brush in front of me. That second shot was close—too close. A foot to the left and I would have bought it then and there. Maybe he was just playing with me. Maybe he had a telescopic sight on that thing and was putting his rounds just where he wanted to. But I wasn't prepared to lie there and find out. I pushed over on my side and worked the .38 out of the holster. At least it was a standard Smith and Wesson Police Special and not some snub-nosed popgun; I had at least half a chance of hitting what I aimed at across the fifty yards that separated us.

What I aimed at was the upper pane of that window. I squeezed off two rounds. The first one thwacked against the window frame lower than I'd intended. The second broke the window glass, just where I wanted it.

Whoever shot at me wasn't used to drawing return fire. There was a muffled yell of surprise from the house, and the rifle barrel abruptly disappeared from the window.

That was all I needed. I scrambled to my feet and ran along the side of the driveway just as fast as I could in a crouch. I made the thirty yards to the Ford in record time. I was inside,

198

had the engine started, and was slamming the lever into reverse when there was a sound, a weird sound like nothing I'd heard before, something between a howl and a moan from somwhere close. Then another shot from the house ripped across the roof of the Ford. I didn't stop to assess damage. Let Hertz deal with it. I raced backward along the road until I was out of sight of the house. Only then did I slow down and make a reasonably orderly entrance onto White Ridge.

It shook me up. I don't like getting shot at. As I sped along, keeping an eye on the rearview mirror, just one thought cheered me: at least I knew I had the address right.

But what was that noise I heard? It seemed barely human. Had I hit someone shooting through the window? Was the castle monster loose?

Eighteen

There's this old joke about a rich man who happened by a shop window that was done in exquisite taste. There was, on a covering of black velvet, a beautiful circle of matched pearls and, laid diagonally across them, a single red rose. His heart swelled at the simple beauty of the offering. He went inside the shop and was met by a thin man dressed in black. "I must have that strand of pearls," he said. "Money is no object." The man in black replied, "I'm sorry, but we don't sell pearls here." "Well, the rose then," said the rich man. "It's simple. It's perfect. My sweetheart will love it." The shopkeeper shook his head and said, "We don't sell roses, either." The rich man, confused, asked, "Why are they in the window? What do you do here?" The shopkeeper shrugged and said, "We castrate cats. What would you expect us to put out there?"

I don't know when it was I thought of that, maybe the moment I walked inside the sporting goods shop just off the main street there in Shasta City. Outside, you might have taken it for a clothing store. There were dummies in the window, dressed in all kinds of heavy hunting gear. Rows of boots filled one side. Another featured camping equipment—everything from a tent to a charcoal broiler.

Inside, it was a different story. Oh, sure, off to the left the clothes were there, piled casually on the counter, boots laid out behind. Another dummy dressed in camouflage jacket and pants stood in an awkward attitude of attention in one corner. And so on. But across the long aisle—that was what it was all about. The whole right side of the shop was a kind of arsenal. The wall behind the counter was one big gun rack—shotguns at one end, lever-action carbines at another, and in between just about anything you could imagine in the way of long-range destruction. There were handguns in the display case and piles of cartridge boxes. You could outfit a small army out of that shop. That's what the motel manager had told me. But that was only after a long, involved tale about how he'd had to shoot a bear in his backyard, where he used to live, in the hills above Modoc.

"How do'." It was a woman of about forty who came out to see what I might want. I hadn't expected a woman. She was followed out from the back by a big, goofy-looking dog that looked part collie and part who-knows-what. His tail was wagging vigorously, and the woman was smiling a nice, big small-town smile.

I gave one right back to her. "Yes, ma'am," I said, "I'm looking to buy a rifle."

"What you got in mind?" she asked. "Deer? Elk?"

"Bigger than deer," I said. "Bear-size, I guess."

"Oh?" That seemed to interest her.

"See, I've got this problem. I moved into this place up around White Ridge. Nobody told me there were bears up there."

"There are," she agreed. "Black bears, whole tribe of them."

"Well, they come down and go after the garbage. My neighbor said to get a gun and just shoot in their direction, and that would scare them off. But something tells me you don't go shooting at a bear to scare him off unless you've got something big enough to kill him if he doesn't scare."

She thought that over and nodded. "Right on both counts. I mean, your neighbor's right they'll probably just turn tail first time you let go with a shot. But you're right, too. Once in a while they get annoyed and head at you instead. You wouldn't want a twenty-two for that—or a shotgun. You're going to need a thirty-ought-six, I'd say, something in that range."

"That's what I thought."

The dog came over and gave me a friendly sniff. I riffled him behind the ears. He liked that.

"You ever shoot before?" She looked sort of skeptical.

"Some," I said. "Mostly in the army."

She brightened at that. "Well, then, I might have just the rifle for you."

With that, she went behind the counter and unlocked the gun rack. Then, down the line, she pulled out a piece bigger than the rest. I noticed, as she returned with it, that she handled it with ease and authority. By the time she put it in my hands, I'd recognized it.

"This is the first thing I ever shot," I said. It was an M1 Garand rifle, the basic U.S. Army weapon in World War II and Korea. "That was way back in ROTC at UCLA." I gripped and regripped it, feeling the familiar bulk of it in my hands. "By the time I actually went into the army they'd converted to M16."

"I could sell you one of those—an M16, I mean. Well, it's an Armalite, same thing really, fixed for semiautomatic. But I really think thirty caliber is right for what you want it for. You can hunt with it, too."

I swung the M1 up to my shoulder and took a sighting at an imaginary target out the front door. It was solid and substantial. "Yeah, I think so," I said. "I'll take this one."

I found a deserted patch of woods out beyond Everett and went through three clips—twenty-four rounds—adjusting the sights and getting used to the thing again. It felt right. Six of the last eight I fired went right where I wanted—into a cluster about eighteen inches in diameter at a distance of about one hundred yards. I was satisfied.

There was quite a pile of brass around me by the time I finished. I picked up after myself and got ready to go. That first shiver I got the afternoon before up on White Ridge Road was just a preview of coming attractions. From the moment I got up that morning, the temperature had been falling. As I walked back to the Ford Bronco, M1 in hand, pockets jingling with brass, I studied the sky. I didn't like what I saw there. All but the base of Mount Shasta was obscured in a thick quilt about the color of dirty dishwater. The clouds were rolling in low from the west. It looked like heavy weather coming over the mountains from the Pacific. By the time I got the Ford out on the road, it had started to rain. Nothing subtle about it. The first drops hit my windshield with a resounding splat. Was it going to be a thunderstorm or what? No, once I got the wipers started and could see what I was heading into, it looked to me like it would be one of those driving, dismal daylong rains, the kind they say are typical of that part of the country. There hadn't been a thing about it on TV that morning, but the TV came from Redding, and Redding was a long way off.

Once back in Shasta City, I parked just down the street from the sporting goods shop and dashed inside. I stood a moment wiping my feet on a mat that had appeared at the door since the last time I was there. The dog sat nearby, looking at me questioningly. The woman was behind the counter on the left rearranging the piles of clothes. She regarded me with the same quizzical expression the dog wore.

"You're back," she said.

"Looks like it."

"I hope that doesn't mean there was anything wrong with that M1 I sold you."

"Not a thing," I said. "It shoots better than I do."

"What can I do for you then?"

"You can sell me a pair of those rubber boots—the kind that lace up."

A knowing smile spread over her face. "Yeah," she said, "you'll be needing those."

"It looks like an all-day rain, doesn't it?"

She pulled what looked like a big shoe box out from the piles behind the counter. "No, the rain won't last till evening."

"Glad to hear it," I said.

"That's when the snow will start. Welcome to winter, friend. Those bears won't bother you until next spring."

203

She called it about right. I'd spent the night before planning all this. I had sat on the bed writing down every detail I could remember of that house off White Ridge Road and the grounds surrounding it. Then I drew a map. After an hour of that, I studied the sheets of paper around me on the bed and tried to work out something that made sense. I had made out a shopping list. The rifle was the top item. The rest of the stuff I could get at any hardware store or filling station. Considering I'd made a pretty hurried visit to White Ridge, I thought I'd done a pretty good job of planning this raid. But the one thing I hadn't factored in was bad weather—not rain, and not snow in the first week of November.

Because I'd done all my shopping and had hours to kill before dark, I tried to take a nap that afternoon. I stretched out on the bed and lay there, listening to the rain with my eyes shut, breathing deeply and regularly, waiting for sleep to happen.

It wasn't working. My mind raced on to what I'd planned for that night—and what I hadn't. I had visions of myself sliding in the mud, slipping on ice, screwing up royally. And there was Petko's ugly face, leering at me. It was a lot like a bad dream, the kind of nightmare where every move you make is the wrong one. Except I knew I was awake.

I made an effort to regain control. I fixed my mind on that moment the day before when I stopped by the roadside and looked back at Mount Shasta. I was just climbing back into the car, wasn't I? I got this big shot of self-confidence, just standing there. Remembering it, thinking about it, I was trying to bring it back. But it wouldn't come. What did come, surprisingly, was sleep.

There was a dream. Maybe there was more than one, but there was one I remembered. Have you ever noticed how dreams are like movies? Or, anyway, mine are. They go from shot to shot—you know, medium shot, close-up, and so on; sometimes an insert on a hand to show you something important you might otherwise miss; and once in a while a line or two of dialogue, more often than not voice-over.

Well, that's how this one was. I remember there was this long view of Shasta—at night, moonlit, more or less the way I'd seen it from the interstate when I drove up here from Redding. Only I wasn't driving. It was just there, like an establishing shot, putting me on notice to pay attention to what followed. Then I was up on the mountain—yeah, I was there, seeing this. There was snow all around, except for a few outcrops of rock. The wind blew, shifting thin clouds of snow across the picture. It must have been cold—it *looked* cold— but I didn't feel anything. I was there, just watching, waiting for something.

When it came, it was just a dark spot moving down the mountain toward me. But somehow I knew what it would be. And yes, there it was—in a closer shot—a bear, a black bear, padding down in a kind of shuffling run, moving closer and closer until only yards of snow separated us on a short flat space. Then he stopped and looked at me for a long moment, and he did what I've only seen bears do in still photos: he reared up on his hind legs, stood upright, and began to roar. Two things struck me then—first, that I didn't need to be afraid because I wasn't threatened, and second, how much, in that posture, he was like a man.

He kept right on roaring, only that roar turned into a ring— and it came from the telephone on the nightstand next to the bed. I grabbed at the receiver, dropped it, then picked it up again. It was the motel manager with the wake-up call I'd asked for. I thanked him and hung up, then pushed up to a sitting position and put my legs over the side of the bed. Was I listening? If I was, I didn't hear anything. That was just it. There was nothing to hear. The rain had stopped. I jumped out of bed and padded over to the window. Parting the drapes, I looked out into a great swirl of white.

The coffee tasted good. I'd had three cups already, but when the waitress came behind the counter and asked me if I wanted more, I let her pour me another half cup. The remains of a half-eaten steak lay on the plate in front of me. I'd stopped because I figured I'd had enough. There ought to be something

205

in my stomach, and red meat seemed right, but it would have been dumb to go where I had to go with a full belly. I finished off the coffee in one last big gulp, tossed down a tip, and headed for the cash register.

Just as I was tucking away four Mars bars, thinking I might need them later on that night, I felt a strong hand on my shoulder. I whirled around, maybe a little too quickly. Maybe I half expected to see Ferdy there. But no. It was that cop I'd talked to my first night in Mount Shasta City, the night-duty man. He'd just come in and was shaking the snow from his jacket as he smiled a greeting at me.

"You're the movie fella, ain'tcha?"

"That's me."

"Didn't know you were still in town."

"Yeah, well, I'll be leaving tomorrow," I said. One way or another.

"Wish I'd known where to find you," he said. "See, I ran into Ferdy just this afternoon in town. I told him you were around looking for him, that it had to do with his boss, that English fella, being in a car accident and all. He was sure interested in that. I said he ought to try to call you at that movie studio—Majestic, wasn't it?"

"Yeah. Majestic."

"Then he asked me who you were, and I had to tell him I couldn't remember. I just plain forgot. Didn't have your card with me, either. I told him I thought you were a Mexican fella, though, and you had a Mexican name. That is right, ain't it?"

"Right. Mexican-American."

"He seemed to know who you were, said he'd call you up in Hollywood." The cop seemed annoyed with himself. "I was so sure you'd gone, I guess, I didn't even think to ask him where he lived, like you wanted to know."

I gave him a nod I meant to be reassuring. "Don't worry," I said. "It's going to work out."

One way or another.

When I got back into my room at the motel, the message light on the phone was flashing. Jimmy Albright of the Ventura

206

County Sheriff's Office had called. He wanted me to call back and had left two numbers just to make sure I did. I found him at the first one, still at the office.

"Yeah, I was just leaving," he said. "Thanks for getting back right away."

"Something new?" I asked.

"Yeah, I thought you ought to know. Somebody got into the Weston house and tore it all up, just like you said they would."

"Didn't the cops in Ojai have the place staked out?"

"Oh, well, hell, you know. There's not many of them up there, and they've got a whole lot of territory to cover. They figured it'd be okay if they just drove by pretty often and eyeballed the place."

I sighed. "I'm not surprised. When did it happen?"

"Last night sometime, must've been. Mrs. Weston was back in the daytime yesterday, and it was okay. Then this morning she came to pick up some clothes for her kids, and the place was just totally wrecked. I took a look at it myself. Whoever was in there wasn't just looking for something, they were out to do damage."

That sounded like Ferdinand Petko's modus operandi. And it worked out about right, too. He would have had plenty of time to catch the morning plane up to Redding and meet that cop on the street in Mount Shasta City.

"You didn't happen to talk to the LAPD about this, did you?" I asked.

"Yeah, as a matter of fact I did," he said. "I called your friend Detective Pell right after I came back from the Weston house. He was interested, but not enough to reopen that case at the movie studio." Albright hesitated, than asked, "How you doin' up there?"

I decided to tell him everything. I might not have the chance to tell anyone else. I gave him the location of the house as precisely as I could without a map. He was taking down the information as I gave it to him.

"You're sure that's the place? Wouldn't that fella Petko be

207

down here now? I mean, if it was him broke into the Weston house?"

"No, he was seen here today. Just got into town. And, yeah, I'm sure that's the place, all right. When I went up to knock on the door I got shot at."

"Well, what do the cops up there say about that?"

"Nothing. I haven't told them."

A brief pause while Albright took that in. Then: "Just what're you up to, anyway?"

"I'm going in."

"What does that mean?"

"It means I'm going in."

"Just like Rambo, huh?" He sounded exasperated. "You used to be a cop. You ever hear of probable cause?"

"Well, I'm not a cop any more, and I'm going in."

And I hung up on him.

It took nearly an hour to change, get everything together, and pack the Bronco for the run up White Ridge. I'd intended to delay my departure until sometime around midnight—but that was before the snow started. The way it was coming down, if I didn't get started soon, I might not get there at all. Remembering that road running precariously along the cliff, I had to admit that was a definite possibility, anyway.

After I had stowed the rifle and the backpack I'd bought, I went back into the motel room for one last look to make sure I hadn't left anything. I stood for a moment, now dressed in plastic wet-weather gear, staring at the telephone. I knew I had a call to make. I couldn't put it off any longer. I walked over and picked up the receiver. Still standing, I dialed home.

Why had I put it off so long? Because I didn't know what I'd say to Alicia. And why was I calling now? Because I knew that, under the circumstances, I had to say something. Maybe a last will and testament.

Pilar answered. That didn't seem right. I looked at my watch—a little after eight. Why was she still around?

Alicia was out celebrating.

"Oh, sí, Senor Cervantes. It's a very big deal. Senorita

208

Toller pick her up in a big limo. You should have seen! The baby and I, we wave good-bye."

"What are they celebrating?" I asked, though I was sure I knew the answer.

"Oh, she got the part! She got the part! A big contract! Her agent negotiates it now. But is settled, really. Agreement in principle, they say, huh?"

"Her agent?"

"Sure, she got an agent now an' everything. Mister Bernie. I talk to him on the telephone. Very smart man. He talks very fast."

"Yeah, I'll bet," I said, probably sounding a little less than totally enthusiastic. Why couldn't I let go and be happy for Alicia? Maybe because I had other things on my mind just then. And maybe it went deeper than that.

"But isn't it wonderful?" Pilar sang into my ear. "She's gonna be on TV, Senor Cervantes! She's gonna be a big star!"

Maybe she would be at that. "Yeah," I said, "that's terrific, Pilar. Just tell her I called and I said it was terrific news."

"You bet. I tell her. Too bad you're not here to celebrate with her."

"Yeah, too bad." And then we said good-bye, and that was the end of it.

Nineteen

It wasn't a blizzard. You could see through the stuff, and the wind wasn't really that strong. But what wind there was blew against me, and the way the snow piled up on the windshield, it was almost more than the wipers could handle. I probably wouldn't have made the turnoff onto White Ridge Road unless I'd taken an odometer reading the day before. But I found it, made the turn, then pulled over and cleared the windshield. The way it looked, there was about four inches on the ground then—soft and wet.

Then I drove, nosing along slowly and steadily in four-wheel drive, just keeping those wheels moving along. At this rate, it was going to take a couple of hours to drive what I'd made in not much more than half an hour before. Well, nobody said it was going to be easy.

I hugged the left side of the road, sensing the void off to my right. There may have been some danger I'd meet a car or a truck coming around a curve, but the chances that anyone else would be out on a night like this seemed pretty slim. I kept going as long as I could, then stopped to clear the windshield again. The snow was deeper up here but packed a little harder. I wasn't sure if that was good or bad.

Then, about halfway to the sign that marked the entrance to the Shasta Trinity National Forest, a small miracle happened: the snow began to slack off. I guess I became aware of it gradually. The headlights seemed to penetrate farther into the darkness. The darkness wasn't quite so white. And the windshield wipers really began to do the job. Overconfident again: I sped up, just a little heavier on the right foot. But on a curve a little wider than the rest, I found that the hard-packed snow up there on the ridge held an added danger. I went into a slide. My right rear wheel came dangerously close to the shoulderless embankment, but I brought it back, controlling the slide, driving out of it. Breathing hard, I eased off on the accelerator and decided I wasn't really in such a hurry to get up there, anyway. Nobody said it was going to be easy.

I stopped about a quarter of a mile from the logging road. I'd worked it out from yesterday's odometer reading, and I knew this was about as far as I wanted to go. So when I came to a wide spot half-sheltered by snow-covered trees and brush, I eased the Bronco in and shut off the engine and the lights. I sat there behind the wheel with my gloves off, inhaling and exhaling, breathing deeply, resting from the ordeal before getting on to the next phase of the operation.

I wasn't sure whether the house was situated high enough so that they could have seen my lights coming up the ridge road. And I wasn't sure whether they could have heard the Ford engine chugging along—the wind was blowing against me, and that was in my favor; sound was carried down the ridge behind me. But one thing was likely: they were pretty sure I was coming, and they'd be waiting for me.

I slipped out of the car, hauled out the backpack after me, and struggled into it. Then I pulled the M1 out of its canvas case, adjusted the sling, and put it over my shoulder, stock up and barrel down. Then I shut the car door just as quietly as I could and set off down the road.

The snow had slacked off, but it hadn't stopped. There was now a constant light sprinkle in the air, and from time to time the wind sent showers of the stuff down from the trees. I was dry enough with my rubber boots, plastic overpants, rain hat, and rawhide coat—and God knows I was warm enough. It wasn't long before I was sweating. The trouble with all the stuff I'd bought at the gun shop was that it was camouflage-colored—great for creeping through the woods in the fall, but even in the dim light of a few stars above I must have stood out like the black bear that had tracked through my dream.

At last I reached the entrance to the logging road. I almost missed it. If they had tried to hide it before, they had built a barrier across it this time, a snow-covered wall of brush and branches nearly up to my chest. I could hardly tell it from the dense line of growth I'd been following along the ridge road. The difference was that there were no trees behind it. An empty white corridor led up from behind the barrier. The house was about a quarter of a mile from here.

Even though I couldn't see it, lights would have been visible through the trees—if they had left any lights on. The fact that there weren't any made me certain I was expected. I stood there listening, but I heard only the wind. Kneeling into a half-crouch, I eased the M1 off my shoulder and listened a little longer. Nothing. A tree cracked. Another groaned. Wind. Nothing.

Leaving the barrier undisturbed, I backtracked a little, then worked my way through the brush and up through the trees that ran along the logging road. The idea was to move as quietly as possible. The only way to do that is to go slow, moving boughs and branches before you, sliding by, then moving them back. It's exhausting. You get just as tired going very slowly as you do going very fast. And you sweat just as hard. That's why I sank down at a point I thought would be about halfway to the house to take a rest.

Just because the lights were off and they were waiting for me didn't mean they were huddling in fear inside. No, there was probably at least one guy out walking the perimeter. And if Ferdy was an ex-marine, the way I'd been set straight by that blonde back in Modoc, then he may have prepared a dirty trick or two for me. This was jungle warfare in the snow.

Just as I was getting up, ready to push on, I was stopped suddenly, half-up and half-down. It was that noise, the one I'd heard the day before. It rose in the night, a moan, a howl, a moan that ended in a howl, something inhuman in its misery. Yeah, not human. Animal.

212

And then, spoken clearly, not whispered or shouted: "Shut up, you son of a bitch." That was Ferdy, I was sure. Then there was a bang, like a door closing.

Answered by a low, rumbling sound, a growl in the deepest bass.

Maybe I was closer to the house than I thought, or maybe the wind had carried the sound to me. There was only one way to find out. I moved out again, even slower than before, my feet probing with each step. If I hadn't been moving like that, I might have hit the trip wire.

As it was, I only touched it with my foot and drew back quickly. You couldn't see the thing. It was covered over with snow. But I knelt down, took off a glove and uncovered it, and I saw it was just as I'd supposed—taut and waiting. I struggled out of the pack and hauled out the bolt cutter I'd bought at the hardware store that day and was about to clip the wire when I thought better of it. Where did it lead? What would it do? Ferdy wouldn't, couldn't, set an explosive charge out here so close to the house. Probably just a pile of tin cans at the other end of the line set to shake, rattle, and roll at the first good, strong tug. In that case, sudden slack might have the same effect. I put the bolt cutter back in the pack, then hoisted the pack up and over my shoulders. Then I stepped carefully over the trip wire.

I continued through the trees at the same painfully slow, cautious pace. It would be just like an old jungle fighter to set trip wires in sequence: if he missed the first time, he'd catch me the second or the third. But, no, Ferdy had a couple of other surprises in store.

About fifty yards from the trip wire, I came up from under the low boughs of a spruce, snow showering down on me, and sliced my coat on razor wire. If my arm hadn't been up, protecting my face from the snow, I would have caught it right across the cheek. I took a step back and flopped down under the tree. Lying there, the M1 tucked under me and the backpack weighting me down, I looked over the situation. This hadn't been put up just to keep me out. It marked a permanent boundary, a perimeter of some sort. Even in the dim starlight

213

I could tell that the area beyond the barbed wire had been cleared, and that the big shape looming there ahead and to my right was the house. I'd reached it at last.

There was a post about five feet away and four strands of wire wound around it at about one-foot intervals. I was trying to decide whether or not I could get by just cutting the lowest strand of wire. If I tried going under wearing the backpack, I wasn't sure I'd make it. Maybe I should just push it through ahead of me.

I was starting to squirm out of the backpack when the entire area exploded into bright light. It blinded me. I ducked my head and shut my eyes. If I'd been out there, I would have had no place to hide.

I heard a door open.

"Goddamn it, Alex, all right. I'll go out and take a look."

"I'm sure I heard something."

"Where? Was it the tin cans?"

"No. Oh, I don't know. Out there somewhere. Look."

Squinting against the bright, luminous bulbs that pointed outward from the deck, I raised my head slowly and saw Ferdy standing on the steps, looking more or less in my direction and not seeing me. His eyes swept the area, then moved on to another corner. I was well hidden by the low boughs of the tree above me.

Ferdy took a few steps away from the stairs. He wasn't wearing a coat, so it was pretty clear he didn't mean to stay out there long. But on his hip he balanced what looked like a Winchester or a Marlin, some kind of lever-action gun, anyway. He would make a good target himself, standing right there. I was half-tempted to ease the M1 up and out and let him have it right where he stood. Separated by only thirty or thirty-five yards, I knew I could put a pretty tight cluster in his middle. He deserved it.

Alex Wakefield stuck his head out the door. "Do you see anything?"

"Not a damn thing."

"Well, keep looking."

"I will *not* keep looking. I'm tired and I'm hungry, god-

214

damn it. You want somebody out here all the time, you send your boyfriend out. You said he wanted to help out. Thinks he's a real tough guy, don't he?"

"My dear, he *is* tough, believe me."

"Well, then, send him out. He oughta be able to handle that little Mexican—if he ever shows up. I told you, the cop thought he left town."

"Oh . . . all right." Wakefield stuck his head back inside the door and called, "Larry?" Almost sweetly.

Then a big noise—not the moan-and-howl I'd heard before, but an angry roar followed by another. Where had it come from? Then Ferdy strode off to the far corner of the yard, cursing every step of the way. I saw he was headed for a big, low structure covered over with tar paper. He threw back one of the panels and was greeted with a growl. I couldn't really see inside, but whatever was in there was black and big.

Ferdy jabbed in a couple of times with the barrel of the carbine. I couldn't hear exactly what he was saying, but the general idea was, shut up. More growls, then Ferdy threw down the flap and walked back to the house. A moment later he was inside, and the lights went off.

I waited in the dark.

A couple of minutes passed. I pushed backward in the snow and managed to get at the bolt cutter without hauling off the backpack.

Then I heard the door open. I could see them dimly. There was probably a fire going inside.

Alex: "It's only for a little while. Ferdy needs a rest."

"Yeah, okay." Then: "Jesus, it's cold out here."

"Button up, dear. Sure you don't want to take a rifle?"

"No, I got my magnum. You know I took this off a cop?"

"Really?"

"Really."

"Thrilling."

The door closed. The figure moved off the deck and down the stairs and then was lost in the darkness. I could hear him moving out deep to my left. He'd walk the fence. Would he head in my direction? No, he looped over to his right, toward

215

the cage, if that's what it was. I don't know if I sensed him or
heard him. What I did hear was a lot more growls, and the
sound of the tar-paper flap going up, and then a roar.

"Don't you fuck with me." That came quite distinctly. He
was talking louder than he needed to. Acting tough. "You
know what you are? You're bear meat. Yeah, that's right.
We're going to cut you into steaks and eat you up. I hope you
taste better than you look, you ugly fucker. You smell bad,
too. Ferdy says you'll taste great, but I don't know." He
drawled out the last three words, and then broke into a laugh,
like he'd really said something funny.

Then the guy stood there and lit a cigarette. He tossed the
lighted match into the cage. As the howl went up, I heard the
flap go down.

Larry, if that was his name, wasn't hard to follow after that.
The glow of the cigarette moved at an easy speed as he ambled
around the yard, then disappeared around the other side of the
house. Some jungle fighter he was.

I cut the lower two strands of the razor wire, pushed the
ends away carefully, and crawled under and through. It all
took less than a minute. Up and on my feet, I moved about as
swiftly and quietly as I could. The snow muffled my steps. I
passed close beneath the windows of the house, ducking low,
beneath the level of the deck. It might be too dark to see me,
but you can detect movement even in pitch dark—and it
wasn't quite that. I could hear voices inside.

I was following Larry. I reached the far corner of the house,
paused, listened, then moved cautiously along the side. There
was no cigarette glow ahead, just the dark. But, no, as I
reached the front of the house I spotted the glow down the
long driveway. He'd been down to the road and was returning.
As I moved in a crouch behind the brush next to the Jeep,
Larry threw away his cigarette, sailing it off to the side. But the
way he was stamping around, it wasn't hard to follow his
movements.

I sensed that they would take him pretty close to me. But
close enough? Here I was with the M1 in one hand and the bolt
cutter in the other. I had to choose my weapon.

He picked a path between the Jeep and the brush off to one side of the house where I squatted in hiding. Lucky for me, unlucky for him. As he stepped past, I rose up, took one step after him, and let him have it on the side of the head with the bolt cutter. But he didn't go down right away. He stood there swaying on his feet. So I hit him on the other side of the head, and he toppled over into the brush.

I grabbed at his hands. No gun there. He had it in his pocket—and, yeah, it was a magnum, a .357 Colt Python. I tucked it in my own pocket and turned him over. The bolt cutter had cut one ear pretty badly and opened a gash on the other side of his neck. He'd need stitches, but he wouldn't bleed to death. I shrugged out of the backpack and pulled out the clothesline, another item from my shopping list. Using the bolt cutter, I cut the pieces I needed, then tied him hand and foot. I used one of his gloves for a gag. Just as I was jamming it in, I recognized him. He was the guy from Alex Wakefield's office, the one Alex called his "personal secretary." Well, whoever he was, he was out of the way for a while. I dragged him a decent distance from the Jeep and left him, still inert, under a tree.

Now the Jeep. I returned to the pack and from my bag of tricks pulled out the two quart-cans of 10W-40 I'd picked up at the Chevron station across from the motel. I opened them both up with my pocket knife. One of them I emptied on the rear seat and floor of the Jeep. The other I emptied over two towels I'd swiped from the motel room. Then I pushed them in a big wad under the rear of the vehicle. I lit the oil-soaked towels. Sure, oil burns, but it's not as volatile as gasoline, so it took me about three matches to get the fire started under the car. The one in the backseat started up right away.

Here was the plan: I'd start this slow fire in front—slow enough to let me get around to the back. When they saw it burning—or better yet, when the gas tank blew—they'd go running out the front, and I'd come crashing in the back. Brilliant? Well, maybe not brilliant, but it was a plan.

I grabbed up the M1, thinking I wouldn't need the bolt cutter anymore, and I'd emptied the backpack, so—

Wait a second! The backpack *wasn't* empty.

I got the craziest idea I've ever had in my life.

I picked up the bolt cutter and the pack and ran for the backyard. I went right to the cage. Larry was right about one thing. It smelled pretty bad, all right. I threw up the tar-paper flap, and, yes, just as I figured, there was a black bear of uncertain large size in there. He growled a greeting.

How do you make friends with a bear? You feed him. I didn't try to sweet-talk him. I didn't try to reason with him. I just reached into the backpack and pulled out one of the four Mars bars inside and dropped into the cage. He went down on the floor of the cage and stuffed it into his mouth, wrapper and all. When he did that, I saw his teeth flash, and I almost walked away. But, no, he was chewing, making contented sounds.

"You like that, huh? Well, I've got some more for you."

The padlock on the door of the cage was good and sturdy, but the bolt cutter took care of it. I got out of the way just as quickly as I could. I guess I expected him to come running, but he didn't. He pushed tentatively against the cage door. When it opened, he seemed puzzled. He moved out at a slow walk, looking right and left and then at me. I saw he was wearing a chain. I hadn't expected that. I'd have to deal with it. He came to the end of the chain and stood looking at me suspiciously. God, he looked big, probably not full-grown but solid and thick.

I tossed another Mars bar down in the snow within easy reach. He scooped it up with his paws, sat down, and shoved it into his mouth. As he did, I circled around him and cut the chain. Then I tossed the bolt cutter aside and made straight for the back stairs. He was up and after me, even before I was ready. But I managed to get a third candy bar down right at the foot of the stairs. Then I backed up, step by step, watching him.

He poked at it this time and sniffed; then, satisfied, he gobbled it up. We stood, him looking up at me and me looking down at him. What about that Jeep? When were they going to

218

notice it was on fire? Maybe it *wasn't* on fire. Maybe my little oil blaze had just sputtered out like a spent candle.

I leaned the M1 against my hip and hastily unwrapped the last Mars bar. I held it up to him. I wanted him to smell it. I wanted his mouth to water for it. Backing away from him down the deck, I passed what must have been a small kitchen window. He started up the stairs after me and what I held out in my hand.

Glancing behind me, I saw that I was about five feet from a big picture window. Through it, I could hear voices.

Woman's voice: "How long we gonna keep the lights off? It's creepy with just this fire going."

Alex: "I think it's cozy, don't you, Ferdy?"

The bear was up on the deck with me, moving in my direction. He stopped when I stopped.

Then, again, the woman's voice: "Hey, I think there's somebody out there on the deck."

There was no putting it off now. I blessed myself, as fast as I used to do it when I was a kid.

Then I whirled around and with the butt of the M1 I began bashing in that picture window, all eight feet of it. A scream, noise, confusion, for about three seconds. But I held onto that Mars bar.

When I looked back, panting, the bear was still standing there looking puzzled. I was probably lucky he hadn't been frightened away by all the noise. But I had his attention, so I tossed the Mars bar right through the broken glass, and into the room.

He hesitated just an instant, then dived in after it.

I followed him in, leaping, grazing my knee on a glass shard, landing in a crouch on a floor slippery with broken glass. I let go three rounds from the M1, firing high—*Blam-Blam-Blam*—and the sound of it exploded against the walls like cannon fire.

The bear raged around the room, roaring and slapping out. The woman fell away from him, yelling out something in fright. He moved away from her indifferently, then pushed up on his hind feet and lumbered forward like a man with bad knees.

219

Jesus! Somebody was shooting at me! Something whizzed by—a dull pop and another one, and something with the force of a hammer blow hit my left shoulder. I dropped down on the broken glass and saw that it was Alex, silhouetted against the fireplace, pumping away at me with a small automatic he held extended in both hands.

"I got him, Ferdy! He went down!"

He fired again. I managed to get the M1 up and out and pointed at him, not aimed, at about twenty feet, then I pulled the trigger twice, big booms, and Alex fell back into the fireplace and began screaming. He managed to roll out of the fire, yelling to Ferdy for help. His pistol went skittering across the floor.

Ferdy wasn't going to help anybody. He was busy trying to save himself. My guess is that when that bear jumped through the window and got the scent of his old tormentor, he forgot about that Mars bar. He forgot about everything except getting even.

The bear had Ferdy backed into a corner. Ferdy was taller. The bear was only about five and a half feet, standing upright, but it looked like the two were about even in weight.

Ferdy had a knife. I saw it glint in the firelight.

Struggling to my feet, I left the M1 on the floor and pulled Larry's Colt Python from the pocket of my coat. My left arm was fairly useless. It sort of dangled and flopped around by itself. I went over to pick up the pistol Alex had lost. He lay there moaning, a bullet in his thigh and burns on his back.

As I was bending down to retrieve the automatic, I caught movement to my left and saw that the woman had got hold of Ferdy's carbine and now had it pointed at the bear's back. She looked like she knew how to shoot.

"You pull that trigger, and you're dead," I yelled at her. I had the Colt angled in her direction. Without either lowering the gun barrel or swinging it toward me, she moved her head and looked at me. When she did that, I recognized her. It was the blonde from the bar in Modoc.

There was sudden activity in the corner. Grunting. A yell.

A bump. It took a lot of concentration to keep my eyes fixed on the blonde, but it paid off in the end.

"Lay that thing down on the floor real slow," I said.

I don't know if it was my stare or the Colt Python that convinced her, but she did it just the way I told her to.

I walked swiftly over to her, pushed her down on the sofa, and kicked the carbine clear across the room.

Then, and only then, did I dare to take a look at the brawl that was under way in the corner.

I guess you hear about combat like this once in a while up in the wilds of Alaska or the Yukon: "I Fought a Grizzly and Survived." Stuff like that. But this was no grizzly, just a black bear. The man had a knife. The bear had his teeth, his claws, and his hate. They were pretty evenly matched.

Ferdy had scored him on the flank with the knife. You could see blood in the black fur. But it looked like he hadn't cut him in the belly, where he needed to. Ferdy would come around with the knife, and the bear would slap it away with his big paw. Then—bam!—the bear would slam him into the wall and give him a blow to the head with his other paw. They'd been at it this way for a couple of minutes. Ferdy's shirt was in tatters over his arm, and the hand that held the knife was cut and bleeding. How long could he hold on to it?

How long could the bear stay erect? He was tottering, his paws on Ferdy's shoulders, trying to wrestle him down to the floor. Ferdy dug his knife into his side. The bear howled, then chewed at Ferdy's face. Ferdy howled. I'm not sure which of them got the worst of it. The two began staggering around together in a grotesque waltz.

"For God's sake, shoot that thing," the blonde screamed at me. "He'll kill Ferdy."

"Shut up," I said. "The bear's on my side."

It was true. I never expected it, but there it was. I wanted the bear to win.

There was light in the room, more than there should have been from that fire in the fireplace. Then I saw that it was coming from outside—the Jeep! It *was* on fire! You couldn't see the fire directly from the window, but the flames lit the

221

room from one side, illuminating the struggle, flickering in shadow and light over the walls.

Meanwhile they danced on, crashing about the place, bouncing off the walls. On and on, until the bear, exhausted by all he had endured in that upright posture, crashed down onto all fours and stood for a moment, panting, sizing up his opponent. Ferdy staggered backward, free at last of that corner where he had been trapped.

It was just then that the gas tank on the Jeep blew.

I was prepared for it, hoping for it, and still it caught me by surprise. The big, whooshing explosion, followed by the sound of breaking glass. Two windows in another room blew in. The rest of them rattled hard against their frames. Simultaneously the room was bathed in a weird orange glow.

In that illumination the figures froze for a long moment. Then the bear shifted and turned from the light. Ferdy, about eight feet away from him, recovered, saw his chance, and ran. He went just as fast as his thick body would take him, past Alex in front of the fireplace, nearly tripping over the M1 where I'd left it on the floor, running blindly for the window I'd come through. He leaped through it, stumbled on the deck, and kept right on running.

But the bear was after him, moving in that same shuffling run I'd seen somewhere before, bounding past me up to the window and out. There were yells from out in the back, the sounds of hurried, desperate movement.

The blonde looked at me. I shook my head no. Then I walked over to take a look at Alex. I'd done more damage than I thought, and I guess more than I wanted to do. That long, sharp slug from the M1 had gone right through his thigh, and it probably broke the bone, but it must have also passed through the femoral artery. He was pumping blood through the wound.

"Help me," he wailed. "I'm bleeding to death."

"Yeah," I agreed, "you might be." I waved at the blonde. "Come over here."

She came, straining to see out the broken window into the back. There was nothing to see out there. It was too dark. The

222

yells had ceased, but there were bear sounds—snuffling, growling, and a roar. Then there was a loud "Help!" from Ferdy.

She stood, looking at me coldly. "You're going to let that bear kill him, aren't you?"

"Let's worry about this guy. You know how to do a tourniquet?"

"I might. I took first-aid once." She looked down at Alex. "What'll I use for a bandage?"

"Try your shirt."

"Get your jollies, huh?"

"Not from you, babe. Do it—or I'll put one through your foot."

There was another cry for help, louder, sustained. She turned to the sound, then back at me, and saw that the Colt was pointed right where I said.

Then she pulled off her shirt—yeah, don't get excited, she had a brassiere on—and bent down over Alex. I tucked the Colt under my left armpit and managed to hold it there while I fished out my pocketknife. I tossed it down to her. "Cut away his pants and wrap your shirt tight on his skin right above the wound," I told her. "Then slide the knife back on the floor. You got that?"

She did what I said. I walked over to the fireplace and tossed her a stick of kindling, and in a moment she'd put it all together the right way and had started twisting. And in another few moments the bleeding had stopped.

"Hold it there with both hands," I told her. "I'll tell you when to release."

"I know how it goes."

Alex looked bad. I wasn't feeling so good myself. The automatic I'd picked up off the floor was a .25 caliber Beretta. That was the slug I had in my shoulder—in the meat just under the joint. It was throbbing, and there was sticky stuff on my arm. The room swayed a little. My pulse was thundering. I wanted to sit down, but I didn't dare do that.

Then from the back: "Help! Goddamn it, help me!" Well, Ferdy was at least still alive, up a tree maybe, but still alive.

223

Now it was time to collect what I'd come for. "Okay," I said, "where's Osborne?"

"Where's who?" She drawled it out contemptuously. Alex mumbled something to her. I didn't get any of it.

"Right in your foot. You know what a magnum hollow-point will do to your foot? Probably cripple you for the rest of your life."

She glanced from me to Alex, then back at me. "Downstairs in the basement. They're locked in down there—dead bolt on the door."

They? But I didn't have a chance to ask about that.

A powerful set of headlights and a flashing dome light came barreling up the driveway. Cops! I wasn't sure whether I was glad to see them or not. Maybe I ought to get out the way I came. Could I make it all the way back to the car?

The blonde seemed to sense what was going on in my head, and Alex, too. They looked at me expectantly. If they wanted me out of there, then there was no question, I had to stay.

I heard voices, footsteps. I walked to the door and handed over the Colt Python to the first Siskiyou County cop through the door. To the next I gave Alex's Beretta, to the next my .38 Smith and Wesson, and to the fourth I said, "There's an M1 and a carbine on the floor. Better collect them, too."

He seemed to be in charge, and he was looking at me like I was crazy. "What in the hell went on in here, anyway?"

"Well, it's going to take a while to explain," I said.

The blonde jumped up and started screaming: "Arrest him! Arrest him! That crazy Mexican, he's a killer."

The other three cops started through the room, picking up the weapons. One of them yelled, "Hey, there's somebody out back."

"Uh, yeah," I called back. "That's Ferdy. Ferdinand Petko. There's a bear out there, too. Please don't shoot the bear. He's on my side."

The cop in charge looked at me in dismay. "Jesus," he said.

"And there's a guy in front, too. He's tied up in the snow."

"Did you do all this?"

"Well, the bear helped," I said, "a lot."

Then Alex piped up from the floor, managing somehow to muster a tone of authority. "You may arrest this man, officer. He's a criminal. But then, unless you have a search warrant, I must ask you and your men to leave."

"Mister, the way this place looks, we don't need a search warrant." The cop said it with equal authority. He turned to me then like we were in this together. "What is it he doesn't want us to find?"

"Downstairs," I said, "there's a bolt lock on the door, and . . . and . . ."

Then I fainted.

Twenty

I passed in and out of consciousness a couple of times during the next few hours. The first time I was just lucid enough to realize that there were a lot more people around, cops and paramedics. I was still in the big living room. I seemed to be lying on the sofa. My sweater was off and my shirt was ripped away from my shoulder. I was under a blanket, but I was cold.

When I came to again, I was in a moving vehicle, an ambulance, I guess, because I had an IV in my arm. We seemed to be going along pretty fast, so we must have been off the mountain. There was a man and a woman riding in the back with me. The woman leaned over me and saw that I was conscious. She had white pants on under her parka—a paramedic.

"How you feeling?" she asked. She was looking at me like there might be some doubt.

"I'm okay," I said, only I couldn't get up much voice to say it. Just a whisper.

The guy leaned over me then. It was a cop—not the one I talked to before I passed out, one of the others.

"We're almost there," he said encouragingly. Then he gave me a big country-boy grin. "Hey, you sure knocked the shit out of that place! I never saw such a mess in my life."

I tried to concentrate. There were things I wanted to know.

Finally all I could come up with was, "Downstairs . . . the basement."

He nodded. "Oh, yeah, sure. We got 'em out of there—the crazy guy and the little girl. And that ain't all we found down there—two keys of coke, a whole lot of crack, and other stuff we'll have to send out to a lab to find out what it is. I'm telling you, it's the biggest drug bust we had in Siskiyou County in a while."

It took me a while to get all that straight. Only I didn't have it all straight. There was something I needed to know. "The girl?" I asked. "Who's she?"

He told me her name. It sounded vaguely familiar, but it didn't really register. Then he started to tell me all about her, eager to talk, and I wanted to listen, but somehow I slipped away again.

Do I remember going into surgery? Not really. All I was aware of was the rattle of the gurney and the lights in the ceiling going by, one by one.

When I woke up—really woke up, this time—it was day, the sun was shining, and there was somebody sitting by my bed. I blinked and focused my eyes. He was a big, heavyset guy, dressed in a suit and tie. He leaned over and looked at me closely. He was smiling. I'd never seen him before, but he looked friendly—and right then I felt like I needed a friend.

"You been out a while," he said. "Think you can talk?"

"Yeah, maybe. Who're you?"

"I'm Jimmy Albright. We been talking on the telephone. I flew up from Ventura in the morning to see you."

"What time is it?"

He looked at his watch. "Two-thirty-five."

I nodded. That hurt my shoulder. "I've never been shot before," I said. "Is it always like this?"

"No, well, you got hit in an artery. You lost a lot of blood."

"That's where I hit him—the other guy, Alex."

"Yeah, but you can't put a tourniquet on a shoulder wound, so you just bled and bled."

"Oh." I was thinking a lot more clearly now. "Hey, save

227

that slug they took out of me. I'll bet it matches the one in Clay Weston."

"I'll bet it does." he agreed with a big, broad smile. "Yeah, that's why I came up to see how much of this I could put together with what we got in Ojai. We want them for that. I figured I could expedite paperwork if I was here on the spot. And also, well, I wanted to get a look at you."

"Yeah, well, here I am. I'm a mess."

"Naw, Cervantes, you're a hero. The cops here think you are. And there's reporters up here from Redding and Sacramento and Los Angeles. You're a hero. Listen, they got drugs from that place. They got that girl in there, and—"

"Yeah, who was she?"

"Oh, some little runaway kid, name of Karen Valesko. Her parents were up here looking for her, posted notices, went to the cops. She just disappeared. Seems that guy Petko picked her up so that sicko up there could have a playmate. They kept her prisoner in that big house. She ran away once, and they put her in the cage with the bear."

"What about the bear? They didn't shoot him, did they?"

"No, oh, no. How'd you get him to go in there with you, anyway?"

"That's a long story—in a little while maybe."

He nodded. "No, your bear came out of it all right. See, what happened, when that Petko guy got chased around the yard, he went the only place he could to get away—right into the bear cage. The cops up here said they never saw anything like it. The bear's pawing away at the door, trying to get it open. Petko got it secured with a chain some way or other, and he's just sitting there in bear shit, all chewed up, bawling for help."

He started laughing, and I did, too. It hurt.

"But that wasn't all," he continued. "The weird part was, well, they had on these bright lights, so they saw it all real plain. The cops come up pretty cautious behind him, and the bear turns around, takes a look at them. He seems to decide the situation's under control, and he walks away, just like that.

Didn't run, just went to a hole in the fence and crawled out. That's the last they saw of him."

I nodded and laid there without saying anything for about a minute. Suddenly I was exhausted.

"Well, look," said Albright, "I don't want to wear you out. I got things to talk about to the county cops, anyway."

"I'm sure glad they came up there. They weren't just passing by. How'd they know?"

"Oh," he said, pushing up from the chair, putting his rumpled suit in order, "that was me. See, after we talked on the telephone, I called them up in Yreka and sort of filled them in on the situation. You gave me a pretty good idea where that house was, so I just told them what you told me. Even so, they wandered around some until that Jeep blew up. "That gave them a pretty good fix on the location." He laughed again. "You are one destructive little Mexican person, aren't you?"

"When I get pissed off, I am." He was putting back the chair where he thought it should go, getting ready to leave. "Just one more thing," I said.

"What's that?"

"That *was* Tommy Osborne in there, wasn't it?"

Jimmy Albright sighed and nodded. "Yeah, that was him, what was left of him—brain all burned out, can't hardly put two words together. I took a look at him myself. He looks all bloated and sick. But I guess he could still sing. That's what this was all about, wasn't it?"

"More or less," I said, "more or less."

They kept me up there the better part of a week. The county prosecutor came in the third day with a court reporter and took my deposition. There was a lot to tell, and it took all morning and most of the afternoon to tell it. They'd figured there had to be a murder twenty years ago when that Corvette went off White Ridge Road, and so they wanted to hear all about Tommy Osborne and what Alex was up to. He told me they were working on the blonde and getting stuff from her. Such as? Well, it seemed Tommy Osborne had had other

229

playmates in the past. She thought she knew where the bodies were buried.

They had Osborne under observation in some state facility in Redding. I never saw him. I never wanted to.

I got the full treatment up there in Siskiyou County. My last couple of days in the hospital the cops brought in dinner from the local steak house. It was the prosecutor's idea. He said he had to have me good and healthy for my return trip when the trials came up. The only person who gave me a hard time was the doctor. He threw a fit when I told him I was going back to Los Angeles, said I wasn't ready to travel and he wouldn't be responsible. You know how doctors talk. Anyway, I went.

I got driven to the Redding airport in the Ford Bronco by a deputy sheriff. As a matter of fact, it was the same guy who was with me in the ambulance. We talked about that.

"Man, there was a while there I thought we'd be hauling you out of the county in a box," he told me. "Most of the guys I've seen in your condition never made it."

I looked over at him. He had his eyes on the road and had a sober expression on his fleshy face. "Pretty serious stuff, huh?"

He nodded. "Pretty serious. But that little paramedic, she was on you all the way with her stethoscope. And one time, I guess she didn't like what she heard, and she gets over you and wham, wham, wham, she gives you three big ones right on the chest, the way they do. I thought she was going to kill you that way. But it wasn't long after that you came around, and we talked a little bit. You remember that?"

"I remember," I said. I thought of my ex-wife, the emergency room nurse. I wondered how many times she'd done that. "Say, listen, would you find that paramedic and thank her for me? Better yet, give her a big kiss."

He looked over at me and grinned. "Will do."

I think it was then that I turned around and took one last look at that mountain. It was just as big out of the back window of the Bronco as it was the first time I'd seen it through the windshield.

The county paid the Hertz bill, and the deputy explained the

230

bullet crease on the roof to the girl at the desk. Then he said he'd like to wait with me there, but he had to catch a ride back in about ten minutes' time.

While I was there in the hospital I tried about a dozen times to call Alicia. Different times of day, different days. Nothing. The only message left with my answering service was a recent one from Heinrich Toller: I was to call him immediately. I figured "immediately" could wait until I got back to Los Angeles.

I came home to an empty apartment. Somehow that didn't surprise me. There was a note from Alicia telling me she'd signed a contract with Majestic and had money of her own now. She would no longer have to impose on me and thanked me for my kindness.

Short and sweet, just like it had been dictated by Ursula Toller.

Later that day, I got around to calling Ursula's father.

He didn't pussyfoot around: "You're fired," he said.

"Okay."

"Well, you expect to work for the studio after this? You leave us with a picture we can't release. You make a monster of this person who is the big hero of the movie. What do you *expect?*"

"I said, *okay*, didn't I?"

"Now we have nothing for Christmas. So what do we do?" The thunder at the other end of the line ceased for a moment. "I understand you were shot," he said. "Near death."

"I didn't feel so good," I admitted.

"I'll give you severance pay."

"Okay."

"Is that all you say, 'okay?' You could thank me, you know."

"Thank you."

"Ach, Gott im Himmel!" And he jammed down the receiver.

The doctor was probably right. I guess I should have stayed in the hospital a couple of more days. But I was in a hurry to come down and get that pie in my face from Alicia. I thought

231

I deserved more than a note from her, but a note was all I got.

I hung around the apartment about a week, recuperating and feeling sorry for myself. A couple of days after I got back, I went to my own doctor on Wilshire in Santa Monica to get the dressing on the wound changed. He was fascinated. He said he hadn't treated a gunshot wound since his days in the emergency room as an intern. Looking around at his patients on the way out, I could believe it.

When I got back from the doctor's office, I checked with my answering service and found I had a message from Pilar, asking me to call her at home whenever I wanted. I dialed her number right away.

"Ah, Senor Cervantes, is you, huh? How do you feel? Your cousin, he said he read in the paper you were hurt bad, but you're a big hero now, verdad?"

"Yeah, I'm okay now, Pilar. What's up?"

"Well . . ." She hesitated and then plunged on: "I just want you to know, Senor Cervantes, I think she did wrong to go the way she did. I tell her that. We have a big fight. I say to Alicia, 'How can you go after the way Chico take care of you, after what you been through together?' You know what she say to me? 'Chico can't make me a star.' Just like that. It make me sick. That woman Ursula, she cause it all." I could hear the tears in her voice.

"That's okay, Pilar. I'll get along all right, but it's good to know how you feel about it. Me importa, sabes?"

She sniffled. "Sí."

"But how come you're home? You got the baby there? Is everything okay with her?"

"Oh, sure. That Marilyn, she so cute, so smart. You two made a good baby. But, no, they take her away from me, too, Senor Cervantes. Alicia got an ahper girl now."

What was she talking about? "An ahper girl?"

"Sí, you know, like when they come over from Europe and they baby-sit for eating and sleeping."

"Oh, an au pair girl."

"I pronounce it wrong?"

"No, I just wasn't thinking in that direction."

"This one, she's from Germany, and she think she know everything."

"Well, no matter how much she knows, she can't take care of Marilyn the way you can."

"Gracias, Senor Cervantes—and you right, too." There was something more, I could tell. Finally: "How about you come over here, and I cook for you? Frijoles, enchiladas, carne asada, anything you want."

Somehow the idea appealed to me. "Well, that'd be nice, Pilar. Only I don't really feel up to it right now. Maybe in a few days, a week, okay?"

"Oh," she said, "so you really not all better now! I tell you what, I come over tonight, and I cook for you there. I bring everything with me. You just sit and eat. Let me do this for you. Please."

"Yeah," I said, "sure, that'd be nice."

So she came and cooked—well, she cooked enough for the rest of the week—and we ate, and we talked. And after she left, around eleven, I was lonelier than ever. Couldn't sleep at all that night.

One of these days soon I'm going to drive up to Ventura County and see Jimmy Albright and look in on Rachel Weston and her kids. It looked to me like that daughter of hers was going to have a big load to carry. I hope she can handle it.

And of course I'll be going back to Siskiyou County in a while. I got a package from the county sheriff's office up there just the other day. It was a big, oblong thing that came UPS. I opened it up, and you know what it was? That M1 I had there for just one night. Now, what am I going to do with a U.S. Army M1 semiautomatic rifle in Los Angeles?

But who knows? I may find some use for it.